What Would Wimsey Do?

What Would Wimsey Do?

Guy Fraser-Sampson

FELONY & MAYHEM PRESS • NEW YORK

WHAT WOULD WIMSEY DO?

A Felony & Mayhem mystery

PRINTING HISTORY
First UK edition (Urbane, as *Death in Profile*): 2012
Felony & Mayhem edition (first US edition): 2019

ISBN (trade cloth): 978-1-63194-225-9
ISBN (trade paper): 978-1-63194-222-8

Manufactured in the United States of America

Library of Congress Cataloging-in-Publication Data

Names: Fraser-Sampson, Guy, author.
Title: What would Wimsey do? / Guy Fraser-Sampson.
Description: Felony & Mayhem edition. | New York : Felony & Mayhem Press,
   2019. | "First UK edition (Urbane, as Death in Profile): 2012"--Title page verso. |
   Summary: "A series of ugly killings has shattered the orderly workings of the
   Hampstead police station. And truth be told, they have shattered the confidence
   of the lead investigator on the case, who has long taken pride in his old-school
   "copper's nose." When yet another body turns up, he's forced to give way
   to a new chief with fancy new detecting techniques. But when those, too,
   prove unequal to the task, the police are stymied. So they reach back to the past,
   invoking the skills of one of the great Gentleman Sleuths. Is this nutty? No
   doubt. But Lord Peter Wimsey always got his man"-- Provided by publisher.
Identifiers: LCCN 2019029074 | ISBN 9781631942259 (hardcover) | ISBN
   9781631942228 (trade paperback) | ISBN 9781631942235 (ebook)
Subjects: LCSH: Wimsey, Peter, Lord (Fictitious character), 1890---Fiction.
   | Hampstead (London, England)--Fiction. | GSAFD: Mystery fiction.
Classification: LCC PR6106.R454466 W47 2019 | DDC 823/.92--dc23
LC record available at https://lccn.loc.gov/2019029074

The icon above says you're holding a book in the Felony & Mayhem "British" category. These books are set in or around the UK, and feature the highly literate, often witty prose that fans of British mystery demand. If you enjoy this book, you may well like other "British" titles from Felony & Mayhem Press.

For information about British titles or to learn more about Felony & Mayhem Press, please visit us online at:

www.FelonyAndMayhem.com

Other "British" titles from

FELONY&MAYHEM

What Would Wimsey Do?

Chapter One

Boyo was a border collie cross, which was how he had come by his name. The crackhead who had given him to his owner, Ben, as a puppy had been convinced that Boyo was a proper noun much in evidence among Welshmen, rather than an anti-quated form of address. Not that Boyo himself was particularly worried one way or another, for two reasons. First, he was on the whole preoccupied with satisfying his pressing need to find something to eat. Second, as a dog he was incapable of abstract conceptual thought.

Ben was currently lying blind drunk on an old blanket in a shop doorway in Wood Green. Unlike Boyo, he *was* capable of abstract conceptual thought, but it was an intellectual ability that he rarely chose to indulge. For one thing, any rational assessment of his situation would have prompted deep depres-sion and possible suicide. For another, he was frequently either drunk or drugged to the eyeballs, and occasionally both at the same time.

Having been awake for some time, Boyo had been viewing the corpse-like appearance of his master with stern disapproval. For some days now, since the last night they had spent in a hostel, Ben had been smelling so strongly that even other humans had begun to notice. From the stertorous noises drifting towards him, Boyo knew that it would be impossible to wake Ben until he recovered consciousness of his own volition, and this fact was rapidly becoming most inconvenient, since his bladder was sending him urgent messages. He experimented with a few plaintive yaps but found that, as expected, these produced no response.

He gave a little pull on his lead, and found to his surprise that it yielded slightly. Ben had forgotten to tie it around his wrist, as he usually did when bedding down for the night, but it was trapped beneath the snoring bulk of his sleeping body. Getting up, Boyo threw his weight onto his back legs, braced his front ones, and pulled mightily. Slowly but surely the old cord gradually emerged, and suddenly he was free. With the lead dragging along the ground behind him, he sped round the corner into a small alleyway, and urinated contentedly against the wall.

After answering the call of nature, he became aware that a woman was lying on the ground further back in the alley, shortly before it gave onto a service area behind the shops. He approached her and sniffed, cautiously at first but then more eagerly. It was apparent that this woman was just as immoveable as his master. He licked her face, but this produced no response. He had a sudden instinct that something was wrong. Her eyes were open and staring unblinkingly upwards towards the grey North London sky. He drew back and whimpered uncertainly. Then he trotted back to the entrance to the alley, sat on the pavement, and began to bark determinedly.

Arriving on the scene some time later, Detective Chief Inspector Tom Allen found that both the alleyway and a stretch of pavement on either side had been fenced off with blue-and-white police tape. He pushed his way through the inevitable small crowd of onlookers that always formed on these occasions.

Didn't these people have lives of their own to lead? Perhaps it was simply his persistent head cold that prompted this feeling of resentment, but in truth Tom Allen was a man who found little in the world of which he truly approved, and much towards which he was deeply antipathetic.

The young constable did not recognise him, but once he had peered at Allen's identification he lifted the tape to allow him to duck underneath it, and pointed to where a little knot of people, some in white boiler suits, had gathered around two or three vehicles that were parked ostentatiously on a double yellow line.

"Morning, Bob," he said as Detective Inspector Metcalfe saw him coming, and walked towards him. "What have we got?"

It was a private joke between them that they often resorted to clichés from old police films and television shows. A couple of years previously, a drug dealer whom they had pursued through the streets of Brixton had been surprised, as he lay prone on the pavement being cuffed, to hear Allen say, "Book him, Danno," at which Metcalfe had lent over him and said, in a passable imitation of John Thaw in *The Sweeney*, "Right, sunshine, you're nicked."

"SOCO thinks it's the same guy," Metcalfe replied, "but of course they won't commit to anything until they get the body back to the lab and do their stuff. Single head wound, no knickers, and he's pretty sure there are chloroform burns around the mouth."

"Sounds the same," Allen agreed. "Let's take a look."

Together they walked the few yards into the alley. Seeing the Chief Inspector, the group of people around the body parted and fell back. Allen was relieved to see that the duty pathologist was Brian Williams; he knew his job and, what's more, he had already worked on at least one of the previous victims.

"Morning, Brian. What do you think?"

"Morning, Tom. Officially, you'll have to wait for my report. Unofficially, I'm pretty certain it's the same killer. Same MO, anyway."

"Time of death?"

"Sometime after midnight, I'd say, and that's good because it hasn't rained, and nothing's disturbed the body apart from the dog that found it, so this is our best chance yet of getting some good forensic samples."

"It's time we had a break," said Allen dourly. He squatted down on his haunches to inspect the body. He saw an ordinary-looking brunette, body twisted, legs apart, eyes gazing sightlessly at nothing in particular. He knew without even having to look that there would be a savage hammer wound at the back of the head. Some poor sod's daughter, he thought. Then he saw the rings; some poor sod's wife.

He stood up. "On a night out, do you think?" he asked nobody in particular.

"Unlikely, I'd say," said Williams. "She's not wearing any make-up or perfume as far as I can tell without my lab equipment. More like a chance encounter, I'd say."

"I agree, guv," Metcalfe chipped in. "She's wearing flat shoes, not heels, nothing fancy. Anyway, there are no bars in the immediate area."

"Always assuming this is where she was killed," countered Allen, "or met her killer, at any rate."

"Again, I'll need to examine her properly in the lab," Williams said, "but for what it's worth, Tom, I'd say she was killed here. There's nothing I can see with the naked eye to suggest that she's been moved after death. The position of the body's all wrong for that, as well. I'd say that not only was she killed here, but raped here too."

"Hmm," said Allen. "That would be consistent with the others, anyway—rape, I mean." He pulled a packet of throat lozenges out of his pocket and put one in his mouth absentmindedly while he carried on looking at the body.

"Any ID?" he asked Metcalfe.

"Driving licence in her handbag. Also credit cards." He held up two or three sealed and tagged plastic bags. The Scene of Crime Officers had worked quickly. "Katherine Barker, home address Lyndhurst Gardens in Hampstead. I had the station run a computer check—her husband tried to report her missing at 4 a.m."

"Tried? Oh yes, of course." Allen rubbed his eyes tiredly. Police procedures did not allow an adult to be treated as missing unless they had been unaccounted for over at least a twenty-four-hour period.

"Got Mr Barker's address?"

"I have. It's Dr Barker by the way. He's part of a group practice in Belsize Park."

Allen leaned back against the wall and wished for the thousandth time that he had never given up smoking. Sometimes the relentless grind of the job threatened to overwhelm him.

"Well, come on, Bob," he said quietly. "Let's go and give the good doctor the news."

"Have you finished here, Tom?" Williams asked. "If so, can I take the body? We've finished with photos."

"With pleasure," Allen replied, as he blew his nose for the umpteenth time already that morning. "Let me have something as soon as you can."

Colin Barker looked as though he had not slept for some considerable time. He also looked heavily hungover. Certainly he had not shaved, and the hand with which he had motioned them into the ground-floor flat after they had identified themselves at the front door was trembling perceptibly. They followed him into the living room and as he sat down so too did they, perching awkwardly on the edge of the sofa. Bob Metcalfe already had his notebook out.

"I presume," said Barker, after the briefest of pauses, "that when two senior detectives come knocking on your door in these situations, it's not good news." He managed a grim smile.

"I am very sorry, sir," Tom Allen began. "Very sorry indeed." He stopped for a moment. It was funny how in these situations he always found himself thinking about Mary. His colleague eyed him sympathetically. He was all too aware that Allen had never properly come to terms with his daughter's death. On a previous occasion during this very case Allen had been forced to leave the room briefly while breaking the news to another bereaved spouse.

"I am afraid to have to inform you, sir," Metcalfe said, cutting in smoothly as though Allen had simply stopped to allow his partner to pick up the story, "that we have discovered the body of a woman whom we have reason to believe is your wife."

Total silence greeted his announcement.

"Is there anyone we can call for you, Doctor?" asked Allen with a hint of desperation. "Anyone you would like to have with you?" God, how he hated these situations.

"No—no, thank you." Barker gazed at them dully. "Is that all you can tell me?"

"We still have a lot of enquiries to make," Allen temporised formally. "Until you've identified the body we cannot say for certain that it is your wife."

"Is there any doubt?" asked the doctor with sudden hope in his voice.

"It's unlikely, I'm afraid, sir. Not unless somebody stole her handbag and everything that was in it."

As he spoke, his eyes were moving around the room. As with so many small London flats, there was a curious sense of impermanence. There were chairs and a sofa; a mirror and some prints on the walls. Yet while they filled the room they somehow did not furnish it. It was as if the entire contents of the room, including the people, might be swept up into large cardboard boxes at any moment, ready to move to their next location. At last Allen found what he was looking for. He heaved himself off the sofa and picked up a framed photograph from a side table by the window.

"Is this your wife, Doctor?"

"Yes, that's Kathy."

Allen and Metcalfe looked at each other.

"Then I'm afraid there really is no hope, sir. The identification will only be a formality, for the coroner's records."

"Is this a recent photo, sir?" asked Metcalfe.

"Pretty recent—six months or so back, I think."

"Do you mind if we keep it? You'll get it back, of course."

"Yes, do, if you think it will help."

"Thank you, sir." Metcalfe placed it carefully in a plastic wallet and slipped it underneath his open notebook on his knee.

"Now then, Doctor," Allen said. "If you're feeling up to it then, there are some questions we need to ask. Only if you're feeling up to it, mind. We can easily do this tomorrow if you prefer."

"No, no, let's do it now," Barker replied at once. "By all means, let's get it over with."

"That's the spirit," Allen said encouragingly, "but might I suggest we let my colleague slip into the kitchen and make us all a cup of tea while you and I begin?"

This was a well-practised ploy that the pair had used before. Metcalfe would make a great noise about filling the kettle and then slip away quietly for a look round.

"Yes, of course. By the way, how did she die? You never said."

"No, we didn't, did we?"

Another meaningful glance passed between the two detectives. They had both been wondering how long it would take him to ask. Failure to do so could be ascribed to shock, but sometimes had a more sinister explanation.

"We're treating the case as one of murder, sir," Allen said carefully. "I'm afraid I really can't say any more than that at this stage. You'll appreciate that our enquiries are only just beginning. Now, when did you last see your wife?"

"At about 11.30 last night. She went out at about that time."

"Went out?" asked Allen blankly. He heard Metcalfe slip out of the room behind him and close the door. He opened his own notebook and started jotting things down. "Did she often go out so late? Did she work night shifts?"

"No, nothing like that," Barker said. He seemed embarrassed. "If you must know, we'd had a row."

"Did you often have rows with your wife, sir?" Allen was careful to keep his voice non-committal.

"It's happened before," the doctor said drily. "You can check with her sister. She lives in Wood Green. Kathy usually goes to her when she storms out late at night. She must be getting pretty tired of it by now—" He caught himself using the present tense and stopped.

"And yet you tried to report her missing at"—he consulted his notebook—"about 4 a.m. Why was that?"

"What do you mean?"

"I mean, if you thought she was safe and sound at her sister's, then why did you try to report her missing to the police?"

"I know it sounds strange, but I had a queer feeling that something was wrong, that something had happened to her. I can't explain it; it was like an instinct or something. I tried phoning Angie—that's her sister—but couldn't get any reply."

"Was that unusual?"

"Not really. She's a nurse and has to work some strange hours. That's why Kathy has a key to her flat. It's supposed to be if anything happens while Angie's away, but really it's so Kathy has a bolt-hole available whenever she wants to get away from here."

"Would Kathy have answered Angie's phone?"

"I wasn't sure. Certainly she's done so before when I've called the flat and she's been on her own."

"So, having called, you were still worried?"

"Yes. I waited for a bit and brooded some more—I was, er, drinking actually. I'd had a few. Then about two I tried again. This time I let it ring twice and then rang off, then did the same thing again. That's a sort of code we've used before, to let the other know that it's you who's calling. Then I let it ring quite a long time, but there was still no answer."

"But that was two hours before you called the police."

"I know. I tried to watch a film on TV after that, but I was getting more and more twitchy so eventually I phoned the police. They said they couldn't do anything at this stage except log the call."

"Yes, sir," Allen said evenly. "Procedure, I'm afraid. Had it been a child, it would have been different. Most adults turn up sooner or later, you see—and usually sooner."

He looked up from his notebook. "Don't take this the wrong way, Doctor, but do I take it from what you tell me that there isn't anybody who could vouch for your movements between, say, 11 p.m. last night and 7 a.m. this morning?"

"No, of course not. I was here alone after Kathy went out, like I told you. Why should I need an alibi? I'm not a suspect, am I?"

"Just routine, sir," Allen said soothingly. "I'm sure you'll appreciate that we have to ask these questions, if only to have something for the file."

Bob Metcalfe came back into the room, pushing the door open with his elbow and holding a tray with three mugs of tea on it. He broke the awkward silence by saying "Here you are, sir," as he handed the doctor one.

"This is another difficult question," Allen went on as Metcalfe flipped his own notebook open again, "but I'm afraid I have to ask. Were you aware of your wife seeing anybody else, another man, I mean?"

"No, not at all." There was a short silence. "Not as far as I was aware, anyway."

"Any family, other than the sister?"

"Her father died some years ago. Her mother lives in South London, but they're not close. Hardly ever even speak, let alone see each other. So far as I know, Angie's all there is. Certainly nobody else from her side came to the wedding, apart from a few girlfriends from work."

"So she did work at one time, then?"

"Yes, but she gave it up when we got married a couple of years back."

"What was it—her work, I mean?"

"She was a secretary with a firm of solicitors—a big one in the City. Or executive assistant, I should say. She was always very insistent about that. Executive assistant to one of the partners."

"Did she miss not working?"

"She claimed not, but actually I'm pretty sure she did. She'd always liked the idea of being a 'lady of leisure' as she called it, but she was used to being busy at work all day, and when she was at home she didn't have anything to take its place. I sometimes used to think that was part of her trouble—boredom, I mean. Sitting around at home all day with nothing to do, and then giving me a hard time when I got in."

"Did she drink at all?"

"Not during the day, I don't think. Unless perhaps she was meeting a girlfriend for lunch. But definitely a bit too much in the evenings. That's when the rows usually start—started, I mean."

"How would you describe your relationship with your wife, sir?" Metcalfe asked very politely.

"Very good." Barker gave a quick snort of a laugh that turned into a gasp. "I suppose that must sound pretty funny coming after what I've just been saying, but we've always loved each other. It's just that she has—had—a very quick temper, which has always been made much worse by booze. Every time she's gone off at night, she's always come back some time the next day, suitably apologetic."

"But not this time," murmured Allen, almost to himself.

"No," said Barker flatly.

"I'm sorry, sir, I didn't mean to distress you, nor with all these questions, neither. I think it's time we left you in peace. Just a couple of points to go over with you first, though."

He glanced at Metcalfe, who sat with a ballpoint poised in readiness.

"First, could you please let DI Metcalfe have your home and surgery phone numbers. As I said, we will have to arrange a time for you to identify the body, but there's no hurry about that. Second, we'll also need your sister-in-law's address and telephone number so we can find out if your wife really did attempt to go there last night."

There was a pause while this information was found and recorded.

"Just one more thing, Doctor," Metcalfe said, with a glance at Allen. "Do you happen to know if your wife kept a diary? There wasn't one in her handbag."

"Yes, she did. I think it's in the kitchen."

"I thought as much, sir. To tell the truth, I came across it while I was making the tea. Would this be it?" He showed a blue pocket diary inside a plastic bag to Barker, who nodded.

"Do you mind if we hang on to it for the moment, sir? Again, you'll get it back."

"Yes, of course, no problem."

"Thank you, sir." Metcalfe slipped the bagged diary into an inside pocket of his jacket.

As they walked through the hall, Barker suddenly asked where his wife's body had been found.

"I'm not supposed to answer that question, really, sir," Allen replied. "But since it'll be all over the newspapers and the telly by lunchtime, I don't think there's any harm in you knowing. She was found in Wood Green, and, if my geography is correct, very close to her sister's flat. I should also tell you, since you'll find out anyway, that we believe she may have been the victim of a serial killer who we've been hunting for some time."

As he exited the flat through the front door, he thought sardonically that Metcalfe would have said "whom."

Lyndhurst Gardens was not far from the operations room at Hampstead police station. The location was a source of some inconvenience and much black humour, as the station was slated for closure under a raft of proposed economy measures, and

Allen was constantly being called to attend committee meetings, both within the police and at the local authority, to discuss if and when his team should be moved. This would have been irritating enough in itself even if he had not been in the middle of trying to catch a serial killer.

A search, moreover, which seemed to be going nowhere, a fact which had of late had him metaphorically looking over his shoulder. There would be an obvious reluctance on the part of the powers-that-be to disturb the team while in the middle of a serious case, and such a high profile one into the bargain. Yet as the investigation had dragged on into its second year, voices began to be heard, both in seriousness within management, and in banter within the operations room, that if things were to carry on like this indefinitely then perhaps a change of leadership should be postponed no longer.

At the same time, there were those within the local authority and the wider community who opposed the closure of the station on principle and who seized on any excuse, including the ongoing murder inquiries, to delay the inevitable. Frequent demonstrations outside the station by local residents in support of the "no closure" lobby only complicated matters. While Allen bitterly resented the time all this took up—time which he would far rather have spent on the investigation—he accepted reluctantly that such commitments were an inevitable part of modern policing.

There was an incongruous air of gaiety about the exterior of the police station, looking as it did like a perfect cardboard model in a toyshop window. The exterior, with its decorative brickwork, was almost too perfect. Inside the operations room, however, the mood was sombre. Morale was already close to rock bottom after nearly eighteen months of pursuing a serial killer with no real lead to go on. This new murder threatened to plunge the team into whole new depths of despair. Despite all their training, remaining detached and objective just wasn't possible when they felt powerless to stop this maniac loose on the streets, killing women seemingly at will. As far as they were concerned, this was personal, and they felt each new failure keenly. Had they been able to catch the killer already, this young woman would still have been alive today.

There was no need for Allen to call for silence. The room was still, and the dozen or so occupants sat waiting for him to begin. He stood in front of a large whiteboard onto which the photos of the first four victims had been fixed.

"Well, you'll all have heard the news, but yes, it looks like we could have victim number five. DI Metcalfe will brief you on what we know so far. Bob?"

"Our fifth victim is Katherine Barker, known to all as Kathy, married to a Dr Colin Barker, who lives right here in Hampstead, in Lyndhurst Gardens. Body found in an alleyway beside some shops in Wood Green early this morning by a passing workman, who was alerted by a dog barking. Dog belonged to a homeless guy, who has been interviewed but had nothing useful. He'd been sleeping round the corner all night, drunk and possibly on something as well."

"Same MO?" came a voice from the back.

"As far as we can tell, yes, but as usual we need to wait for the formal forensic report before we come to any firm conclusions. Still, I think we can work on the assumption for the time being that this was indeed the work of our friend the Condom Killer."

"Do we know what she was doing in Wood Green? Assuming she was killed there, that is?" Detective Constable Karen Willis had joined the team recently.

"The husband says that she left their flat after a row about 11.30 last night, most likely to go to her sister's flat in Wood Green to cool off. Apparently that was quite a common sequence of events. We have the sister's details and obviously the first thing on the list is to interview her and find out whether she heard or saw anything of our victim last night. The husband believes she was out, probably working a night shift, but that doesn't explain why the victim was out on the streets, since she had a set of keys to her sister's place."

He picked up two plastic bags on the table.

"Two sets of keys found in her handbag. We checked one of them on the front door of Lyndhurst Gardens and they fitted. We assume the others are to the sister's flat, but we'll need to check that. Andrews and Desai, you can arrange to interview the sister later today and check the keys at the same time."

"As to the place of death," cut in Allen, "the pathologist's first impression is that she *was* probably killed at the scene, and that brings us to the next point. That alleyway leads down into a service area, which is behind a load of flats over the shops. There's a good chance that someone saw or heard something, so I'm asking the local nick to lay on as many uniforms as possible for house-to-house enquiries, starting at four this afternoon. Apart from Andrews and Desai, we'll leave one person here to man the phones, and the rest of you will get over there to join in. We need as many bodies on this as possible."

There was no response to this. House-to-house enquiries were one of the most boring and frustrating aspects of police procedure, and for this reason usually left to the woodentops, as detectives customarily referred to their uniformed colleagues, but they all knew that it was necessary. Somebody out there might have witnessed the one little detail that could open up a new line of enquiry, without which they were dead in the water. All their previous ones had led them nowhere.

"We should also," suggested Metcalfe, "check with the neighbours in Lyndhurst Gardens to see if anyone witnessed Kathy leaving home last night. It's a quiet road, so someone may have heard something, particularly if they were shouting at each other—their upstairs neighbours, for a start."

"Agreed," said Allen. "But let's go quietly on that one, Bob. After all, it's not that we disbelieve what the doctor said, only that we need to have it confirmed if possible. A couple of plain-clothes knocking discreetly on doors ought to do the job. But after we get Wood Green sorted; that's our priority right now."

"Excuse me, sir." A uniform from the front desk put his head round the door. "Superintendent Collison from the Yard is downstairs. Wonders if he could have a word?"

"Oh, hell," Allen replied resignedly. "OK you lot, off you go. If I've got to stay anyway I can just as easily man the phones as anyone. Report back here at 0900 tomorrow, got it?"

The team shuffled from the room, and Allen asked for his visitor to be brought up.

Chapter Two

"Hello, Tom." Detective Superintendent Simon Collison edged into the room. He was a slim man, and young for his rank.

"Hello yourself, Simon," Allen said in some surprise. "I didn't know you'd made Super. It seems only yesterday I heard you were a DCI."

"It was nearly three years ago, actually," said Collison, slightly awkwardly. He was conscious that, as a law graduate, he had been one of the first Met officers to be fast-tracked for promotion. "I've been on secondment in Manchester for a while, and when I finished up there the Chief Constable was kind enough to recommend me to the Commissioner for a leg-up."

"Well, congratulations anyway." Allen had been a DCI for seven years, a DI for five years before that, and knew very well that he was unlikely to progress further. He reached into his jacket for a cigarette and then remembered both that this was now a no-smoking building, and that he was supposed to have given up. The hardest thing, he found, was knowing what to do with his hands. He stuffed them into his trouser pockets and perched on the edge of a desk.

"So what brings you here?"

"Mind if I close the door?" Without waiting for an answer Collision crossed the room and did so. Then he moved opposite Allen and also sat on a desk, facing him.

"I hear you've found another one. What does that make it now—six?"

"Five," Allen responded defensively. "And this time we have some hope for forensics. She was found quickly, and it hadn't been raining."

There was a pause. On Collison's part because he was thinking how best to phrase what he had to say next. On Allen's part because he was beginning to realise, with a sick feeling in the pit of his stomach, what it might be.

"I'm afraid I'm here officially," Collison said, answering Allen's unspoken question. "I was with the Assistant Commissioner Crime yesterday evening. He's asked me to take a fresh look at this case. No criticism implied, Tom, but it's been dragging on for a long time now. The ACC wants to be sure there aren't any other angles we should be considering."

"What other angles? This is a serial killer we're hunting, Simon, for Christ's sake. All we can do is look for clues and then follow them up—and by the way, this guy doesn't believe in leaving clues."

"I know, I know," Collison said soothingly. "Absolutely no criticism of you is intended, Tom. I want to make that clear. I'm sure the ACC thinks you've been doing a great job here. But he's under pressure to show some results, unfair though that may seem."

"You mean the press," Allen said heavily. It was a statement, not a question. Two leading Sunday newspapers had independently run stories on the hunt for the killer in recent weeks, in each case setting out the timeline to date and, while being careful not to single anyone out for express criticism, implying that the case might not be being handled as well as it might.

"The press have played a part, I'm sure." Collison was careful to be diplomatic. "I did say it was unfair, Tom."

"So what does he want, precisely? Me to brief you on the case and let you sit in on all our team meetings?"

"Ah," said Collison, with more than a hint of embarrassment. He was hoping that the older man would have caught on by now, but clearly he hadn't. "No."

"No? What do you mean, no?"

"No, that's not what he wants. He thinks a fresh pair of eyes would be a good idea. You've been working on this for a year and a half now and you haven't taken any leave in that time—he's checked. You must be tired, Tom. I can see you've got a bad cold, for a start, which is a classic sign of being run down. Any rate, you're due a break. He wants you to take it, with his thanks for all your efforts."

Allen was staring at him dully. "You mean you're here to fire me?"

"I certainly wouldn't put it like that," Collison said briskly. "For one thing, it's totally untrue. The ACC is simply rotating command of a case to prevent people going stale. Actually, these days it's regarded as good practice in policing circles. There's been a lot of research in America, for instance—"

"Sod America," Allen cut in quietly but intensely. "What it comes down to is that I'm off the case. You can call that what you want. I call it being fired."

"Tom," Collison pleaded gently. "I know how upset you must be, but please be reasonable. Believe me, the ACC wouldn't be doing this if he felt he had any choice. I shouldn't be telling you this, but he's under pressure himself from upstairs."

There was no answer. Allen was staring off into the distance in an unfocused sort of way, somewhere over Collison's left shoulder.

"And for goodness' sake, don't use the word 'fired,' Tom. The only person it can damage is you, particularly if the press get hold of it. You're simply taking some long overdue leave, after which you will report back to CID for assignment to a new case in the usual way. I assure you, there's nothing more to it than that."

Slowly, Allen got off the desk and reached for his raincoat. "There's a team meeting at 0900 tomorrow," he said without any emotion at all. "You can introduce yourself to the troops then. In the meantime, all the files are in this room. I assume you'll want to study them."

At the door, as he was shrugging himself into his raincoat, he turned to look at Collison. "You've done well, Simon," he said reflectively. "I always knew that you would. Good night." With that, he left the room.

He was halfway to Hampstead tube station before he became fully aware of where he was or what he was doing. The High Street was, as usual, thronged with people and he turned off into a little alleyway on the right to try to collect his thoughts. He took out his mobile and thumbed the speed dial for Metcalfe.

"Bob," he said as soon as Metcalfe answered. "I'm off the case."

"What d'you mean, guv?"

"Just that," Allen snapped curtly. "Look, there's a little cafe in Belsize Park that opens for breakfast. Opposite the station and down the hill to the left."

"Yes, I know it."

"Can you meet me there tomorrow at 8? That'll give me time to think things out."

He rang off without waiting for an answer and headed on up the hill. Almost without thinking about it, he turned right again and wandered into the Flask. Somehow he knew that what he needed was a beer.

Phrasing that desire in the singular was undoubtedly misleading, however, which Metcalfe was quick to notice the following morning as he burnt his mouth on a red-hot cup of coffee.

"Bloody hell, guv," he said, "you look awful."

It was meant sympathetically, but whether Allen took it in that vein or not was unclear. "Never mind about that," Allen said abruptly. "Tell me what you found."

"In a word, nothing. Nobody seems to have seen or even heard our victim. Mind you, that's not entirely surprising. It's the sort of neighbourhood where most people sit around their tellies all evening, and have them blaring at full volume too, even late at night."

"So we have no independent verification as to whether Kathy made it to her sister's flat or not?"

"No, but I think it makes it highly likely that she was killed where she was found. There is a much more obvious access path into the courtyard from the local bus stops and tube station further up the road. My guess is that we'll find she got a taxi from somewhere around here—probably a bit further up Haverstock Hill—and had it drop her by the end of the alley where she was found. It *is* quicker, but most of the locals we spoke to said they would never use it on their own after dark as it's badly lit and one or two people have been mugged there."

"Surely Kathy would have known that? Her sister lived on the estate, after all."

"But we have the husband's word for it that she was pretty tanked up, and we know that makes us a lot less risk-averse than is good for us. We'll have to wait for confirmation from Forensics, of course, but I don't see any reason why Dr Barker should lie to us about that—do you?"

"No, I don't," Allen conceded.

Metcalfe gazed at him compassionately. He was unshaven and, he suspected, unwashed. He looked as though he had fallen asleep on his sofa fully dressed after a hard evening's drinking and was now nursing a hangover—all of which was in fact absolutely true. To add to the picture of woe, a red cold sore had spread above his mouth and he was dabbing at his nose ineffectually from time to time with a handkerchief which was clearly already saturated.

"I know you must feel gutted about being taken off the case," Metcalfe said carefully, "but you really do look as if you could do with a break. I know you haven't taken any leave for ages. If you go on like this you'll just make yourself ill."

"I've got a cold, that's all," snapped Allen, "and it's nothing to do with the case. It's just a bug, a simple bug, and I caught it—probably on the tube or something. I'll be OK in a few days."

"All the same, why don't you just take yourself off to the travel agents and see what they have for a couple of weeks leaving today. You can get some fantastic bargains if you book at the last minute."

Allen gave a brief snort. "Leave it out, Bob. Can you really see me going away on my own to sit on a beach somewhere?"

This was unanswerable. Metcalfe knew that Allen's last girl-friend had tired of their desultory relationship during the opening months of the current investigation, when the time he was able to spend with her had dropped from minimal to nil. All he had ever heard his colleague speak about, apart from the odd casual refer-ence to football, was the job. He wasn't even aware of him having any hobbies or interests outside the police, let alone any friends.

"Isn't there anyone you could go and stay with—family, perhaps?"

"No there isn't," Allen said shortly. "Never mind about me, anyway. It's the case that worries me."

"But, guv," Metcalfe reminded him, "you're off the case now, aren't you? I'm not even sure that I should be sitting here talking to you about it."

"Stuff that. As far as I'm concerned it's still my case, whoever's nominally in charge of it. I know more about it than anyone else. I've been thinking about it twenty-four hours a day, seven days a week for eighteen months. If anyone's going to get that bastard, it's me."

"But you're *not* in charge of it, are you?" Metcalfe's concern was mounting. "Christ, you're not even a member of the team anymore. So what can you do? I'm sure DS Collison would be happy to hear all your ideas, but basically it's up to him now, isn't it? What we do, I mean, and how we proceed."

"I've been thinking about that," Allen said with a sour smile. "I can take my leave all right, but there's nothing to say that I can't carry on working on the case in my own time, is there? I've got it all worked out. You can keep me abreast of everything that comes up, and I'll feed back my ideas to you, plus any results I get from my own enquiries, of course."

"What enquiries?" asked Metcalfe with alarm. "Look, guv, I know you're upset, and I appreciate your feelings and every-thing, but you know damn well there are rules, and rule number one is that you can't discuss the case with anyone who isn't on the team. Now, please, take some leave like they want, and try to forget about all of this. I'm worried about you—it's making you ill and you'd be far better off right out of it."

Allen stared at him. "You mean you won't help me?"

"Can't, not won't. Surely you can see that?"

For a long moment Allen stared hard at him, his hands thrust deep into his raincoat pockets and his legs stretched out under the table. Then, without saying a word, he pulled a handful of change out of his pocket, put it on the table, and walked out. Metcalfe made to follow him after throwing a fiver on top of Allen's coins, but the DCI was heading down the hill towards Chalk Farm at a brisk pace, while a glance at his watch revealed that Metcalfe needed to head equally briskly up the hill to Hampstead if he was not to be late. He sighed and headed in the opposite direction. While he was walking he came to a deci-sion; like it or not he was going to have to note his conversation with Allen in his diary, and report it to Collison.

"All right, everybody," said that very person a little while later as he stood at the front of the incident room. "I'm sure you'll all have heard by now on the grapevine anyway, but just in case there's anyone here who doesn't know, I'm DS Collison, and I'm assuming command of this enquiry on the direct orders of the ACC."

He scanned the expressionless faces around him. There was not a single one that he recognised. Luckily, he had memo-rised a few names.

"I'll be meeting with you all individually as soon as possible," he went on, "but in the meantime I'll ask DI Metcalfe to brief me on the background now and bring me up to speed on your enquiries so far with regard to victim number five."

Metcalfe stepped forwards, and said uncertainly, "I'm not sure just how much you know about the case already, sir…"

"You may assume," Collison replied crisply, "that I have read all the files." He did not add that in consequence he had not gone to bed last night, going home at about 7 a.m. only to shower, shave and change his clothes before returning to Hampstead.

"Then you'll know, sir," said Metcalfe, addressing the room at large, "that we are hunting a serial sex killer whom we believe has so far struck five times, most recently in the case of Kathy Barker, whose body was found in Wood Green just over twenty-four hours ago, and is believed to have been killed where she was found several hours previously. The MO appears to be the same as with our other victims, but as we are still awaiting the forensic report on her, I'll concentrate on what we know for sure about the others."

He glanced at Collison as if to check that this was indeed how the Superintendent wanted to proceed, and received a nod of approval in reply.

"All four bodies to date have been found in open spaces. All had traces of chloroform burns around the mouth and nose, from which we assume that they were anaesthetised first, and since it seems difficult to imagine a woman tamely allowing a man who is facing her, quite possibly a stranger, to put an ether mask over her face, it seems possible that in each case the victim was surprised by someone who came up behind her."

"In at least two of the cases, numbers one and three, we cannot be sure that they were killed where they were found. Their bodies lay undiscovered for some time in fairly remote spots and Forensics were inconclusive on the point. However, if we can't be sure of "where," we can be pretty sure of "what." In each case the nature of the attack seems to have followed the same pattern. First the victim was chloroformed and presumably rendered unconscious. Then she was raped by someone who took the trouble to stop and put a condom on first, following which she was hit violently on the top or back of the head with a heavy blunt instrument, which we are assuming may be something like a hammer."

"Now, let me see," Collison interjected, riffling through the notes he had taken earlier that morning, "victim number one would be Amy Grant, found in privately owned woodland near High Wycombe, and victim number three was Joyce Mteki, found in a conduit on Hackney marshes."

"Exactly, sir," Metcalfe confirmed. "Victim number two was Jenny Hillyer, found, almost immediately we think, at Moat Mount near Apex Corner, which is also open space, while victim number four was Tracy Redman, found by the railway near Paddington. All four had been raped and killed in exactly the same way."

"Similarities?" queried Collison. "Points of interest? Connections between the victims?"

"Other than the MO, sir, the victims seem to have little in common apart from the fact that they were all female and all presumably out on their own when they were attacked. All reasonably young, between eighteen and thirty-eight, anyway."

"One point of interest there perhaps, sir," ventured DC Willis diffidently.

"Go on," Collison said, looking at her encouragingly.

"Well, sexual killers often target prostitutes. Partly perhaps because they are so much easier to trap and kill, having to put themselves into positions of extreme danger every time they go on the street. But also sometimes because they kill from warped religious or sexual impulses, and deliberately target prostitutes either because they see them as figures of evil, or as examples of projected female sexuality which can be used, for example, to take revenge for real or imagined sexual slights in the past."

There were a few smiles and fidgets at this point, even a few murmurs. Analysis of the case within the team was usually succinct and colloquial, while Willis sounded as if she was reading from a book. Collison felt the ripple of amusement and moved to quell it. He swivelled and stared ostentatiously at Detective Sergeant Andrews, who stopped muttering to his neighbour just too late to escape detection.

"Do you have something you would like to contribute?" he asked. It was a heavily contrived moment, he acknowledged to himself, but he knew it was necessary to stamp his authority on this team—Allen's team—straight away. He held Andrews's gaze and forced him to look down.

"No, sir," he admitted.

Collison turned back again to face Willis. "In this case, only one of the victims so far has been a prostitute, at least as far as we know," he said.

"Exactly, sir, Tracy Redman, who incidentally lived out in Essex but came into London and mostly worked around Paddington station. And even with her, we don't whether she was targeted because she was a sex-worker, or just because she was handy."

"Good point," acknowledged Collison. "Well done." He wished he knew her name but resolved to find it out afterwards; it seemed she was one of the brighter members of the team.

"And just to remind ourselves," he continued, looking down at his notes again, "Amy Grant was a student at Birmingham University whom we believe, but have never been able to establish for sure, was hitch-hiking her way back from a weekend in London. Jenny Hillyer was a secretary who shared a flat with some girlfriends in West Hampstead. Joyce Mteki was a nurse at a hospital in Shoreditch and lived in a nurse's hostel in Dalston, while Kathy Barker was a housewife who lived right here in Hampstead."

"So, no apparent connections, sir," Metcalfe pointed out. "Not even physically. One victim was black, the others Caucasian. Of them, one was blonde, the others brunette."

"What does that suggest?" Collison mused aloud, gazing around the room. "A random killer perhaps? An opportunist, who seizes his chance when he sees it?"

"If so," Karen Willis said, picking up the thread of his thoughts, "then he must carry his kit around with him."

"It would seem so," Collison agreed. "Normal people don't wander around with a bottle of chloroform and a pad of cotton wool concealed about their person, not to mention a hammer."

"Which suggests a car, or at least some kind of vehicle," Metcalfe conjectured. "A delivery driver perhaps, or a patrol vehicle—maybe a breakdown mechanic or a security guard?"

"All avenues worth considering," Collison agreed. "Now, what else strikes us as peculiar or significant?"

He looked around the room again. This was starting to assume the cosy atmosphere of a university tutorial, he thought.

"The condoms," Metcalfe said. "How many rapists wear a condom? It's weird."

"Unusual, certainly," Collison agreed. "Surely rape is an act of violence, often intended by the attacker to humiliate the victim by way of revenge for some actual or imagined slight, as we heard." He nodded in Willis's direction. "Doesn't that suggest that the sensation of ejaculating into the victim, of forcing her against her will to be invaded by the attacker's bodily fluids, with consequent terror of pregnancy or infection, might be part of the whole sensation of revenge? An essential part, perhaps, without which the revenge would not be complete?"

There was a silence around the room. It was clear that this was a level of discussion to which they were unaccustomed. Metcalfe looked thoughtful, but Collison was not surprised that it was Willis who answered.

"I've been wondering about that myself, sir," she said. "With your permission, I'd like to do some research on the point."

"Agreed," he said. "In fact, I think it's essential. Give whatever else you are doing to other members of the team. DI Metcalfe can juggle assignments as necessary."

Metcalfe nodded as he jotted notes down on a pad. Then he looked up and said, "Then there's the absence of underwear, of course."

"Yes," Collison agreed. "Though that's not *so* unusual, is it? What do we think about that, people?"

"We've been assuming that they're taken as trophies, sir," said Metcalfe, a trifle uncertainly.

"A sound assumption, I think, Bob. Sound enough to proceed with, at least, unless or until we know different. It's quite common for serial killers to take a trophy—often much more gruesome than a pair of knickers."

"Makes life easier for us, anyhow, sir," said Andrews, making his first contribution to the discussion. "Find the missing knickers and we find our killer."

"True, Sergeant," Collison acknowledged, "though not precisely accurate. We can use the knickers to *identify* the killer. We have to find him first, and we can't go around stopping male members of the public and asking them to turn out their pockets in the hope of finding several items of unwashed ladies' underwear."

A telephone rang abruptly on Priya Desai's desk and she answered it self-consciously. She listened for a moment and then said, "Hold on, please." Covering the mouthpiece with her hand, she spoke to Collison. "Excuse me, sir. Dr Williams would like to brief you on his forensic examination. Any time this morning, he says."

"How far away is it?" asked Collison.

"About twenty minutes by car, sir."

"OK, tell him I'll be there in thirty minutes."

He walked up to the board, which took up most of the front of the room. It was horribly cluttered, with many scribbled notes, most of which had subsequently been ticked or crossed out. Only the photos of the victims had survived more or less unscathed. He looked across at Metcalfe.

"Bob, let's make a fresh start here. Please detail someone to photograph this so we have a record of it, and then clear everything except the victims' photos and personal details. I'll leave you to organise today's assignments, and I'll meet you downstairs in ten minutes. You'd better come with me to the pathologist."

"Very good, sir." Metcalfe hated to admit it, but already there was a new atmosphere about the investigation. He was beginning to see why the ACC should have wanted a fresh mind in charge. That reminded him that he needed to speak to Collison about Tom Allen.

"OK folks," he called out as Collison left the room. "Listen up, please."

Chapter Three

"Now tell me," Collison said to Metcalfe, "provided you don't mind talking and driving at the same time. Who was that female officer who spoke up in the meeting?"

"Karen Willis, sir, Detective Constable. Joined the team a few weeks ago, so I'm only just getting to know her."

"Lucky you!" opined the Superintendent. "I bet half the male coppers at Hampstead nick are trying to get to know her as well."

An uneasy laugh came from the driving seat. Without knowing it, Collison had touched upon a sensitive subject; Metcalfe had been struggling to think about anything other than DC Willis ever since he had first met her.

"Actually, I'm pretty certain she's got a boyfriend," he said ruefully.

"Ah, well," replied Collison with all the insouciance of a happily married man. "Attractiveness aside, she seems pretty switched on."

"She's very bright, yes," Metcalfe agreed. "Degree in law, like yourself, and then went on to do some sort of post-graduate thing in psychology, I think."

Collison looked across in surprise. "You been looking me up?"

Metcalfe smiled. "Just a bit of essential background, you might say."

Collison could feel them both relaxing and realised that they were going to enjoy each other's company. That was good. On a murder enquiry you could end up spending a lot of time together.

"What about the rest of the team, Bob? Personal assessment. Confidential."

"Well, the only other permanent members are DC Desai and DS Andrews. You met them this morning. They've both been on the case from the beginning, so you have to make a few allowances for that. It's been tough."

"Agreed. But still...?"

"Priya is bright too. Not as bright as Karen, maybe, but when she says something, which isn't often, mind, it's worth listening to. She's hardworking and has great attention to detail. Personality-wise she's maybe a bit introverted—needs to come out of her shell a bit. But she's still young and I'm sure she'll develop."

"And Andrews?"

"Ken's a traditional police officer," Metcalfe replied evenly.

"Now why do I feel you're suddenly choosing your words carefully?"

"I *am* choosing them carefully," Metcalfe said, "precisely because I don't want to be misunderstood. Ken's a perfectly sound copper, but he's forty-odd years old and he's still a Detective Sergeant. Even he's worked out that he's not going any further, and he's not the brightest thing on two legs. Good for routine leg work, but don't expect imagination or flashes of inspiration."

"OK. And the others?"

"The others are really just ships that pass in the night, and that's been part of the trouble. They drift in for a month or two, and then they drift away again as they get re-assigned or go on leave. To be honest, I don't think any of them really fancied being part of a long, drawn-out investigation that's going nowhere. Some of them couldn't wait to get off the team. And that all added to the problems for the guvnor—DCI Allen, I mean."

There was silence in the car while Collison digested this, and Metcalfe realised it might be his best chance of broaching a sensitive subject. "Listen, sir, about Tom Allen. I've got something I should tell you."

"Go on."

"He rang me yesterday to tell me he'd been taken off the case. Asked me to meet him this morning for breakfast on the way to the nick."

"I don't see anything wrong with that," Collison said mildly. "After all, you're friends, aren't you?"

"There's more I'm afraid, guv, or I wouldn't be troubling you with it. Fact is he seems to have taken all this pretty badly. He's insisting that he wants to stay involved with the case, in his own time if necessary. The real point is this, though: he asked me to be his source of information from within the team. Passing on anything we come up with."

"Oh dear," said Collison after a pause. "To which you said no, presumably?"

"Of course," Metcalfe averred. "Plus I decided to log the incident in my diary and report it to you as the officer in charge of the investigation."

"Then you've done exactly as you should have done," said Collison. "Thank you for telling me. I'll put it in my diary as well.

"You know," he went on, "I feel very sorry for Tom. He was damned unlucky to end up in charge of a high profile enquiry, which was stuck for lack of evidence. Once the bloody newspapers started with their fun and games it was inevitable that the Home Secretary would lean on the Commissioner, that he in turn would lean on the ACC, and..." He let the thought trail off.

"The real irony," he continued, "is that he should never really have been in charge in the first place."

"What do you mean, sir?" asked Metcalfe, sounding confused.

"Oh, come on, Bob, a serial killer rates a superintendent, maybe even a DCS. The problem was, of course, that it wasn't apparent that it *was* a serial killer until the second victim turned up. There was apparently some thought at that time of putting a more senior officer in, but the official line was that there was a shortage of experienced case-handlers."

"The official line, sir...?"

"Yes. My theory is that none of the available candidates fancied taking over what was already looking like a difficult case, with the very real possibility of falling flat on their face in the full light of national media coverage, so they all invented good reasons why they couldn't possibly leave what they were already working on. So, like I said, Tom was unlucky. If someone had been put in at that stage he would have continued on the case as second in charge, with a more senior officer over him. As it was, he had to carry the full load himself. I'm only surprise he hasn't cracked up completely under the strain."

"He may have done, guv. At least, I'm worried that he may have done."

"Hm," said Collison. "Have you thought what you'll do if he asks you again?"

"I really don't know. To be honest, I'd welcome your guidance. What do you think I should do?"

"Well, the rules are very clear. You are not allowed to discuss the case with anyone who is not a member of the team. Tom is no longer a member of the team *ergo* you cannot tell him anything about it. I appreciate it's a difficult situation, since you're good friends. Perhaps it's better if you agree not to see each other again until after the case is closed, but really it's a matter for your own personal judgment."

"Suppose he just comes wandering into the incident room, though, or starts hanging around the canteen? The team need to know how to handle the situation, I think."

"I agree." Collison thought for a while. "I think I can handle that. Now he's off the case he's got no official reason to need access to Hampstead nick. After his leave he'll revert to his central posting at Scotland Yard pending reassignment to a new case. I'll speak to IT and get his Hampstead access cancelled. Remind me as soon as we get back, will you?"

Conveniently, they arrived at the mortuary yard at this point, thus drawing the conversation to a close. Brian Williams was waiting for them in the pathology room, which was insulated from the day-to-day business of bodies coming and going by a locked security door.

"Good morning, Doctor," Collison said formally, "we haven't met. I'm Superintendent Simon Collison. I'm standing in for Tom Allen, who's off on leave."

"Pleased to meet you," said Williams. "I didn't know Tom was going on leave. He didn't mention it yesterday."

"No, he wouldn't have done," said Collison awkwardly. "It was all rather sudden."

He wondered whether to go on, but decided that whatever else he said could only possibly make the situation worse.

"I see," said Williams, though he wasn't at all sure that he did. "Ah well, police business, I suppose…"

"Quite," Collison concurred.

"Well, let's get on anyway," said the pathologist, leading them across the room to where Kathy Barker's body was already uncovered.

Although they knew what to expect, both men swallowed hard. Collison, who had seen these things less often, comforted himself as he had on every previous occasion by the reflection that it was very difficult still to think of a body as a person once it had been opened up down the chest and round the head. Much better to regard it simply as a piece of meat, like a side of lamb hanging in a butcher's shop.

"All pretty much as expected," Williams was saying. "Definite signs of bruising around the vagina, consistent with rape and, as with the others, there are traces of a spermicide commonly used in condoms. It seems reasonable to assume that she was raped before death by a man wearing a condom."

"Any thoughts on that, Doctor?" Collison asked. "As to why he does it, I mean?"

"Not my area, dear boy," Williams said briskly, with all the bonhomie pathologists traditionally exhibit when in close proximity to a mutilated body. "You need a psychiatrist for that one."

He pointed with a gloved hand to the face. "Chloroform burns around the mouth and nose consistent with the application of a pad covering both. A few strands of cotton wool in the nostrils seem to confirm that. Again, it's exactly as with the previous victims."

His hand now gestured to the top of the head. "You can't see it now because I had to saw the top of the skull off, but I took plenty of photos for you first: a single deep and jagged wound to the upper part of the back of the head. That's definitely the cause of death."

"Any thoughts on a weapon?" enquired Collison.

"Nothing definite. If I had to conjecture, I'd say a hammer of some sort. Not a big, thick thing like a sledge-hammer. Something smaller perhaps, but used with some considerable force."

Collison digested this. "More force than was necessary, you mean? Necessary to kill her, that is."

Williams looked at him in surprise. "Yes, I suppose so. Why? Is that relevant?"

Collison shrugged. "You never know," he said vaguely.

"Anything else, Brian?" Metcalfe said as a formality, already closing his notebook.

"Oh, yes," said Williams with a positive twinkle in his eye. "There is indeed. Take a look at this." He held up a sealed plastic laboratory packet, which at first glance seemed to be empty. "If you look very carefully, you will observe a few grains of fine, sandy-coloured powder. I found them while rummaging through our victim's pubic hair."

"From the killer?" Metcalfe's eyes lit up.

"I would think it's highly likely, wouldn't you?"

The two policemen exchanged glances. Collison had been on the case for less than twenty-four hours, but he could feel the exultation surging through the other man. A year and a half of dead ends. A year and a half of sitting despondently in the incident room trying to think of anything you may have overlooked. A year and a half of door-to-door enquiries trying to get something, anything, out of people who opened the door grudgingly, who were anxious to close it again as soon as possible, disavowing any knowledge of anything that might ever have happened, anytime, anywhere. A year and a half of misery, of slugging your guts out to no good purpose, of arguing with the girlfriend when you got home because you were two hours late and had forgotten to tell her, and now suddenly the break-through that made it all worthwhile.

Metcalfe was smiling and Collison felt his own spirits lift as well. "So, what is it?"

"We don't know," said Williams carefully.

It took a few moments for this to sink in.

"You don't know?" echoed Metcalfe stupidly. He had the weirdest feeling that he was watching one of those comedy sketches that features a big build-up to get everybody excited, only to deliver a real sucker punch at the end, leaving the fall guy standing there with a dumb expression on his face.

"No," Williams said calmly, and then after a pause, "but we will," and then after a slightly longer one, "hopefully."

"Hopefully," Metcalfe repeated slowly.

"Yes, there's no guarantee of course, but we can usually track something down. It's just a matter of chemical analysis and then trying to find a match for the results. We have a comprehensive database of household and industrial products. I'm sure we can come up with something for you in a few days."

Metcalfe looked down at the corpse. "Let's hope so," he said quietly.

Williams handed him a few pages of notes. "Here's a copy of my official report for your file," he said. "You'll see that the only other point of note is the alcohol level in the blood. Even allowing for the time factor, she must have had a considerable amount to drink earlier in the evening. I reckon she would have been about three times over the limit for driving. There were also indications of the early stages of some liver damage, so it looks like she was an habitual heavy drinker."

Back in the car, Collison was silent for a while. Then he stirred and said, "Do you think we might be missing anything with this latest victim? You saw the husband—what did you think?"

"We're checking his story, of course," Metcalfe replied cautiously. "We're interviewing the sister and also making some discreet enquiries of the neighbours in Lyndhurst Gardens, but it had the ring of truth about it for me. Anyhow, the MO is clearly the same as the others, so it's rather irrelevant, isn't it? We're looking for a serial killer, not a domestic dispute that's got out of hand."

"Agreed," Collison concurred, "but we still need to make sure we've covered all the bases."

"Well, we should have our answers by the end of the day. Priya should be interviewing the sister right now. She got off a night shift at the hospital an hour or two back."

"Good. Then let's have an update meeting before we finish today, and see where we are."

At five in the afternoon the team gathered again in the incident room. As Collison came into the room, Metcalfe slipped a couple of sheets of paper into his hand. Glancing at them, Collison saw that they were briefing notes on the team itself. Each member's photograph was reproduced together with their name, extension number, radio call sign and mobile phone number.

"Thanks, Bob," he said warmly. "That's just what I need."

"Yeah, well, I thought it might come in useful."

Putting the details on the table beside him, Collison addressed the room. "I thought it would be useful to have an update meeting to review what we have learned today," he began. "But before I do that, there is a procedural matter I need to raise."

He paused briefly, thinking of how best to phrase what he had to say.

"I would like to remind you all of the rules regarding the confidentiality of criminal investigations. In particular, I would like to make it clear that, without my express permission, it is absolutely forbidden to discuss any aspect of this investigation with anyone who is not a member of this team. A *current* member, that is."

The stress was deliberate and, looking round the room, it seemed to him that they had got the message. "OK, let's move on. Pathology—Bob?"

He moved to one side to allow Metcalfe to stand before the team.

"The guvnor and I saw the pathologist this morning, as you know," Metcalfe began. He realised with a shock that it already seemed natural to refer to Collison, rather than Allen, in this way. "Same MO as before. Identical in fact. One very interesting new development, however. They found traces of a powder of some kind on the victim's body. It seems probable that it was deposited there, possibly inadvertently, by our killer."

A murmur of sudden excitement ran through the team.

"Yes, this could be the breakthrough we've been waiting for, but let's not get carried away. We don't even know what it is yet. Forensics will let us know as soon as they find out."

He checked the notes he had jotted down before the meeting. "Priya, where are we on the sister?"

"I saw her this morning," Priya confirmed. "I've just done a note which you'll find waiting for you. Basically, she confirms the husband's story in every detail. Kathy had a bit of a drink problem, and it had a tendency to make her aggressive or upset. This in turn led to major tiffs with the doctor. Angie, the sister, says it wasn't pretty to watch. Kathy used to needle him and, when eventually he rose to the bait, she'd start a major shouting match. I got the impression that she and Kathy weren't that close, and that she resented the fact that her sister used her place as a bolt-hole whenever she felt like it."

"What about the sequence of events on the night she went missing?" asked Collison.

"Angie was on duty, so she can't help shed any light on what actually happened. She couldn't confirm whether Kathy had phoned or not, as she isn't allowed to have her mobile switched on when she's working in intensive care, and her home answering machine is on the blink."

"We could check with the phone company," Metcalfe pointed out.

"I already have, sir," replied Desai. The note of reproof was unmistakeable. Collison caught Metcalfe's eye and gave him a wry smile.

"The phone company confirms that Kathy made two calls on her mobile, one at 23.41 and one at 23.43. The first was to Angie's home number, and the second to her mobile. There were no calls to anyone else, by the way. Those were the last she made."

"So, we're no closer to actually tracing her movements," said Collison heavily.

"No, we're not. But Angie did confirm that Kathy had a key to her flat, and it was in her handbag when she was found—I checked. She would have had no reason to go to the flat and then go out again. She could have crashed there for the night."

"It's probable that our victim took a cab," Metcalfe said. "The most likely place at that time of night would have been Haverstock Hill around St Stephen's Church and the Royal Free Hospital. Let's make enquiries. We need to find the driver who picked her up, so we can know exactly when and where he dropped her."

"Yes, let's put that on the list for tomorrow," agreed Collison.

"Neighbours?" asked Metcalfe.

"I managed to speak to three or four who were there during the day," Andrews reported. "You'll all get my note tomorrow, but basically the husband's story checks out. One lady heard a door slamming and a woman shouting sometime after 2300. She remembers, because it woke her up and she looked at the alarm clock beside the bed. She and others also confirm that sort of thing had happened before."

"Anything else?" Collison asked.

"Yes, guv, the condoms," Karen Willis reminded him.

"That was quick," commented Collison approvingly. "What have you got?"

"Nothing that gets us very far, I'm afraid," she said. "Initially I thought it was pretty unusual for a rapist to use a condom. In cases of gang rape in America it seems it's now quite common. Not out of concern for the victim, naturally. Apparently each gang member is afraid of being infected by the others."

"Ironic," Collison commented, "in a nasty sort of way, that is."

"Yes. But even so, I don't want to give the impression that this is a universal trend. In Johannesburg, for example, which is the gang rape capital of the world, rapists typically use no protection at all, even though the proportion of adults who are HIV positive is dramatically higher than in America."

"Also ironic," Collison said, suddenly feeling rather sick. "I suppose."

"Well, general attitudes to condom use are very different in Africa," Willis replied. "Hence the rapid spread of AIDS in the first place. I suppose, if they know they're already HIV positive in the first place then they just don't care."

"Bastards," muttered Desai, looking close to tears.

"OK, let me see if I understand this," Metcalfe broke in hurriedly. "Condoms may or may not be used in cases of gang rape, seemingly dependent largely on geography. But in cases of a single rapist it *does* seem to be pretty unusual."

"So far as I've been able to find out in the course of a few hours trawling the internet and making a few phone calls," Willis qualified. "But I think there may be something more to this."

"I think I agree," Collison said slowly. "After all, I assume nobody is suggesting that we're looking at more than one perpetrator here?"

He looked round the room as people shook their heads.

"There's certainly no indication of that, guv, with any of the victims," Metcalfe said doubtfully. "Why? Do you think we might be missing something?"

"No, not at all," Collison replied. "The profile is that of a single sex killer. But it's important that we ask every possible question, even if we think we already know the answer."

He walked up to the newly cleaned whiteboard and gazed for a moment at the five photographs pinned across the top. Then he picked up the marker pen and wrote:

OPPORTUNIST?
VEHICLE / DRIVER?
RAPE—REVENGE? WHAT FOR?
CONDOMS?
MISSING UNDERWEAR—TROPHIES?
POWDER ON VICTIM #5—WHAT IS IT?
CHLOROFORM—WHY?
MURDER WEAPON—WHAT IS IT?

He turned and stood back so that everyone could see what he had written.

"Anything else?" he asked. "Thoughts? Questions? Issues?"

"Movements of fifth victim," proffered Desai.

"Yes—good," said Collison, writing it down. He waited a few moments for other suggestions, but nothing else was forthcoming, so he put the top on the marker pen deliberately and laid it back in its plastic tray. "Let's all think about these points overnight," he suggested. "Maybe they can help focus where we're going with this. OK, let's leave it there for today. Thank you all for your efforts."

Desai and Andrews promptly sat down at their computers and started typing, Desai determinedly and Andrews with a hint of resignation. Collison had been meaning to ask one or both of them for a private chat in an effort to get to know them, but thought better of it. They clearly had things to do. He turned to Willis instead. "I was wondering if you might be free for a chat, Karen," he said. "Maybe a quick drink in the pub, or something?"

"Thank you," she said straight away. "That would be nice. Not the Flask, though, guv, if you don't mind. I think half the nick go there after work."

"Whatever you like," he said with a smile. The thought of being surrounded by drinking coppers did not appeal to him either. "Where would you suggest?"

"There's the Freemason's Arms just down the road," she replied. "Our lads stopped going there when they took the sawdust off the floor. Or, if you don't mind a bit of a walk, there's the Wells Tavern up in the village. That's a gastro-pub too, but they still do decent bitter, if that's what you're after."

Collison realised that a decent bitter was exactly what he was after. "A walk would be great," he said decidedly. "The Wells it is."

Bob Metcalfe, who had observed this exchange, felt a quick pang as though someone had given his intestines a brief but firm squeeze, coupled with a sudden shortness of breath. It was not until some time later that he was able to admit to himself what had caused it.

Chapter Four

O nce upon a time the Wells Tavern had been a traditional London boozer but it was one of the first pubs in the area to strip out the jukeboxes and fruit machines. Pared back to its original Georgian fabric, it was an undeniably elegant building, with an open plan bar area on the ground floor, and a restaurant above. As Collison and Willis climbed Christchurch Hill it became increasingly grey overhead, so they abandoned any thought of sitting outside. They had just bought their drinks and sat down when it started to rain, gently but persistently, the occasional gust of wind throwing drops against the windows.

Collison glanced round appreciatively. "Lovely place," he said.

"Yes, isn't it?" Karen agreed, as she stowed her bulky handbag beside her chair. "We come here a lot, my boyfriend and I. The restaurant upstairs is good too, though rather pricey. They're open every day of the year, you know. We had Christmas lunch here."

"So you know this area pretty well, then?"

She laughed. "I should do, guv. I only live about fifty yards away."

"Did you grow up around here?"

"Colindale, actually," she said with another laugh. "Not exactly the same thing, is it? No, in fact I couldn't afford to live round here, and nor I suspect could any copper—not one below the rank of commander, anyway. It's my boyfriend's place."

Collison wondered whether to pursue this line of conversation, and decided against it. He took a thoughtful pull at his pint of Adnams. "So you've only just joined the investigation, Karen? Hard luck. I think most of the Met is trying hard not to get involved with this one. A lot of people are saying it has career-ending potential written all over it."

"You're joking, right?"

"Only partly," he conceded.

"Well, I was delighted when I was assigned to the team," she said firmly. "As a matter of fact, I requested it."

"Really? Why?"

"How often do you get the chance to help catch a serial killer? And anyway, I was ready for a change from filing burglary reports and giving the good folk of north-west London reference numbers for their insurance claims."

"I can understand that," Collison remarked. "I've never had to do it myself, but I'd imagine it's pretty soul destroying."

"It is," she said shortly. "Anyhow, I felt I deserved better. I put a lot of hard work into getting my qualifications and I want a chance to use my brain—you know, stretch myself intellectually. This is just the sort of case I want to work on."

"Well, that's good," he said calmly. He felt instinctively that they were going to be friends, though he could understand the effect that she had on Metcalfe. She was not obviously beautiful but there was something about her that seemed to draw men's attention, and hold it. Her dark hair and fine-boned features gave off the suggestion of the classic girl-next-door while also exuding a sassy self-confidence.

"How about you, guv?" she was asking, as he managed, with difficulty, to refocus his thoughts on their conversation. "How did you feel about being assigned to a murder enquiry that's supposed to be going nowhere fast?"

"On one level," he said slowly, "I was assigned by direct order of the ACC. So, since I had no choice in the matter, I suppose I reasoned that I should make the best of it."

He sipped his beer. "On a different level, I've never run a murder enquiry before, and it's something I've always wanted to do."

"And on yet another level?" she asked him, with a hint of a cheeky smile.

"On yet another level, I knew all too well how Tom Allen would feel about being relieved. Whatever anyone says, and unfair though it all undoubtedly is, some people are bound to see it as some sort of implied criticism. Naturally, I found that aspect of it...awkward. I had worked with Tom before, you see, when he was very much the boss. Suddenly here I was, swanning in and taking over, having been promoted over his head. Promoted too quickly, as doubtless he thought."

"Yes," she said quietly. "I can see that must have been difficult."

"It was," he said frankly. "Though I like to think that I handled it more delicately than others might have done. God knows, I tried.

"Not sure if I succeeded though," he added after a while.

She sipped her wine and gazed at him equably. "I'm sure you did your best," she said. "No-one can do more. So did Tom Allen, incidentally."

"I know that," he said quickly. "Nobody respects Tom more than me."

She fiddled with the strap of her bag for a minute and then asked: "Is it all right to talk about the case in here?"

He looked around. They were alone in the bar at present apart from what were almost certainly a couple of estate agents in another corner, and they were clearly much too interested in their own, very loud, conversation to listen to anybody else's.

"Yes, I think so," he said, "as long as we talk quietly and don't mention any names."

"Well, there's an idea I had as soon as I joined the team, after I spent hours and hours reading the files," she said hesitantly. "I mentioned it to DCI Allen, though I felt a bit strange about it, being so new to the team, but he more or less ignored it."

"Try me," Collison said, taking another pull at his beer.

"Well, I feel it even more strongly now, given the way that you are approaching the investigation."

"Feel what?"

"That there must be some sort of important psychological issue lurking here somewhere—maybe even more than one. Now, I've studied psychology a little bit myself, but I've only scratched the surface. What we need is a real expert—that's what I think anyway."

He considered her words carefully. "I think that's an interesting idea. You mean, like a profiler?"

"Yes, I suppose so. I hadn't really thought it through to that extent but, yes, a profiling exercise would make sense."

"To tell the truth," he said, "I had actually begun thinking about something like that myself, though I don't in any way want to detract from it being your idea."

"I don't really care about that. In fact, I'm not sure I want to put myself forward in any way. Some of the team don't really like me as it is."

"That's their problem," said Collison firmly. "It's having ideas like this, and the courage to put them forward, that should mark an officer out for advancement. If others have a problem with that, there's nothing for you to worry about."

She grimaced wryly.

"Don't get me wrong. You should get credit for your ideas, particularly if they lead to a result. However, we need to take into account the possibility that this may *not* work out. It doesn't always, you know. I did quite a lot of reading about profiling a little while ago. And there'll be plenty of folk—the traditionally minded, and those who didn't have the gumption to think of it themselves—all too ready for it to fail, you know. That's human nature for you."

Karen tossed her head, and looked at him with keen determination. "I'll take my chances," she said squarely. "If it's a good idea, it's a good idea. That's all there is to it."

"I was hoping you'd say that," Collison said with a grin. "In that case I'll make sure the record shows that it's down to you. However, there's no guarantee the powers that be will say 'yes.' I don't have to tell you the sort of pressure our budget is under, particularly now that the investigation's been running for eighteen months."

"Actually, that was part of my idea," she said quickly. "I thought it might be difficult to get it authorised officially, but there's a way in which we could get some expertise for nothing."

"I'd like to hear that," Collison remarked sardonically. "How do you plan on getting a professional to give his or her expertise for nothing?"

"It's a little unorthodox, but in this case, the expert is my boyfriend." She could see he seemed a little taken aback, and her expression changed from triumphant to dubious.

"That's what I wanted to ask you, really," she said. "Would it matter if he was connected to somebody on the investigation?"

"I don't know," Collison replied honestly. "I'd have to check. You can't be too careful with the rules, though on the face of it, I can't see why it *should* matter. After all, suppose your boyfriend just happened to be a pathologist who was assigned one of our victims. Would he be required to refuse to perform the post-mortem? I can't believe that he would."

"That's what I was hoping. Apart from anything else, frankly it would be helpful to be able to talk to him about the case. It's very difficult when you go home with stuff whirling around inside your head, knowing you can't share your ideas with anyone until the next morning."

"I know what you mean," Collison admitted. "My wife often accuses me of being distracted in the evening when I'm working on a case, and she's right, though I try to leave my work behind me when I come home. Fortunately for me, she's very good-natured."

"So is Peter," said Karen. "That's his name, by the way, Peter Collins."

"Same as the racing driver."

She looked at him blankly.

"Sorry," he said. "Before your time. Before mine as well, actually. I've just read about him, that's all."

He saw his glass was empty, and got up to go to the bar for a refill. Karen declined, saying she would be drinking wine later over dinner.

"Tell me a little about Peter," he said when he returned. "I'll need some background for my official request. I assume he has the necessary qualifications and experience? Just for the record."

"He's a very intelligent man," she said seriously, "the most intelligent person I've ever met, anyway. He's got three degrees in psychology, including a PhD in criminal behaviour, and he's writing several books, though I'm not sure he's close to finishing any of them. He's interested in so many different things, you see. Quite often he gets a craze for something or other and scours the internet for everything he can find on the subject. Then he decides that the precise book he wants has never actually been written, so he starts writing it himself."

"But?" he queried.

"Before he can finish it, he's usually struck by some fresh craze," she explained resignedly. "Some last longer than others. Medieval history seems to have stuck. So has philosophy. He's been making notes for months now on the Logical Positivists."

"Right," said Collison, feeling that he was in danger of getting rapidly out of his depth, "well, that all seems fine."

He took another sip of beer, hesitated, and then asked: "If it's not prying, how did you meet?"

"He was one of my tutors when I did my criminology diploma, actually. We started going out not long after we met, about six months into the course, which was all a bit awkward, as you can imagine. We had to keep it very quiet until I left."

"Was that difficult?" he asked curiously.

"Horrible!" she said determinedly. "I hated it. I couldn't see how two adults wanting to spend time together could be anything to be ashamed of. I wasn't a child, after all; I'd already done three years at university. But there were all these stupid rules about lecturers not having relationships with students, though in reality of course it happens all the time. I hated having to creep round secretly as if it was some sordid little affair. I used to get quite upset about it."

She smiled at the recollection.

"Why don't you come and meet him now?" she suggested suddenly. "It's only just up the road."

He glanced at his watch and grimaced. "I'd love to, but I can't. We have a deal that I'll always be home by 7.30, unless it's an emergency."

He downed a further gulp of his second beer. "Tell you what, though," he said. "I'll ring the ACC first thing in the morning and ask him personally to sanction bringing Peter on board. My guess is that he'd say 'yes' anyway since he knows he's put me in a bit of a spot, and he seems to like me. And if he doesn't agree straight away, then I'll throw in the added inducement that it's not going to cost the Met a penny. That should do the trick."

"So," he went on, draining what was left of his beer, "why don't you tell Peter that you hope to be able to fix a time for him to come in and see us tomorrow?"

When Peter Collins entered the incident room late the next morning, it was with an air of diffidence, as though he felt he should apologise for being there. Tall, slim and fair, he made a striking figure: he was wearing what looked like a hand-tailored suit of light grey tweed, with an old-fashioned watch chain fastened across the waistcoat. Highly polished brown lace-ups completed the look of a man who was visiting the present as a brief experiment in time travel, but really inhabited the England of forty or fifty years previously.

Collison clapped his hands and called for quiet. "Can I have your attention for a moment please, folks," he said firmly, and waited a few seconds for the hum of conversation to die down. "I'd like to introduce Dr Peter Collins, who has kindly agreed to give us the benefit of his expertise as a psychiatrist. Just for the purposes of full disclosure, I should mention that Peter is Karen Willis's partner. Dr Collins, welcome to the investigation."

Peter blinked at him uncertainly. Then he took a pair of round, tortoiseshell spectacles out of his breast pocket and put them on. "Thank you," he said finally. "I think I should clear one point up, though. I'm not a psychiatrist."

"You're not?" Collison echoed. "But, I thought Karen said—"

"I'm a psychologist, certainly," Peter said. "One who studies psychology. But I'm not a psychiatrist. You have to be a doctor for that—a proper doctor, a doctor of medicine. And they aim to treat people for mental illnesses. I don't do that. I study why people behave as they do—I teach it too, of course."

He noticed that there was a smudge on one lens, and so took his glasses off again and started wiping them absent-mindedly with a clean white handkerchief.

"Though I could have chosen to treat people, you know," he mused. "One can become a chartered psychological therapist. Indeed, the whole thing is really totally unlicensed. There's nothing to stop you just putting a plate up and inviting people to come along and pour out their troubles to you. But somehow that never appealed."

He put his glasses back on and smiled benignly at Collison with a newly focused gaze.

"Not sure why," he went on. "Maybe I disliked the responsibility of having all sorts of good folk depending on me to sort out their problems for them. Maybe I wouldn't want the discipline of keeping regular consultation hours. And anyway, I wouldn't really have had the time. There are so many things which keep me busy, you know."

"Quite," Collison agreed, at a loss as to where this was going.

"Main thing is, I'm not a psychiatrist," Collins emphasised quietly but insistently. "Mustn't call me one, I'm afraid. Very naughty. Criminal offence, and all that, to impersonate a member of the medical profession. Like a policeman, in fact."

Metcalfe's face had borne a curious expression ever since the announcement of Collins as Karen's partner. Now he began to smile, and seemed about to say something. Collison noticed, and threw him a stern glance. "Absolutely," he agreed hastily. "A simple misunderstanding, that's all.

"OK, boys and girls," he said more loudly. "Everyone back to work."

There were quite a few amused faces around the room, which now bent themselves slowly back to their desks. Andrews looked at Desai and raised his eyebrows. She shrugged in reply. Metcalfe noticed that Karen was looking at Peter Collins with a concerned expression, as though worried that he should make the right sort of impression upon the team, and troubled that he had not.

"Now then, Doctor," Collison went on, "let me introduce you to Bob Metcalfe, my right-hand man. He's been on the investigation from the beginning, so anything you want, or need to know, he's the man to ask."

"Pleased to meet you," Metcalfe said formally, shaking hands. Once again he felt that strange feeling briefly in the pit of the stomach, before it disappeared just as quickly.

"How do you do," the other replied. He glanced briefly at Metcalfe and then let his gaze wander over the whiteboard.

"So these are our—um—victims?" he enquired.

"Yes, and we need to bring you up to speed as quickly as possible," Collison said briskly.

"Excuse me, guv," Metcalfe proffered diffidently, "but I thought Dr Collins might find this useful."

He passed across a slim folder. "That's only a summary, of course, it's no substitute for reading through the files, but I thought you'd be interested in particular in the circumstances of each murder, so far as we have been able to piece them together. How the victim was attacked, that sort of thing."

"Great idea, Bob," said Collison warmly.

"Yes indeed," Peter agreed with a sudden smile. "I'm sure that will be very useful, thank you. Thank you very much."

"Perhaps," Collison suggested, "we could direct you to one or two points in particular that we'd like you to think about?"

"Go ahead." Peter perched himself on a table, still gazing at the photographs of each murdered woman at the top of the whiteboard.

"Number one," said Collison, "the killer uses chloroform to subdue his victims: is there any significance in them being unconscious or semi-conscious when he rapes them?

"Number two," he continued, marking them off on his fingers, "what about the use of a condom in each case? Is this at all usual, especially in a rape by a single perpetrator? Might it tell us something useful about our killer?

"Number three, the missing underwear. Is it taken as a trophy, do you think?

"And generally," he wound up, a little lamely, "can you spot any sort of pattern or common thread which runs through these murders connecting them in some way, other than the obvious fact that the MO is the same in each case?"

"Not straight away, of course," Karen broke in, a little anxiously. "Nobody's expecting you to shoot from the hip, Peter. Least of all Mr Collison, I'm sure." She glanced at him for confirmation.

"Absolutely!" he agreed. "The last thing we want is a snap impression. Ask us for anything you like, study the material, and then let us know when and if you have any tentative conclusions you'd like to share, OK?"

"There you are, Peter," Karen said, making sure that he was not about to leave the folder behind. "Now, is there anything you need?"

"Yes, please. I'd like a map of Greater London."

"I'll see what I can do," she responded with a smile. "Why don't you wait downstairs while I get it?"

As they left the room, Collison buttonholed Metcalfe. "Bob, any luck tracing that cab driver?"

"Not so far, guv. We've tried all the radio cab dispatchers, but nobody has any record of a call coming in for Wood Green from the Hampstead area any time after about six. We're working our way through the list of individual black-cab drivers, but it's a long job. We could use some more bodies, ideally."

"I'll see if I can charm a few from uniform just for one shift," said Collison dubiously, "though heaven knows they've already done more for us than we have a right to expect. They're just as stretched as we are."

"I can ask for volunteers to put in some overtime this evening," Metcalfe suggested.

Collison hesitated. On the one hand, he was conscious that the team had already put in a lot of overtime over the past eighteen months. This was undesirable for two reasons. First, they were clearly jaded, and tired people make mistakes. Second, the ACC had told him, and none too subtly, that concern was already being expressed in high quarters about the impact the spiralling costs of this case were having on the overall CID budget. On the other hand, it was vital that they find the cab driver fast, before the trail went completely cold.

"Alright," he said at last, "but use your discretion. I'd rather it was some of our short-term brethren. You old lags are knackered enough already."

"OK, sir, if you say so." Metcalfe sounded uneasy.

"Something on your mind, Bob?"

"Nothing specific. It's just that there are some I'm not sure we should trust with anything too important, if you know what I mean."

"Then use your discretion, like I said. And as for you, Bob, you'll leave at 5.30 this evening and try not to even think about the case again until tomorrow morning—that's an order. We'll none of us be any use if we're exhausted."

❊ ❊ ❊

An hour or two earlier that same morning, Tom Allen was standing by the cab drivers' cabin on Haverstock Hill, sipping cautiously a mug of tea which was scalding hot and composed of roughly equal parts sugar and tannic acid. His stomach, troubled by the effects of too many beers the night before, rebelled at the prospect and attempted to engage his gag reflex, so he put the mug down and stared hard at the chipped counter while he waited for the moment to pass. Apart from anything else, Len had insisted it was on the house, so he could hardly leave it.

"What brings you out of the nice warm cop shop then, Chief Inspector?" Len asked cheerfully. "Business, is it?"

"'Fraid so, Len," Allen replied. "Looking for a cabbie who picked up a lady somewhere round Lyndhurst Gardens—probably here or hereabouts—shortly after 11.30 two nights ago, and took her over Wood Green way. Pass the word, would you? Here's my card with my mobile number should anyone remember anything."

"Right you are, Mr. Allen. Always happy to be of assistance, you know me. I'll put it up here on the board here, to remind me to ask."

He slipped the card behind an elastic band wrapped around a piece of cardboard, which was in turn pinned above the tea urn.

"'Ere," he said suddenly as he turned back, "it's not that poor girl 'oo was done in, is it?"

"'Fraid so, Len," Allen said again. "Make sure you pass the word, will you? It's important."

He turned his head aside and sneezed loudly.

"That's a nasty cold you've got there," Len said sympathetically.

"Yes, I know—can't shake the damned thing," Allen replied, blowing his nose vigorously.

"You work too 'ard, Chief Inspector, that's your trouble. Spot of leave, that's what you need. Nice long 'oliday. On a beach somewhere, maybe."

Allen grunted, and managed to tip most of his tea away on the pavement without Len noticing. He swallowed the remaining contents, hoping that the mug would hide his grimace.

"Got to go, Len," he said. "Thanks for the tea."

"Back to the nick, is it?" Len asked as he dunked the empty mug in a bowl of soapy water.

"St John's Wood," Allen replied with a shake of his head. "Next cabbies' hut on my list."

"Nice one, that," Len purred appreciatively. "One of the original nineteenth-century shelters. Listed building now, you know."

Chapter Five

The next day was an unproductive and therefore depressing one. At the wrap-up meeting at the end of the day, which Collison had now instituted as routine, there was little new to report. There were still no firm reported sightings of Kathy Barker on the night of her murder. Nor had they found the driver of the cab which they felt sure must have picked her up. There was nothing new from Forensics, and nobody had called in response to any of the cards which the door-to-door team had pressed into reluctant hands "just in case you remember anything later, no matter how unimportant it may seem." As Metcalfe went round the room, the response "Nothing to report" began to sound like a ritual incantation.

It was a Friday, and Collison had decided that he did not want anybody working over the weekend. He wanted the team, the whole team, to stay as fresh as possible.

"That includes you, Bob. For God's sake take a proper break from the case, even if only for a couple of days."

"Understood, guv," Metcalfe replied dutifully, but they both knew he would probably be sneaking guiltily into the station.

It wasn't that he didn't have a life of his own, he told himself as he pushed a trolley round Sainsbury's on Saturday morning, wondering vaguely, as he did every time, whether he might encounter Karen Willis similarly engaged. However, by the time he had put two washes on, one white and one coloured, quickly vacuumed the carpet, and then done the ironing in front of the television, he was beginning to wonder.

It was not yet 9 p.m. on a Saturday night and he knew that he should have been out socialising—but where, and with whom? He didn't fancy a solitary pint in the pub; it might force him to recognise himself for the sad loner that he had undoubtedly become. "Face it," he thought as he brooded over a TV dinner for one, for which his appetite seemed to have disappeared even while he was heating it up, "you don't have a girlfriend, you don't have a hobby apart from the occasional gym session, and you don't even have any mates."

It would have been convenient to blame the investigation. Certainly for the last eighteen months he had genuinely had little free time, often working evenings and weekends; his neighbours had finally complained after he had run the washing machine in the middle of the night once too often. When Tom Allen's faltering relationship had finally given up the ghost, he had been sympathetic; he had reason to be. His own on-again, off-again romance with an air stewardess he had met through an old flame a couple of years back had already preceded it round the U-bend of oblivion.

He fiddled with his food rather than ate it, and drank his way through a bottle of wine. Finally he fell asleep in front of the television, waking at about 5 a.m. with a sour taste in his mouth. Rather than going to bed and trying to sleep some more, he decided to put on his running kit and go for a long jog.

From his studio flat in Golders Green, it was a long, slow pull up the hill, past the Old Bull and Bush and on to Jack Straw's Castle. He deliberately took this as his route, however, relishing the challenge of whether he could make it to the top without pausing. The pain in his legs and the tightness in his chest were a welcome distraction as well as a reminder that he was not spending nearly enough time in the gym. As he fought his way up the last stretch it was a real struggle to keep going, the sweat streaming down his forehead and into his eyes. Finally, mercifully, it levelled off and he slowed to a walk as he waited for the pounding of his heart to subside. He took his pulse, and when it fell back below 150 he set off again, much more easily this time, as the road started to drop downhill into Hampstead. Almost without thinking, it seemed his feet were taking him towards the police station.

This was sad, he thought, *really* sad, and he forced himself to carry on down the hill towards Belsize Park. He could turn down Pond Street and loop back up East Heath Road to Jack Straw's Castle again. He trotted doggedly past the taxi drivers' cafe, down to the traffic lights by St Stephen's Church. An onlooker would have seen him suddenly run three times in a tight little circle at this point, then jog back to the cafe, which naturally was closed so early on a Sunday morning, gaze at it for a few moments and then turn to resume his planned route.

During his three revolutions on the pavement, he was in fact cursing himself fluently and unforgivingly under his breath. While marking time, he was looking for the cafe's opening hours. Noticing that it would now be closed until the next morning caused him to curse some more. Why hadn't he thought of it before? It was so obvious. As he resumed his run, he made a mental note to be there when the cafe opened on Monday.

He had found his rhythm now, and his stamina, had found a pace at which he felt he could jog, albeit slowly, almost forever if need be. The long drag back up the hill past the Vale of Health seemed to clear the fuzziness from his head, though the unpleasant taste remained. The long descent from Jack Straw's Castle came as a well-earned reward, carrying him easily back to the door of his building, which was tucked away in a service yard behind some shops—exactly, he noted automatically, like the one in which Kathy Barker had met her killer a few days previously.

Even after a shower, a shave and a cup of coffee it was still only 9.30 a.m. He tried to read the Sunday paper he had bought, but found himself staring blankly at the page, thinking of nothing in particular. He had to face facts. The investigation had taken over his life. Without it, he had nothing on which to focus. Was that why he had become obsessed with Karen Willis. Obsessed? He forced himself to try to consider the situation as dispassionately as possible.

Surely not 'obsessed.' He had come across one or two stalkers in his professional capacity and knew what it was to be truly obsessed with someone. 'Infatuated' perhaps? That might describe it more accurately. He thought about her frequently, found her disturbingly attractive, and had the utmost difficulty, try as he might, in discerning anything about her that was less than perfect.

Yet 'infatuated' sounded wrong as well—too juvenile, somehow, like a schoolboy crush. He was thirty-two years old, not sixteen. Then again, he could not remember feeling like this about anyone before. His air stewardess had been a good friend to have a drink and a meal with, a convenient squeeze when he needed sex, and someone pleasant to wake up next to in the morning, but he could not summon up any emotion for her which ran any more deeply than that. Nor, he was forced to admit, for any previous girlfriend.

"This is pointless, anyway," he told himself. "The woman has a boyfriend, after all." Yes, now Peter—what was he to make of him? He seemed so—well—strange, and yet she was clearly deeply attached to him. What drew a woman like Karen to a man like Peter? He realized he was still stuck on the same page of the newspaper and stood up abruptly. For a while, he gazed out of the window; Golders Green was quiet at this time on a Sunday morning. Then, as he had known would happen sooner or later, he found himself heading out towards the tube station for the one stop journey to Hampstead. Had it not been starting to drizzle slightly he would have taken the bus; it seemed silly to travel only one station, even though, like all Metropolitan police officers, he went free of charge.

As he wandered down Hampstead High Street he was startled to see Tom Allen coming in the opposite direction.

"I've just been looking for you," he began without preamble. "I thought you'd be at the nick...?"

It was a question, but sounded close to an accusation.

"I do get weekends off, you know," Metcalfe replied defensively.

"Oh come on, Bob, when did you take a weekend off since we started on this case? There's a killer out there somewhere, and every day that we don't catch him is another day he's free to kill some other poor cow."

Metcalfe winced slightly; Allen had a way of expressing himself that was all his own. He looked around for somewhere they could sit down. A coffee shop was just opening up across the road. "Come on, why don't we have a coffee? It'll be nicer than the inside of a cop shop on a Sunday morning."

"All right," Allen said grudgingly.

"And that's another thing," he said as they crossed the High Street, "why can't I get into the nick? My swipe card won't work."

"Well," Metcalfe replied carefully as they sat down. "That's just standard procedure, isn't it? You're not attached to Hampstead anymore, so I expect IT automatically cancelled your access."

"Hm." Allen sounded unconvinced.

There was a break while they ordered coffee.

"And why would you be trying to get into the nick anyway?" Metcalfe asked innocently. "You are on leave, after all."

Allen snorted. "Leave? Do me a favour! I told you, I want to catch this nutter, whether it's official or unofficial."

Metcalfe sighed. "You know the rules as well as I do. I can't discuss the case with anyone who's not on the team. DS Collison has made that a specific order, by the way."

"Charming," commented Allen sarcastically. Yet, thought Metcalfe, he did not seem as upset as he might be. On the contrary, he seemed almost to be suppressing a smile.

"That's charming that is," he reiterated, "considering I've found your taxi driver for you."

Metcalfe gaped. "Our taxi driver...?" he echoed stupidly.

"That's right," Allen said briskly. "The black-cab driver who picked up the victim from Haverstock Hill and deposited her in Wood Green shortly before her death. I assume you *are* looking for him, aren't you?"

"Of course we are," Metcalfe replied uncertainly, "we've been phoning around for a couple of days. But how did you...?"

"Easy enough," came the airy response. "I asked around at a few cabbies' caffs and shelters. Nothing to it really. Just good old-fashioned police work."

"Damn!" muttered Metcalfe in intense irritation. "I should have thought of that. It only occurred to me an hour or two back when I jogged past the cafe down the road."

"Yes, I daresay." Allen was clearly relishing his moral superiority. "It's probably all that sitting around in front of a computer all day. Addles the brain, I daresay. You should get out in the fresh air more often, Bob, ask a few questions. That's what we used to do all the time in CID, you know."

"All right, all right." Metcalfe threw his hands up in surrender and very nearly knocked over the two cups of coffee that were just arriving at their table. He broke off and waited as the Polish waitress, who had leaned back expertly to avoid his flailing arms, put their drinks down and departed with a playful backward glance.

They watched her retreating figure and it was Tom Allen who voiced what they were both thinking. "Nice, eh?"

"Very nice indeed," Metcalfe agreed. It was perhaps progress of a sort that he could admire a woman other than Karen, but he found it difficult to whip up any real enthusiasm. He was still reeling from Allen's news. "So who is he, and how do I contact him?"

"Easiest thing in the world," Allen said, taking a rather crumpled betting slip out of his raincoat pocket and pushing it across the table.

Metcalfe stared at it blankly.

"Sorry," Allen apologised. "It's the only thing I had handy when the call came through. The name and phone number are written on the other side. Some bloke who lives in Kentish Town. Was just on his way home, but agreed to do one last trip as long as it kept him in North London. I'll leave you to take the details."

"Thank you very much." Having smoothed it flat, Metcalfe snapped the piece of paper carefully underneath the band securing his notebook.

"Now then," said Allen briskly, "tell me about the forensic report."

Metcalfe sat up straight. "Sorry," he said stiffly. "No can do."

"What do you mean? Fair exchange is no robbery. I've given you some information you wanted. The least you can do is return the favour."

"Sorry," Metcalfe said again. "It doesn't work like that. You know the rules. I can't discuss the case with someone who isn't a current member of the team."

Allen stared hard at him. "How long have we known each other, Bob?"

"Don't do that," Metcalfe responded. "Just don't, all right? You know the rules as well as I do. There's nothing I can do about it."

He stared back at Allen. "Look, guv," he went on more gently. "Why not just give it up? Go on leave, like they want you to. Properly on leave, not hanging round Hampstead like a ghost or something."

"A pretty useful ghost, wouldn't you say?" Allen said with a sour smile.

"I'm very grateful to you for what you've done. That goes without saying. I'm sure we all are. But you're off the case now. Please just accept it and move on—for your own sake."

Allen looked off into the distance for a moment and seemed to relax a little.

"I know you have my best interests at heart, Bob," he said quietly, "but I can't let this go. There's a nutter out there somewhere who's been getting the better of me for a long time. I can't have that. I can't let him beat me."

"When we get him, and we *will* get him, it'll be largely down to you and all the work you've already put in on the investigation. I'm sure DS Collison will give you credit for that. He's a big admirer of yours, you know."

"Is he now?" Allen drank some coffee and seemed to be getting ready to go, or maybe he was just shifting his weight in his chair. Abruptly he shifted it back again. "I hear you're getting a profiler," he said innocently.

Again his companion could only gape in astonishment. "How the hell do you know that?"

Allen ignored the question. "So it's true, then?"

"I'm not going to comment one way or the other," Metcalfe said primly, feeling suddenly like a politician who has been put on the spot by an unexpected question during a live interview.

"Oh—'I can neither confirm or deny,' is it?" Allen was obviously thinking along similar lines. "I know they give you lessons in PR in the Met these days, Bob. I think yours are paying off."

Metcalfe made up his mind and stood up, putting a five-pound note on the table as he did so.

"I'm ending this conversation right now," he said. "There's only one way you could possibly know what you've just mentioned, and that's from a member of the team."

Allen said nothing, but looked mutinous.

"You must realise, guv, that I'm going to have to report this conversation to DS Collison, that you could be causing huge problems for whoever your source is, maybe even ending their career?"

Another thought struck him, with anger. "And that I'm going to be the prime suspect?"

"Oh, come on, Bob," Allen began, but Metcalfe cut him off.

"No," he said simply.

They looked at each other for a moment, a long moment in which, and they both felt it, something died between them.

"Please don't contact me again," Metcalfe said quietly, hoping that the tremble that he felt did not show in his voice. "Not until after the case is over, anyway."

He walked away down the hill towards the pedestrian crossing. He didn't look back.

Metcalfe was surprised to find the incident room empty when he walked in. There was supposed to be one officer there at all times over the weekend to field telephone calls. Puzzled, he rang the front desk.

"DI Metcalfe," he said curtly when they answered. "Who's supposed to be on duty in the incident room? I've just got here and the place is empty."

"PC Wilkinson, sir. If you'll just hang on a minute I'll check to see where he is."

After a while the desk sergeant came on the line. "You looking for Wilkinson, sir? The computer is showing that he swiped in at 0856, and he hasn't swiped out again, so he must be somewhere in the station. I'm sure he'll turn up again in a minute."

"Right then, thanks."

He checked his watch. It was now just after 10.45. He went downstairs to the men's toilets. The stalls were all open and clearly unoccupied. He went into the locker room and then checked the canteen. It was empty apart from two uniforms, one man and one woman. He didn't recognise either of them but he needed to make sure.

"Excuse me disturbing you on your break," he said as they both looked at him, "but have you seen Wilkinson anywhere in the last few minutes?"

They shook their heads.

As he headed back upstairs he caught a glimpse of a blue uniform slipping through the door of the incident room. By the time he came back into the room himself, a face he did recognise, and with which he could dimly associate the name Wilkinson, was sitting at a table next to a phone with an open notebook ready beside him.

"Wilkinson?" asked Metcalfe.

"Yes, sir."

"Where the hell have you been? You're supposed to be on duty in here."

"So I am, sir," the constable replied uneasily. "I just had to nip down to the bog for a minute."

"Strange, that," Metcalfe said sarcastically. "I just checked down there and there was no sign of you. And we didn't pass on the stairs either."

He waited for a response, but none was forthcoming. Suddenly he felt all the pent-up rage within him swell and burst out. Rage at Tom Allen for being stupid and risking both their careers. Rage at the team for not being able to find the killer. Rage with this idiot for jeopardising the investigation should an important call have come through while he was skiving. Even as he felt his face flush he knew that a lot of this rage was actually targeted at himself, but that realisation did not calm him. Rather, it shamed him and made him all the angrier.

"Don't play the bloody fool with me!" he shouted abruptly, loudly, much more loudly than he had intended and more loudly perhaps than he had believed himself capable of shouting. "I know exactly what's been going on."

He took a deep breath and continued, more quietly but still with an intense anger. "You slipped out through the door into the reception area without swiping your card, and then after you'd been for your coffee or whatever it was, you got your mate on the desk to let you back in again through the same door. That way it looks on the system as though you've never left the building."

Wilkinson's silence was as eloquent as a confession.

"Well, I have news for you," Metcalfe went on. "This is a murder enquiry, sonny, and when you are in sole charge of manning the phones, that is what you do. You do *not* slip out whenever you like just because it happens to be a Sunday morning and you don't think anyone from CID is going to be here."

"I'm very sorry, sir," Wilkinson said at last. "It won't happen again."

"Too bloody right, it won't." Metcalfe picked up the phone again and, when the constable answered, asked for the desk sergeant to come up to the incident room immediately.

"Sergeant," he said when the man arrived. "At the end of this shift you will place PC Wilkinson on a disciplinary charge of being absent from duty without permission."

"Yes, sir," said the sergeant woodenly. He was glaring at Wilkinson but Metcalfe knew that this was at least as much due to him letting the side down by getting caught as to him having been swanning around in Hampstead when he was officially on duty in the station. Uniform stuck up for each other, and could usually get away with something like this. They would view it as unfortunate that Metcalfe had come into work at that time on a Sunday morning; the luck of the draw.

The sergeant stood and looked at him, though whether waiting for him to say something else or not Metcalfe was unsure.

"That's all, Sergeant," he said calmly.

He waited for him to leave, and then pulled the crumpled betting slip out of his pocket. The taxi driver was apparently called Ronnie Hazel. He ran the telephone number through the police database and found that it was indeed registered to a "Hazel, R." at an address in Kentish Town. He cross-checked the name against Criminal Records, and came up blank. "Of course," he told himself, "if he'd had any form he wouldn't have been accepted as a black-cab driver."

He rang the number and after some time it was answered, somewhat drowsily, by a woman. She seemed unimpressed when she heard who was calling, saying only that Ronnie was out in the cab. He arranged for him to call in at the station at 11 a.m. the next morning, stressing that this was urgent and part of a murder investigation. He rang off feeling strangely unfulfilled and more than a little anxious.

It wasn't that Hazel might prove uncooperative. The Metropolitan police effectively acted as the licensing authority for London's black cabs through the Hackney Carriage office at New Scotland Yard. Unsurprisingly, therefore, they usually took every possible step to remain on good terms with 'the law.' But he was far from convinced that his interlocutor had fully appreciated what he was saying, or even that she would remember to pass the message on, despite him having asked her to be sure to write it down.

He sat gazing into space rather moodily, wondering what to do next. He had been intending to spend the rest of the day ploughing through the phone lists of taxi drivers, but obviously that would no longer be necessary. He found himself wondering what Karen might be doing right now. Preparing lunch, perhaps?

He uttered a sigh of exasperation at being unable to discipline his thoughts sufficiently to keep her out of them. Then he realised that Wilkinson might think this was some further criticism aimed at him. He looked round, but the constable was staring fixedly into a computer screen and ignored him.

Without any clear idea of where he was going, he stood up and went downstairs. His life seemed to be falling into a pattern of random wanderings whenever he was not at work. He would decide on a destination, but no sooner would he get there than restlessness would overtake him once more, coupled with an intense irritation at his own feebleness of purpose. What was wrong with him?

He stopped in the downstairs reception area and turned to face the desk sergeant, who looked back at him impassively.

"About Wilkinson," he said.

"Yes, sir?"

"You can forget the charge."

"Thank you, sir," said the sergeant, visibly relaxing. "I'm sure it'll be much appreciated."

Then, as the door closed behind him, he turned and stuck his head back through into the police station.

"But give him a bloody good bollocking," he said viciously.

Chapter Six

Metcalfe buttonholed Collison as soon as the latter arrived on Monday morning. "Sir," he said urgently, "I need a word in private."

"In here," replied the other, leading them both into an empty office.

Metcalfe shut the door behind him. "I almost phoned you at home about this yesterday, but in the end I decided not to disturb you. I hope I did the right thing."

"Well," Collison said calmly. "Once you tell me, doubtless I'll be able to venture an opinion."

"Sorry," said Metcalfe quickly, "it's about Tom Allen, well partly, anyway."

"Go on."

"I ran into him yesterday morning, here in Hampstead. I was on the way in to work, actually. I know you said not to—" He broke off and looked guiltily at the Superintendent.

"Don't worry about that," Collison reassured him. "Just tell me whatever it is I need to know."

"Well, it's good news, bad news, really, sir."

Collison raised his eyebrows.

"Let me tell you the good news straight away. The taxi driver has been identified and will hopefully be here for an interview in a couple of hours."

"Why, that's not *good* news at all, Bob," Collison said with delight. "It's *great* news—well done."

"Ah," said Metcalfe unhappily, "not exactly. You see it wasn't me who found him—it was Tom Allen."

Collison looked dumbfounded. "How did that happen?"

"My fault, I'm afraid. He did exactly what I should have thought to do."

"Which was what, exactly?"

"Spread the word in the cabbies' caffs and shelters—you know those green huts you see at the side of the road. The stupid thing is that it *did* occur to me, but too late. I jogged past one of their caffs in Belsize Park on Sunday morning and got the idea then, but within a few hours Tom Allen was passing me the name and phone number."

"I don't see how that's your fault at all," said Collison after a moment's reflection. "If you should have thought of it, then so should I. If anything, it just shows what a first class copper Tom is. Here we are taking days to go through phone lists and he beats us to the draw with a bit of good, old-fashioned police work."

"I suppose so," Metcalfe said dubiously.

"Well," said Collison clapping his hands together, "if that's all that's bothering you, Bob, forget about it. We've got a result, that's all that matters. Remember to buy Tom a drink the next time you see him, with my compliments."

"I don't think I will be seeing him for a long time, guv," Metcalfe said, in such a strained tone that Collison stopped and stared at him.

"You see," he went on very deliberately, "Tom Allen knows we've hired a profiler."

Collison's jaw dropped. "But there's only one place that information could have come from…"

"I know. From within the team."

There was silence.

"Don't take this the wrong way, Bob," Collison said finally. "But you're one of Tom's closest friends and colleagues…"

"I know," Metcalfe repeated angrily. "That's why I won't be seeing him for a long time. He's dropped me right in it."

"Only if it was you who told him," Collison replied evenly.

"That's what everyone will think, isn't it?"

Collison looked at him levelly. "Did you tell him?"

"No, I didn't."

"Well," said Collison, "then that defines our problem, doesn't it? We need to find the source of the leak, if we can. We need to make sure that it doesn't happen again. We need to make sure no blame attaches to you.

"But not necessarily in that order," he finished, with a smile.

"You mean you believe me?"

"Of course I believe you. I've no reason not to, and anyway you're far too good a copper to do a stupid thing like that."

"Thank you," Metcalfe said, feeling suddenly close to tears. "Thank you. That's a great relief. I—" He stopped, unable to go on.

"I think on balance you *should* have called me yesterday," his boss said briskly. "At least I could have put your mind at rest about this and saved you some worry."

He patted the other man on the shoulder. "Come on, Bob," he said, "let's go and talk to the troops."

As they went into the incident room it fell quiet. It may have had something to do with the expression on Collison's face.

"Good morning," he said routinely. There was not even a mumbled response. It was obvious that he had a great deal more to say. "I am afraid that I have some grave news," he went on. "It appears that, despite my clear warning to the contrary, a member of this team has breached security and disclosed a key piece of information to an outsider. I am going to give that individual one opportunity, and one opportunity only, to own up. If they do, I will take that into account in deciding how to proceed further."

He stopped, and his gaze swept around the room, looking each person in turn squarely in the eye. "Does anyone wish to tell me anything?" he asked finally. There was no response. "Very well," he continued levelly. "This is now a serious disciplinary matter. It may be that I will ask for an internal enquiry, but enough of that for the moment. DI Metcalfe will give us an update on the case. As you will see, there has been at least one encouraging development. Bob?"

Metcalfe stepped forward. "Good news, everybody. Over the course of the weekend we identified our taxi driver and I hope that he will be with us a little later today for an interview. So that's one thing crossed off our list. As to the rest, we are still waiting for a report from Forensics on the mysterious powder found on our last victim."

"Thank you, Bob," Collison acknowledged. "What about our profiler, Karen? When does Peter think he may have something for us?"

"He's been working on it all weekend, guv," she replied. "I think he'd be happy to come in any time. This afternoon, if you like."

Collison reflected briefly. "Better make it tomorrow morning. If that's convenient for him, of course. With a bit of luck, we may have some leads to follow up from our taxi driver this afternoon."

The bit of luck was not to be forthcoming, however.

When Ronnie Hazel finally put in an appearance, twenty minutes late, he was surly and uncooperative. His answers were, so far as possible, monosyllabic. It was only when prompted with a photograph of Katherine Barker that he grudgingly acknowledged that he remembered her at all. He was hazy both about exactly where he had dropped her off, and when. It was almost as if time itself was an alien concept to him. At last, they were able to agree on a location somewhere on Wood Green High Street at some time around midnight.

Collison and Metcalfe, who had interviewed him together, saw him off the premises with barely concealed irritation and went back to the incident room to report to the team.

"Anything useful, guv?" asked Andrews, speaking for them all.

"Not a thing," Metcalfe replied savagely. "A bloody useless witness. It was almost as if he was wilfully refusing to remember anything."

"Maybe he just doesn't like the police," Karen cut in quietly.

"Whatever the case," Collison said ruefully, "there's not a lot we can do about it. It's not as though he's a suspect, after all."

"Excuse me, guv," Priya Desai said suddenly, "but why not?"

There was total silence as everyone in the room turned to look at her. She looked embarrassed, but determined.

"Explain," Collison asked simply.

"Look at the board, sir." She walked to the front of the room and pointed. "You wrote these words yourself. We think our killer is an opportunist who has a vehicle in which he can carry his murder kit. Well, a taxi is a vehicle. A taxi driver meets a lot of lone women, especially at night, and we know that a taxi driver was the last person to see our fifth victim alive."

Collison stared at her. So did Metcalfe. So did everybody.

"God in heaven, why am I such an idiot?" Collison cried. "Bob, find Hazel and get him back here. If he won't come voluntarily, arrest him on suspicion of murder. And find his bloody cab and get Forensics to go over it molecule by molecule."

"Shall I check for previous convictions?" asked Willis.

"I've already done that," Metcalfe answered. "He's clean so far as CRO's concerned. If he wasn't, he wouldn't have got his cabbie's licence."

"Well done, Bob," Collison said. "At least one of us has got his wits about him. Now, get moving. Priya, can I have a word?"

While Metcalfe was giving orders behind him, he drew her aside. "Priya," he said earnestly, "when this case is over, remind me to have a serious chat with you about what you'd like to do in the force."

"Thank you, sir," she replied with a sudden grin. "I will."

❁ ❁ ❁

When Ronnie Hazel reappeared he was, if anything, even more sullen and uncooperative than before. He was also very angry.

"What the hell's all this about?" he demanded as soon as Collison entered the room. "We've just been through all of this. If you can't bloody well remember what questions to ask, that's not my problem, mate. I've got a living to earn."

"We'll try not to keep you longer than necessary," Collison replied mildly while Metcalfe switched on the tape recorder, "but I'm afraid you're not going to be able to drive your cab for a while anyway. We need to take a look at it."

"Look at it? Why?"

"Evidence. After all, the murdered woman did sit in it, didn't she? She might have dropped something out of her handbag, for example. It happens."

"Nah," said Hazel dismissively. Collison and Metcalfe both looked at him quizzically.

"You seem very sure of that," murmured Collison.

"Course I am. I'd have found it when I cleaned it this morning, wouldn't I?"

"How often do you clean your cab?" asked Metcalfe. "Inside, I mean?"

"As often as it needs it. Every couple of days, I suppose, with a proper steam clean once a month, or thereabouts. Just so happens it was this morning—with the steam, that is."

They both stared at him for a few seconds.

"Do you mean to say," Collison asked grimly, "that you knew we wanted to talk to you about a murdered woman and yet you steam-cleaned your cab, thus destroying any forensic evidence that it might contain?"

"Yeah, what of it?" Hazel was growing more belligerent. "Good job I did, innit? If it's no good to you, I can get back in it and start earning some money, rather than wasting my time here."

"I see you don't properly understand the situation, Mr Hazel," Collison told him calmly. "So far as we can ascertain, you were the last person to see Katherine Barker alive. Earlier today we gave you every opportunity to tell us exactly when and where you last saw her, which you were very reluctant to do. That being the case, I am going to detain you for questioning under caution on suspicion of murder."

Hazel went a bright pink colour and subsided abruptly onto a chair.

"Do you wish to say anything at this stage?" Collison continued, delivering the formal caution they all knew by heart. "You do not have to say anything, but that it may harm your defence if you do not mention, when questioned, something which you later rely on in court. Anything which you do say may be given in evidence."

Hazel made an inarticulate gurgling noise.

"We'll take that as a 'no,' I think," Collison said briskly. "Now let's take you to see the custody sergeant. Then we can come back here and have a proper chat."

It turned out their chat was to be somewhat delayed, however. The custody sergeant took one look at Hazel and promptly asked him if he had any history of heart trouble or high blood pressure. When he nodded in reply, the sergeant took Collison to one side.

"Sorry, sir," he said, "but I don't like the look of him, really I don't. He's got 'heart attack' written all over him. I'd like to call the duty doctor to take a look. Once he okays him for further questioning, you can have him back."

"Fair enough," said the superintendent with a sigh. "But see if you can hurry things up, will you? Coffee, Bob?"

"Why not?"

"Damn," said Collison as they sat down in the canteen. "I didn't want to caution him unless I had to. Now the clock's ticking. I was hoping we could shock him into saying something before he thought to ask for a lawyer."

"Worth a try," Metcalfe said sympathetically. "I'd have done the same myself."

"Yes, but it didn't work. Now we have to justify continuing to hold him, *and* we've got a doctor crawling all over him, *and* he's bound to ask for a brief."

"Worth it anyway," said Metcalfe with a smile. "At least it shut the surly little bugger up. Came as quite a shock, didn't it?"

"Yes," said Collison slowly, "which isn't great. Certainly seemed like the reaction of an innocent man."

"Oh, come on, sir, you had no choice but to go for it. He has a vehicle, he's constantly having chance encounters with lone women late at night, we know that he was the last person to see the Barker woman alive. At the very least we need to check his alibis for the other murders."

"That's all true," Collison agreed, "but maybe he would have given us all that voluntarily anyway."

Metcalfe snorted. "Fat chance! He wasn't exactly bending over backwards to help, was he?"

"I suppose not."

"Anyhow, he's all we've got."

"Yes," Collison concurred grimly. "He's all we've got."

They lapsed into silence.

"Tell you what," said Collison after a few moments. "If we've got to wait to interview Hazel anyway let's go back and check his whereabouts for the other killings with his wife, and let's get Peter Collins in this afternoon instead of tomorrow."

Desai was despatched to interview Mrs Hazel but Collison's frustration grew by the hour. It seemed the custody sergeant was having trouble finding a duty doctor. In response to the suggestion that they should simply call a doctor from the Royal Free Hospital, which was just down the road, he muttered darkly that "It has to be someone on my list."

When Metcalfe brought the afternoon edition of the evening paper into the incident room and laid it down before him with a meaningful expression, his stress levels rocketed some more. Spread across the front page was the headline "Cops detain suspect in hunt for serial killer."

"Oh dear God, no." He groaned involuntarily.

"Sorry, guv," Metcalfe said with feeling. "Looks like we have a real problem here—within the team, I mean."

"Agreed," said Collison quietly, "but short of placing everybody under surveillance and tapping their phone calls, what can we do?"

"Excuse me, sir," Willis cut in, "but Peter is here."

"Great!" said Collison thankfully. "Here's one person I can look to for good news, at least." He stood up and clapped his hands for attention. "Gather round please, everyone," he called. "Let's hear what Dr Collins has to say."

Dr Collins, who was dressed in a sports jacket, a watch chain leading into his breast pocket, looked ill at ease.

"Well, er, hello again everyone," he began uncertainly. "I suppose before we go any further I should stress that what I'm about to say is pure conjecture. Personal conjecture, I mean."

"But based on the facts, surely?" said Collison, with a reassuring smile.

"Based on the facts, certainly," Peter replied cautiously, "but you must bear in mind that any two or three psychologists might come up with two or three different interpretations. This is not a precise science.

"In fact," he continued, warming to his task, "Popper even questioned whether it is really a science at all, you know."

He gazed around the team as if looking to spark a debate. Karen intervened quickly. "Why don't you just give us your views, Peter? I'm sure the guvnor can decide for himself what to make of them."

"All right then." He looked around for somewhere to sit down, ignored the proffered chair and perched instead on the edge of a desk. "First and foremost, our killer is most probably a loner. He either lives alone, or has a job which involves him spending a lot of time on his own, possibly travelling."

"So it could be a driver—a taxi driver maybe—even if he was married?" Metcalfe interjected.

"It's possible," mused Collins, "though I really had in mind something like a travelling salesman, or a long distance lorry driver. I don't think our man has any sort of proper relationship with a woman, and if he doesn't live alone then that situation would be difficult to sustain unless he was away from home for quite lengthy periods."

Collison motioned Metcalfe to hold back and said, "Go on."

"I'm having problems categorising him," Collins said thoughtfully. "The serial killer's motivation usually falls into one of two broad groups: punishment or fantasy friendship. In the first case, the killer believes that women are evil and deserve to be punished. Sometimes this feeling is limited to prostitutes, but in more extreme cases it can extend to all women. Killers of this type can exhibit religious mania, even to the point of claiming to hear God telling them what to do. Yet in everyday life they can behave quite normally."

He crossed his arms and gazed down at his brown brogues, as though focusing his thoughts.

"Killers in the second category often kill almost for company, literally so if they live alone they can keep the body for an extended period, as though it were a sort of houseguest. In this case we may be talking about having sex with the body after death, and constructing some sort of fantasy relationship with it. This element of fantasy may play itself out in the rest of their lives too, perhaps pretending to have had some sort of dramatic and impressive past, or knowing famous people, or having fantasy friends and sexual partners."

"So what's your concern here?" Collinson asked.

"Well, to a certain extent we have elements of both types. The killings appear to be the result of random sightings, which argues for the first type, as does the fact that they were all young women on their own, who either were or could be taken by a disturbed personality to be prostitutes. But that's about as far as it goes. In particular, these killings are quite clinical. Punishment killers usually indulge in frenzied attacks with multiple injuries, and often mutilation of the body as well. There's none of that here."

There was a pause as he scratched his head.

"So you think the second type is more likely?" Karen prompted.

"Perhaps," he admitted. "The taking of an item of clothing, particularly an intimate item such as underwear, could be simply a trophy, but could also suggest that he wants some sort of personal reminder for emotional purposes, just as we might keep a photograph of someone close to us when they die, rather than something to gloat over."

"So, what does this tell us?" Collison asked.

"Not a great deal by itself," Collins conceded, "but there are some special aspects of this particular case, which we need to take into account."

He took a sip out of the cup of tea that Karen had placed beside him. An instinctive grimace was quickly and politely suppressed. Peter Collins was not used to tea of the sort on offer in police incident rooms.

"The two things which exercised me a good deal were the manner of killing and the use of a condom. It seems to me, on reflection, that taken together they may tell us quite a lot.

"First, the victims have all been struck over the head by a heavy instrument, which may be a hammer. He either rapes them first and then kills them, or the other way round, we're not sure which. An initial hammer attack argues for a desire to make absolutely sure that the victim is incapacitated straight away with a single blow. Whether before or after, it shows a desire to get things over with quickly and cleanly.

"What can we make of the hammer blow? Our man is uncertain of his ability to overpower a woman quickly and effectively. Therefore he is likely to be of slight build and below average height. He certainly will not have any background of hard physical work, nor come from the armed services (though he may well brag about some fantasy military background) nor be proficient in any physical activity which involves in some way imposing yourself on someone else—rugby, say, or martial arts. In short, our man is a bit of a weed."

Collison was jotting down notes. "Go on, this is very useful."

"I'm not sure the manner of attack tells us too much, except that it definitely points to these *not* being punishment killings. If so, he would want to keep his victims alive as long as possible, not despatch them cleanly. Also, if he hits them first, it argues even more strongly for him wanting them to be completely help-less when he rapes them. You can't get much more helpless than being dead."

"What if he rapes them first, and then kills them?" Metcalfe enquired.

"Well now, that's where it might get really interesting. If he rapes them first and then kills them immediately afterwards, it could suggest disgust either with what he has just done specifi-cally or with sex generally. That's where we start moving from one category into the other. If that were the case, then we would expect mutilation, but there isn't any. Of course, it may be that by this time his overwhelming instinct is fear of getting caught and he just wants to be off and away as quickly as possible. Perhaps if he ever has more time to linger over a killing, then we *will* see mutilation.

"On balance, though, I incline towards a different direc-tion. The use of a condom is most unusual in a rape of this nature. At first I thought that it could just be symptomatic of a horror of sex generally, but if you accept that, then nothing else seemed to make sense. Then I found myself going down a different track."

Feeling the suspense in the room, he rather mischievously broke off to take another sip of tea.

"What we have to explain, to reconcile if you like, is why we are seeing indications of two different types of killer. I believe what we are dealing with here is someone who has the motivations of the first type—anger, revenge, hatred—but the characteristics of the second."

Collison suddenly grasped what he was driving at. "You mean someone who wants to punish women but is too frightened, too pathetic, whatever, to do it properly?"

"Exactly."

"And the condom? Where does that fit into the picture?"

"Ah!" Collins beamed triumphantly. "That's where it all came together for me. I believe you will find that at some stage your man has been infected with some form of sexual disease, certainly by a woman and possibly by a prostitute. He sees the rape as some way of getting his own back—"

"—but is terrified of getting infected again and thus wears a condom," finished Collison. "Brilliant."

A round of applause broke out spontaneously. Collins smiled bashfully.

"Bad news, sir," Priya called out as she put her bag down on her desk. Nobody had seen her enter the room.

"Great—now what?"

"Our suspect has an alibi for at least one of the killings, sir. A coach trip to Wales with his wife. I'll double-check the details with the travel firm, but she showed me her diary and their credit card bills, and I'd say it's kosher."

"Suspect?" Collins looked confused. "I didn't know you had a suspect."

"Don't you read the papers?" said Ken Andrews. "We've got a suspect banged up downstairs right now—taxi driver."

"A suspect we may now have to release," Collison reminded everyone. "If only the bloody papers hadn't got hold of the story. Now we're going to have to explain why we held him for questioning in the first place."

A phone rang on a nearby desk. Karen answered it and then held the receiver out apologetically to Collison. "Assistant Commissioner Crime for you, guv."

Chapter Seven

That evening the police put out a press release regretting premature media speculation and announcing that a man who had been assisting them with their enquiries, and had been briefly held under caution while certain facts were checked, had been released and was no longer a suspect in the case.

Ironically the duty doctor finally turned up just as Hazel was being released, and was none too pleased to discover that his visit had been wasted. He sent the "no longer a suspect" on his way with admonishments to see his own doctor for a check-up.

The ACC had been surprisingly understanding, and was heartened to hear that Collison now had a profile of the killer.

On impulse, Collison called his wife to suggest that they go out to dinner. Eight o'clock saw them at their favourite restaurant in Fulham. However, whether it would remain their favourite was called into question as they were turned away at the door; it was closed for a private function.

As they turned to look elsewhere, someone said, "Good evening, Superintendent." Glancing back, Collison realised that it was Peter Collins, immaculately dressed in a double-breasted pinstripe suit and a hat. Beside him Karen was wearing a fifties-style dark suit with a pencil skirt and high heels. She reminded him strongly of a vintage glamour photograph.

"Hello, you two," he said in surprise. "This is my wife, Caroline. Darling, Peter Collins and Karen Willis.

"I say," he added, cutting through the mumbled greetings, "you can't go in there, it's booked for a private function."

"I know, we're going to it," Peter said apologetically.

"It's a fifties evening," Karen added. "That's why we're dressed up like this."

As if on cue, some Latin American dance music struck up inside the restaurant.

"What a lovely idea," Caroline Collison said. "Simon, we should try something like that."

"Well, there's a website you can go to," Collins explained. "I'm sure Karen could give your husband the link sometime, if you want."

"Hm," Collison said noncommittally, "that would be nice. Anyway, come along, dear. We need to find somewhere to eat. Goodnight, folks, enjoy your rumba."

"Actually, it sounds like a cha-cha-cha," Collins replied as Karen guided him away.

Caroline stared at her husband in surprise. "I didn't know you knew anything about dancing."

"Only a little," he conceded. "It seemed like a good guess but it turned out to be wrong. Story of my life at the moment, I'm afraid."

His wife shook her head and took his arm. "Never mind, Simon," she said quietly. "Let's try Angelo's round the corner."

The next morning's meeting had a new sense of purpose.

"Right," said Collison. "We know what we have to do. I want the medical records of every VD clinic in London, going back three years."

"We'll need a court order, sir," Andrews said.

"I know. Get one."

"Perhaps we should widen the search a little, as well," Metcalfe suggested. "My guess is that if it's only a minor infection it can be cleared up by something on prescription."

"Bloody hell, boss," Desai groaned. "That means every GP in London."

"If that's what it takes, that's what we'll do," Metcalfe maintained doggedly.

"Have you any idea how many doctors' surgeries there are in London?" Andrews queried. "It would take months to go through their records."

"And what exactly are we looking for, anyway?" Desai asked. "All men under a certain height? And, if so, what height?"

"And what if at the end of it all we find ourselves with a list of several hundred blokes?" Andrews said. "We just don't have the manpower to check out that number of people."

"Maybe we can narrow it down a bit," Collison said. "I've had an idea. Karen, see if Peter can come in again. In the meantime, Ken, get onto the Yard's lawyers and get a court order organised."

❊ ❊ ❊

So it was that an hour later found Peter Collins back at Hampstead police station, this time standing in front of a map of Greater London.

"OK, Peter," Collison said. "I've read that there can be a geographical pattern to serial killings. Can you help us with that here, at all?"

Collins stared at the map. "I see you've put pins in each murder location."

"Yes, and a number showing the sequence in time."

He nodded silently and turned back to face the expectant team. "I *have* considered geography and time," he began. "The reason I didn't mention anything about it yesterday is that the research studies are far from conclusive, and we actually don't have that much data to work with. It's only five observations, after all. This sort of stuff seems to work best with someone like a rapist who may have struck ten or twenty times."

"We understand all your reservations," Collison said, "but we're not relying on this in any evidential way. We don't want to use it to prove that someone is or isn't our killer. We just want to find some way of making our task more manageable by starting to look in the most likely places."

"All right, then," he said reluctantly, "but with the strongest possible health warning."

"Noted," Collison acknowledged.

"I should perhaps explain, for those of you who might not know what we're talking about," Collins said, as if addressing a lecture room, "that there is a theory to the effect that serial killers start off quite a long way from home and then gradually, as they grow more confident and/or more desperate, they strike closer and closer to where they live."

"More desperate?" Metcalfe echoed.

"Yes. Some serial killers, the most disturbed ones, kill simply for the pleasure of it. They get a kick out of the excitement. But that kick is like a drug. You need more and more of it to have the same effect. I think we can disregard that possibility here, though. What happens in such cases is that the interval between successive killings gets shorter and shorter, and I don't see that in this case.

"Incidentally," he went on, "that's another reason why I felt, I still feel, diffident about using this particular technique in this case. I'm not sure that our killer *is* growing more confident, except that perhaps the last killing was in the most public place so far."

"Nonetheless..." Collison prompted him.

"Nonetheless, the theory is there if you want to use it. In fact one American academic has even developed a computer programme that claims to be able to place a killer or a rapist within a particular area if you feed in the map coordinates of his crimes in sequence. I've tried it with these murders."

Peter Collins turned back to the map and drew a circle with his finger.

"It would suggest that we're looking for someone who lives within a radius of about half a mile from Camden Town. It's possible that his local tube station is either Kentish Town, Chalk Farm, Mornington Crescent or Camden Town itself."

"Now we're really getting somewhere," Metcalfe said in satisfaction.

Desai's mind was already racing ahead. "We can check Oyster card records for people who start and finish their journeys at those tube stations," she proffered, "and cross-check them with medical records."

"And check whether their addresses are within that circle," Andrew agreed.

"I must stress," Collins tried to insist through the hubbub, "that this really is very *speculative*."

"Don't worry, Peter," Collison said, patting him on the shoulder, "it's only a way of narrowing down the search. We'll carry on keeping an open mind, I promise.

"And well done, again," he added. "Thank you."

In the days to come the team were to realise just how grateful they really should be. First they had to get the court order, which was opposed by the local health authority's lawyers "because we have to." Then they had to serve it not just on the health authority, which submitted with a good grace, but on every single GP practice in the area. Then it turned out that the records in question were stored on various different computer systems, none of which were compatible with the police database. Karen was given the job of taking the various printouts, collating them in hard copy and assigning interview responsibilities.

"And just as an added complication, sir," she reported to Collison, "only the GPs' records have the patient's height. The hospital ones don't."

"So, how many people does that mean we've got to interview?"

"Even if we restrict it to the indicated area, about three hundred."

"Bloody hell," said Metcalfe, who was listening.

"Good old-fashioned police work, Bob," Collison said with heavily overdone enthusiasm. "Nothing like it."

"We have eleven people on the team, sir, so that's only about twenty-five each," Karen said.

"Good," he said briskly. "Bob, you coordinate that with Karen, will you? By the way, I think we should exercise a bit of discretion here. Some of these men may have partners who never got to hear of their—ah—affliction."

"What should we brief the troops to look for?"

"Initial screening should be to look for men of below average height and build, either living alone or with a job that involves them being away from home frequently. Once they can press those buttons, they need to close in for detailed questioning about their whereabouts on the relevant dates."

"OK," Metcalfe nodded.

"Good, let's report back at 1700 tomorrow," said Collison. "I'll be at the Yard in the morning if anyone wants me. I have to brief the ACC."

The next day was Friday; another week had passed, largely wasted in legal procedure. Little success had been encountered in running patients to earth, presumably because most were at work and their patient records listed only their home addresses. Collison authorised voluntary overtime over the weekend for anyone who wanted it. Many did; for the first time in the long investigation there was a feeling that they were getting closer to a result. Karen ran off notes to be left where no answer was to be had, asking the named individual to contact the incident room.

Metcalfe diffidently suggested that the two of them should meet up at Saturday lunchtime and she readily agreed. "I'll be ready for a break," she said. "How about the Wells?"

"Might be very busy if it's a nice day," he demurred. "Why not, say, the King William?"

"OK."

"You're sure you don't mind?" he asked, in some surprise.

"Not at all," she said with a laugh. "It'll make a change from door-stepping VD patients, anyway."

Waiting for her, Metcalfe felt irrationally nervous, like a schoolboy waiting for his date. What was it about her that he couldn't get out of his mind?

Suddenly she was there. "Hello," she said, dropping her shoulder bag on the seat beside him. "How did you get on?"

"Not bad. Not a bad response rate, that is. But nothing that looks interesting. All of them could say more or less straight-away where they were on the evening of the last murder, and most of them for the one before that as well. Of course, we'll have to check the details…"

"Another fun job. Why can't police work be more like all those detective stories?"

"What, you mean like *Prime Suspect*, or something like that?"

"Actually, no. I was thinking more of the Golden Age. Sayers, Marsh, Allingham, all that mob. Peter's mad about them. In fact, he's close to being obsessed with Lord Peter Wimsey."

"Like Agatha Christie's Poirot?"

"Yes, but Peter doesn't really rate Christie. Nor do I, actually, I much prefer Alleyn to Poirot, for example."

"Hm," said Metcalfe. "Not sure I've heard of him—or is it a her?"

"The author's a her, the detective's a him," she said briskly. "Drink?"

"I've already got one, thanks. Let me get you one."

"OK—same as you if that's Diet Coke."

"It is," he admitted ruefully. "Think anyone could guess we were coppers?"

"More than likely. See you in a mo—I'm just off to the loo while you're at the bar."

"I've never been quite sure about real-life policemen reading detective stories," he said when she returned. "Difficult to take them seriously somehow."

"Know what you mean," she said, sipping her drink. "Peter loves them, though. Actually, so does Collison, I think. I'm dreading him and Peter getting going about them one day."

"How do you know?"

"I read something he wrote for one of the Sunday papers a while back. It was about the criminal's need to be discovered, well, some criminals anyway, and he turned it into a discussion about lots of different detective writers."

"I didn't know he'd studied psychology. I thought he had a law degree."

"Yes, he does. I think it's just an interest really. Maybe he did criminology as part of his degree course."

"So, what do you think of him?" Metcalfe asked.

"As a person, or as a copper?"

"Both, I suppose."

She thought for a while. "As a person I think he's intelligent and genuine. I think he tries to do the right thing by people. He's got a good reputation in the force. Of course there will always be people who make snide remarks when you've been promoted so quickly..."

"And as a copper?"

"I think he's good," she said simply. "He thinks really deeply about what he's doing, and he knows all the procedures. What's missing is all those years of grubby, everyday experience that all the old-timers believe you need to be a good detective —copper's nose, copper's instinct, whatever you want to call it. Personally, I'd take intelligence any day."

"I agree," Metcalfe nodded. "It's a horrible thought, but if you could put him and Tom Allen together, you'd probably have the perfect policeman."

"Horrible and quite impossible," Karen said with a grimace. "They're so totally unalike, the mind meld would never work. They'd reject each other."

"Yes," he mused. "Maybe you'd get left with two monsters who'd each taken the worst of each other."

They both smiled and fell silent. A strand of hair, which she normally wore tied back, fell across her face. As she brushed it back, he felt a sudden surge of longing mixed with sadness for what he knew could never be.

"I think he's getting frustrated, though, the guvnor, I mean," Karen went on, "and I can sympathise. He's pressing all the right buttons but nothing's happening. He must feel under a lot of pressure, having been brought in by the ACC to ginger things up."

"I have a theory, for what it's worth," Metcalfe proffered.

"Go on."

"I think serial killer cases are very different to normal murder enquiries, though that must sound very pretentious since this is the only serial killer case I've ever worked on."

"Me too, and I hope to God it's my last."

"Amen to that, but as I was saying…"

"Yes, sorry."

"You see with a normal murder, if that doesn't sound a strange phrase to use, you can generally work out a list of suspects and motives. After all, most murder victims know their killers. Serial killings are different. They're random attacks by a complete stranger, and often at night and/or in remote locations. So unless you have an immense stroke of luck and catch them in the act, or by accident, the odds really are stacked against you."

"What about DNA?"

"DNA evidence has made a big difference," he acknowledged, "but if the killing takes place outside and it's some time before anyone finds the body, then you don't have much chance. Look at Ted Bundy. Most of his victims were badly decomposed when they were found. Some had been partially eaten by wild animals. Some were never even found at all."

"That's a depressing picture you're painting," Karen said quietly.

"Depressing, yes, but realistic I think. We have to face the fact that most serial killers never get caught. Look at the Zodiac Killer, for example."

Karen stared at him. "Do you mean there are serial killers at work all around us, and only a tiny minority ever get caught?"

"Yes, I do," Metcalfe replied resolutely. "Look at the number of people who simply go missing in Britain every year. Generally they either turn up in a matter of days, or they're never heard of again. I've actually been doing some research on it, just for my own interest. Over a quarter of a million people go missing every year. That's one in every 225 members of the population, by the way. Most are found almost straight away, though not always alive, but that still leaves about eight per cent who are never heard of again. That's a lot of people."

"And you think that proves there a lot of serial killers out there getting away with it?"

"I think it's a possible explanation. In fact, I think it's the most likely explanation."

"Sounds logical," she agreed. "You know, you should tell Collison about this. I'm sure he'd suggest you work it up into a formal paper and submit it to the Commissioner."

"I think I'll leave it for the time being," Metcalfe said sardonically. "He's got rather a lot on his plate right now."

"Yes," Karen said soberly. "Poor guy. It's bad for us, but it must be much worse for him. The pressure must be building with every day that goes by. Will we get a break, do you think, Bob?"

"You have to believe so, or you couldn't do this job," he responded after a moment's thought for reflection, "but I have a theory—yes, another one," he added with a smile. As he did so he suddenly realised that she had called him "Bob" for the first time. He brushed the thought away, but still somehow found it absurdly pleasing.

"Which is?"

"That in a case like this you don't find the break, it finds you. Oh, of course you have to do all the work, put the hours in, follow the leads. I'm not suggesting that we just sit around waiting for something to happen. But it goes back to what I was saying just now. The odds against you finding anything that points to one specific individual are enormous, overwhelming. You have to believe that sooner or later the fates will align and an apparently random connection will suddenly click into place."

Karen thought about this. "Like synchronicity, perhaps?"

"What's that?"

"It's Jung. He believed that we are surrounded by much more coincidence than we realise, and so we've become incapable of noticing most of it. It's only when it becomes sufficiently extreme that we begin to recognise it for what it is."

"Wait," Metcalfe said with a sudden rush of recollection, "I'm remembering reading something about this now. But isn't there more to it than that?"

"There was, but it's the bit that most people find pretty weird or cranky."

"Something to do with us being able to control our own destinies, wasn't it?" he asked uncertainly.

"Not exactly. He thought that there was some sort of conceptual framework that is too big and too complex for us to understand, and that things, events even, could be grouped together by some sort of hidden meaning. Where detectives go wrong, I'm sure he would argue, is by being obsessed by cause and effect, rather than trying to tease out apparently random connections...I'm sorry, I'm not explaining this very well."

"Yes, you are, you are," he encouraged her. "Go on."

"Well, that's about it, really. Except that elements of your own life, your own personality, interact with this shadowy conceptual framework, the world of ideas if you like, and that in some cases you may be able apparently—only *apparently*, mind you—be able to cause things to happen just by wishing for them strongly enough."

"Well, then, let's wish for a breakthrough," said Metcalfe fervently. "Tell you what, if it works, I'll even read the book."

Chapter Eight

"You must have been wishing very hard indeed," Karen said with a smile as Metcalfe arrived at work the next morning.

"What do you mean?" he asked, putting his coffee down on his desk and checking his mobile phone for messages.

"I've just had a forensic report in and handed it to the chief. They've identified that powder on the last victim."

Before she could explain further Collison had swept in, and was standing at the front of the room. "Morning everyone! Quiet, please." The room fell silent. Collison was smiling. Suddenly an air of expectancy settled on the team. "I have some news—very good news. Forensics may have taken their time, but they've come up trumps. They have identified the yellow powder that was found at our last crime scene."

He stopped for effect and looked at the piece of paper in his hand.

"It's fish food. But not just any old fish food like they sell in supermarkets or pet shops. This is very expensive food for tropical fish, and it's only sold by a few specialist outlets. The only one around here is in Hendon Central. Ken, I'd like you to check that out this morning, please. See if they happen to keep a list of their customers, though it's a bit of a forlorn hope."

"So how does this help us, guv?" somebody asked.

"Maybe I'm just being foolishly optimistic," Collison said, "but one of my neighbours is a tropical fish buff and he reckons that most people these days buy their stuff online. There are apparently only two main websites, and I have their details here. Priya, you take one and Karen the other. Contact them, make it clear this is a murder enquiry, and get all the names and addresses they have mailed stuff to over the last year and a half for starters. If they won't play ball, get a court order."

"Shall we stop what we're doing, guv?" asked Metcalfe. "With the patient lists, I mean?"

Collison considered the situation. "Don't stop the interview process. It's still highly likely that our man is on one of those lists somewhere. But don't let's take the next step of starting to check their alibis until we know whether this fish food thing is going to take us anywhere."

In the event it turned out that both online businesses were happy to turn over their customer lists though one, based in the Netherlands, only did so after stipulating that they would restrict their list to deliveries made to addresses in the UK.

By Tuesday afternoon Collison was in possession of both customer lists. Rather than inputting all the customer names and addresses, together with all the patient names and addresses into a database, a process which would have taken days, he hit upon the simple but old-fashioned expedient of giving each member of the team a patient list from a different clinic, while he read the names off each customer list in turn. He read through the entire list from the Dutch business without result. Without showing any disappointment, he picked up the second one and started reciting names. About a third of the way through, Ken cried "Bingo!" in a tone almost of disbelief. They had found their match.

An hour later they had gathered all the information they could find on their suspect.

"Our man's name is Gary Clarke, as you know," Collison announced. "According to what we have been able to pull off various sources he has no previous, nor does he appear on any police database in any capacity. However, he was treated for NSU at the Royal Free's sexual health clinic about three years ago, and he lives smack in the area indicated by Peter Collins."

"Are we going to bring him in, then?" asked Metcalfe.

"You bet we are," Collison said warmly. "But I want to do this properly. I want Forensics to go in straight away when we arrest him so there can be no argument later about any contamination of evidence. So, let's get a search warrant first and then pick him up first thing tomorrow morning. Early, in case he's planning to head off anywhere."

"How many of us, guv?"

"Two of us will be enough to arrest him. I'll do that with Ken. Bob, you take charge of the rest of the team. Once Forensics have given you the all-clear, but only then mind, you take the place apart. I want anything and everything that may link him to the killings."

"You think his flat could be a crime scene, guv?" asked Karen.

"It's possible, isn't it? We don't know for sure that our victims were killed where they were found. It's also possible there could be other bodies we don't know about."

"In that case, guv, Forensics are likely to take a day or two, maybe more, if you want them to check every inch of the place."

"So be it." Collison nodded. "I don't want any slip-ups."

Gary Clarke was arrested at six o'clock the following morning by Collison and Andrews and installed in the cells to await questioning. Meanwhile Metcalfe supervised uniform as they sealed off the property, and waited for SOCO to give him the all-clear to enter the flat.

As he was on his way back to the police station, his mobile rang.

"I hear you've got him, then," said Tom Allen.

"I'm not going to talk to you," he said curtly. "Don't call again."

SOCO were thorough, but disgruntled. Having taken over twenty-four hours to pore over every square inch of Clarke's flat, they took pains to point out that their acronym stood for Scene of Crime Officers, and there was nothing to suggest that this was in fact a scene of any crime whatsoever. As it was a small flat, Metcalfe and the team then needed only about two hours to go through every drawer and cupboard. Their haul was disappointing.

"Nothing out of the ordinary, then?" said Collison.

"Nothing, guv," Metcalfe confirmed, "and that's about twenty-seven hours gone."

Collison nodded. He had been able to secure an additional twenty-four hours in custody for Clarke on the grounds that forensic investigations were still taking place, but the clock was ticking. At the end of the extension period they would have to decide whether to charge or release him. "But there is a tropical fish tank?"

"There is indeed, guv, and a couple of containers of fish food which forensic are fairly sure are the same as the sample found on our last victim, but they're checking."

"Hm, well, he fits the profile right enough. He's about five foot seven and lightly built, just as Peter predicted. He works as an IT contractor, so he's always moving around travelling between clients, again as predicted. And he was infected with a sexual disease, though he's not very forthcoming about how it happened. And of course he lives in the right area."

"So he's talking, then?" Metcalfe enquired.

"Up to a point. He wanted a lawyer as soon as we told him his rights, so he's been fairly cagey. However, one thing he has said is that he has an alibi for the night of the last murder, so we need to check that right away. Says his girlfriend stayed the night at his place."

Metcalfe felt disappointment flooding through him. Collison saw his face change and shrugged. "May be something, may be nothing. Only one way to find out. The lady's name is Susan McCormick."

"I'll take it," Metcalfe volunteered. "What's her address?"

"There's something a bit strange about that," Collison replied. "He says he can't remember off hand but he does have her mobile phone number. That's probably better for our purposes anyway, as she's not likely to be home in the middle of the day and we're pushed for time. Here you are—see what you can do."

When Metcalfe phoned Susan McCormick, what she told him prompted him to sit bolt upright and ask her if she could come in to make a statement right away. She agreed to be there by half past six that evening after she finished work, so when Collison and Metcalfe sat down in front of her they knew they now had less than twelve hours left.

"Can I just make sure we've got this right, Ms McCormick," Collison said without further ado. "As you know, we have Gary Clarke in custody helping us with certain enquiries. He has given us your name as an alibi witness, in other words to confirm that he was somewhere at a certain time—"

"Yes, I understand that he's said I stayed the night at his flat," she cut in briskly, "and I didn't. I can tell you that for a fact."

"Perhaps we could just check the dates," Collison began, looking down at his notes.

"The date is irrelevant," she said. "You see, I've never stayed the night at his flat. I'm not his girlfriend; I've never even been properly out with him."

Collison and Metcalfe looked at each other. She set her lips in a tight line and stared at them uncompromisingly, as though strongly disapproving of what they were suggesting.

"Perhaps we'd better start at the beginning, Ms McCormick," Metcalfe said. "Could you explain to us how Gary Clarke is in possession of your mobile number?"

"Oh, I know him right enough. He does some IT stuff at the office where I work. He has my mobile number because I foolishly asked him if he could help me when my home computer crashed. There was some stuff on the hard drive that I wanted to rescue. He did, as well. He's very good at what he does, actually."

"Why 'foolishly'?" asked Collison.

"Because then he asked me back to his place for a drink a few days later. I didn't feel I could say 'no' just like that after what he'd done for me, so I agreed. I thought he was a bit creepy, but I wasn't unduly worried. After all, it was only for a quick drink after work."

"What happened?" asked Metcalfe.

She sat with her wrists pressed together in front of her, perfectly parallel with the handbag she had placed carefully on the table, and glanced quickly around the room, not uneasily but more as if trying to find the right words to frame what she wanted to say.

"I started feeling uncomfortable very quickly," she said tightly. "He was behaving really weirdly, as if he was my boyfriend and had been for years. It was strange, very strange. I got frightened, to be honest. I finished my drink, made my excuses and left."

"And that was that?"

"Yes, but there's something I think I should tell you. I don't know for certain, but I think he may have drugged my drink. I started feeling very drowsy on my way home, and when I got in I just collapsed on the bed and fell asleep without even taking my shoes off. I slept for about twelve hours, and woke up with a splitting headache."

The two detectives digested this. A feeling of certainty was flooding through them, something almost tangible as though it were a mist slowly seeping into the room through an open window. She watched them steadily, nodding slightly as if somehow confirming what it was they were starting to sense.

"What else can you tell us about Mr Clarke?" Collison asked, careful not to let his excitement show.

"Well, I'm not sure if this helps you at all..."

"Everything is helpful," Collison assured her. "We're trying to build up a picture of him. Do you know anything about his past? Whether he has family? Anything at all."

"I've never heard him mention any family," she said. "As for his past, he's full of all sorts of stories, but all the girls at work think he makes most of them up."

"For example?"

"Well, he says he's been in the army, for instance. Talks about having done all sorts of special training—parachutes and unarmed combat and all that sort of thing. But, I mean, it doesn't seem very likely, does it? You've seen him. He's pretty pathetic physically. I suppose that's why I didn't really stop and think before going back to his place. Like I said, he can be a bit creepy but I never felt there was anything, well, threatening about him."

"Right, Ms McCormick," Collison said briskly. "We'll get this typed up for you to sign. Thank you very much indeed for your help."

She picked up her handbag, stood up, nodded briskly, and waited very pointedly for one of them to open the door. Collison did so.

"You've got to hand it to Peter," Metcalfe said admiringly after she left the room, "he got it bang on. Fantasy military service, fantasy girlfriend, the lot."

"We don't know yet that Clarke was lying about the army," Collison pointed out. "Check that out, will you? But yes, I agree, he's done a fantastic job."

"What are you going to do with our suspect?"

"First I'm going to tell him the game's up on his false alibi," Collison said with relish, "and then I'm going to charge him. Why don't you sit in?"

"Thanks, guv, I'd like to," Metcalfe replied. "I can't wait to see what he looks like."

In fact, Gary Clarke turned out to look exactly as Metcalfe had imagined. He was short and slightly built, with a rather weaselly face which took on a distinctly frightened expression as he sat with his lawyer beside him and listened to Collison tell him that Susan McCormick had refused to confirm his alibi. After a pause he said, "No comment."

"Further than that," Collison pressed on, "she says that in fact she has never been your girlfriend at all, that's it all just a figment of your imagination. What do you say to that?"

"No comment."

"Tell a lot of lies do you, Gary?" Metcalfe asked.

"No comment."

Collison could see that further questioning was pointless. "Right, Mr Clarke," he said. "You will now be taken downstairs to the custody sergeant, who will charge you with the murder of Katherine Barker."

He waited and thought he saw a flicker of emotion run across Clarke's face.

"Your lawyer may accompany you. I'm sure he will explain to you exactly what all this means. You will then be remanded in custody. I should warn you that further charges may follow."

"Interview terminated at 2033," Metcalfe announced, and switched off the tape recorder. He nodded to the uniformed constable, who led Clarke and his lawyer from the room.

Collison sat back and rubbed his eyes. "Well, we've got him, Bob," he said. "Now all we have to do is prove it."

"Not difficult, surely, guv? He fits the profile and he's given a false alibi."

"Hm, I'm not so sure. Anyway, sufficient unto the day and all that. Let's try to fix a meeting with someone from the DPP tomorrow and lay out what we've got."

"Excuse me, guv," said Metcalfe, suddenly remembering, "but I haven't had a chance to tell you. Tom Allen called me. He knows about the arrest."

"So our spy is still active," Collison said sadly. "Well, I suppose it's no more than I should have expected. I assume it's the same person who's leaking to the press, either directly or through Allen."

He stood up and then paused for thought. "Which means," he said ruminatively, "we'd better contact all the next of kin of the murdered women. I wouldn't normally at this early stage, but if we don't they'll probably read all about it in the papers tomorrow morning."

"I could do that if you like," Metcalfe offered.

"You can go and see Doctor Barker, since you've met him recently," Collison decided. "I'll do the others by phone. You know the form, Bob, just a simple statement that we have a man in custody on suspicion of his wife's murder. Better do it now, on your way home. Then first thing in the morning please check Clarke's supposed military exploits."

"Right you are, guv."

"Actually," Collison went on reflectively, "let's check everything. We may as well find out everything we can about him. Check out his flat. I suspect he's renting it, so see who the owner is and if he's been any trouble as a tenant. Let's talk to the companies he's done contract work for, and see if we can find any friends or family."

Metcalfe jotted notes down on a pad and nodded. "Tax? National Insurance? Medical records?"

"Everything," Collison repeated, "and let's set up the meeting with the DPP for the afternoon. I want to get an independent view on the evidence."

He noticed Willis sitting at her desk, looking tired but happy. The same feeling was pervading the whole room, as if the team had just finished running a marathon and were recovering, but savouring their achievement at the same time.

"Go home everyone, and thank you," Collison called. "We'll reconvene in the morning."

Then, to Willis, he added, "And please pass on my special thanks to Peter, Karen. I'm going to see if we can't get him some sort of commendation for this. He's done a great job."

"Thank you, sir," she said. "I'll certainly tell him."

Chapter Nine

"Right, everyone, great work," Collison said next morning. "We've got our man. The challenge now is to be able to prove it so it stacks up in court. Bob and I will be discussing that with the DPP's office this afternoon. Your job is to make sure absolutely everything is ship-shape and beyond reproach. I want everything properly filed, cross-referenced and tabulated. We have to sift all the material we have and turn it into a prosecution file.

"Ken," he continued, "I'm going to put you in charge of that. You've done it before so I don't need to tell you what's required. Karen and Priya, you carry on with gathering background on Clarke. Bob, you check out his army claims with the Ministry of Defence, and then come with me to the meeting this afternoon. I have to go and report to the ACC now, but I'll meet you back here about midday."

By the time he returned, the team had made two significant discoveries.

"Good news and good news, guv," Metcalfe greeted him. "I'll give you mine first and then you can hear Karen's."

Karen was sitting on Metcalfe's desk and, as he had come into the room, Collison had experienced a fleeting suspicion that whatever they were discussing, it was not the case.

"OK, go ahead."

"Our man did enlist with the territorials several years ago," Metcalfe said, "but he dropped out almost at once. He never even completed his probationary training."

"So much for that—pretty much as expected. Karen, what have you got?"

"Something pretty explosive, I think," she said with a smile. "You were right about Clarke renting his flat, sir. The owner is listed at the Land Registry as Colin William Barker of Lyndhurst Gardens. I rang him to double-check and it is indeed our Dr Barker, husband of Katherine."

Collison sat down heavily on an adjoining desk. "Bloody hell!" he gasped.

"There's more," Karen went on. "He told me that they didn't use a letting agent and that Kathy did all of that sort of stuff herself. It was almost like a hobby, apparently, gave her something to do. I asked if that included showing prospective tenants around and he said yes, absolutely. He confirmed that she had met Clarke several times; there were some plumbing problems to sort out after he moved in, he said."

"So our suspect knew the last victim," he said, still dazed by this revelation. "Is that good or bad, I wonder?"

"Good, surely, guv?" Metcalfe said, puzzled.

"I'm not so sure." Collison looked at his watch. "Let's give Peter a quick ring before we leave. We can put him on the squawk box so we can all hear. Karen, see if you can get hold of him."

They gathered around her desk as she got through and switched on the loudspeaker.

"Peter," said Collison. "We've had a bit of a surprise here. It turns out that our suspect actually knew the last victim. He rented a flat from her. What do you make of that?"

Whatever Peter made of it obviously took him a bit of time to think about, because there was a long silence before he responded. "It's rather surprising," he said at last. "Serial killers are on the whole opportunists, and usually target complete strangers, people they've never seen before. The Yorkshire Ripper would be a good example."

"So serial killers aren't generally stalkers as well?"

"No. There was a case in Florida a while back, I think, where someone who had been stalking women ended up killing three of them, but no. It certainly isn't usual."

There was another long silence.

"Thoughts?" Collison asked eventually.

"My thoughts would be as follows," said Peter slowly. "First, do we know that he *did* actually stalk her? Surely she would have noticed if he had, and might have told someone—her husband, for example. It's quite possible that the fact that they knew each other was coincidental. It just so happened that the opportunity which presented itself featured someone he knew."

"Good thinking," Collison said. "Karen, you'd better speak to Dr Barker again, and check whether Kathy mentioned anything about Clarke in the weeks before her death."

"There is one other possibility," Peter's disembodied voice added. "It's most unlikely, but I mention it for the sake of completeness."

"Yes, go on."

"I appreciate this would mean you re-investigating all the other murders," Peter said cautiously, "so I hesitate to raise it, but it is a logical alternative."

"Go on," Collison said again, glancing impatiently at his watch.

"What if he stalked them *all*?" Peter asked. "I rather think it has to be all or none. I could get comfortable with either, but I'd be dubious about one murder being completely different to all the others...I'm not sure how you find the answer, though," he trailed off.

"That's our problem," Collison said briskly. "Peter, many thanks again. Come on, Bob, we must be off."

It turned out that the case team from the DPP's office already felt in need of counsel's opinion, so that afternoon's meeting was scheduled to be held in the Temple, that network of gardens and Victorian tenements which sits behind the Strand, unsuspected by most yet waiting to be discovered. At its eastern end stands King's Bench Walk, and it was to one of these doorways, adorned with a simple list of barristers' names, that Collison and Metcalfe made their way.

After sitting in what seemed to be a rather cramped hallway for some time, they were ushered into the august presence of Mr Alistair Partington, a young man trying to give a convincing impression of being middle-aged. Neither this attempt nor the august atmosphere survived very long, however, as Collison realised as soon as he walked through the door that the two of them had sat through lectures at King's College London together. The two men exchanged introductions.

"So, Alistair," he said after they had rehearsed the case against Clarke, "what do you think?"

Alistair Partington brushed from his waistcoat some crumbs of a certain type of fruitcake that can be found only in barristers' chambers and the Long Room bar at Lord's Cricket Ground. "I'm sorry to say this, Simon," he said quietly, "but I don't think it's much. It's all circumstantial. I agree what you have is consistent with him being the killer, but none of it actually proves it."

"But he fits the profile..." Metcalfe urged hesitantly.

Mr Alistair Partington fixed him with that benign smile which barristers tend to reserve for their instructing solicitors but which, it appeared, would do service for detective inspectors as well.

"The profile is an ingenious piece of work, but it's not evidence," he explained. "In fact, if I were defending Clarke, I would object to it being mentioned in court at all. I would argue that its prejudicial effect outweighed any possible evidential impact." He nodded approvingly at his own eloquence and his hands strayed dangerously towards his lapels. Collison, in whose opinion Partington had been the pompous type even as a first-year law student, smiled briefly.

"All right, Alistair," he cut in. "Let's assume you *are* defending and you successfully persuade the judge that we're not allowed to mention the profile at all. What do we have?"

"You have the fact that chummy knew the last victim," Partington said, telling the points off on his fingers. "You have the fact that he gave a phoney alibi and so cannot account for his whereabouts on the night of her murder. You have the fact that he seems to be an habitual fantasist. That's all interesting stuff, but hardly compelling. If I *were* defending I'd be on my feet at this point arguing that my client had no case to answer.

"Indeed," he went on, after allowing this to sink in, "I have no wish to teach my grandmother to suck eggs, Simon, but were I in your place I'd be wondering whether I could even properly keep him in custody."

"So what do we need?" said Collison calmly.

"You need something that places him at the scene of at least one of the murders. The closest you have to that is the fish food powder. It's good, but it's nowhere near enough."

"Even taken with everything else?" asked Metcalfe hopefully.

"Ah," Partington said, darting a glance at the man from the DPP's office, who had so far said absolutely nothing, but had sat trance-like through the conference, "that's another thing you have to think about. The courts and"—another glance at the silent prosecutor—"as I understand, the DPP, have become rather sensitive to allowing cases based entirely on circumstantial evidence to go before a jury, for reasons of which I am sure we are all aware."

The man from the DPP awoke from his trance at this point and started scribbling furiously. Collison sighed. Partington was of course alluding to the Dando murder, in which an innocent man had been sent to prison for several years purely on the accumulated weight of circumstantial evidence.

"There's no forensic evidence to link him with any crime scene or any victim, I understand? No, I thought not. Well, then, in the absence of any confession, I'm really not sure what I can suggest."

"Suppose we could establish a motive for him murdering Katherine Barker?" Metcalfe said.

"That would be different. It would be something, at least. You mean if he had become obsessed with her or something like that?"

"Something like that, yes."

"Is there something like that?" Partington asked, looking at Collison.

"No," he said shortly, "there isn't. Come on, Bob, we've got some thinking to do."

As they walked back through the Temple they made a gloomy pair. The man from the DPP had bolted outside chambers after cautiously proffering the limpest of handshakes, as though they were both infected with some contagious disease. He would doubtless shortly be shuffling his paperclips in an agitated fashion and composing a memo proposing no further action.

As they came out into the Strand, Collison came to a decision. "Do you have the keys to Clarke's flat?" he asked.

"They're at the nick, in my desk," Metcalfe replied.

"Then let's go and get them," Collison said, hailing a cab. "We're missing something, Bob. We must be. You can't murder five women in cold blood and not leave any traces anywhere."

After two hours' painstaking searching, though, Collison was forced to admit he was wrong. They had levered off the skirting boards, removed the backs of kitchen units, taken the panel off the bath and lifted floorboards, yet they had found nothing except angry house-spiders, scurrying woodlice and water pipes.

Closing the door of the flat behind them, he stood on the landing and took out his mobile phone with an air of resignation. "Alright," he said sombrely, "I'll tell the nick to release him." He pressed the speed dial for the police station and gazed up at the ceiling while he waited for them to answer. "Never mind," he said when they did, and cut the call off without taking his eyes off the ceiling. "Bob," he said. "Tell me what you see up there."

Metcalfe's gaze followed his. "A trapdoor," he said slowly. "Presumably into the loft space. This is the top floor flat."

They looked at each other, and then Collison took the keys out of his pocket again and re-entered the flat. He remembered having seen a ladder in the hall cupboard.

"It doesn't really reach, though," Metcalfe said, after they had erected it outside.

"It's good enough," Collison said curtly. "I bet if you stood on the top rung you could open the trap and pull yourself up, Bob."

Metcalfe realised that this was a command, rather than idle speculation, and did as he was bid. "I can't find a light switch anywhere," he called down.

"Wait," Collison said. "I remember seeing a torch in a kitchen drawer." He retrieved it and handed the torch up to his colleague. "What can you see?" he asked as Metcalfe switched it on and shone it around.

"A light switch," came the reply, followed by a sudden illumination, which revealed a space directly under the roof, presumably left over when the top floor flat had been carved out of what had originally been a house.

Metcalfe pulled himself up so that he was sitting on the coaming around the trapdoor, and then said "Ah, wait a minute."

"Gloves, Bob," Collison cautioned. He took two new pairs of plastic gloves out of his pocket and threw a packet up to Metcalfe, who caught it deftly, ripped open the plastic and pulled them on.

"There's a box up here," he said. "Not very big. Here, I'll hand it down—careful, there's something heavy in it."

Collison laid it carefully on the floor as Metcalfe switched off the light and dropped back onto the ladder. Closing the trapdoor, he climbed down and the two of them stood looking at his find. It was plain brown cardboard, the sort of box that might once have contained an electrical appliance.

Collison checked that his own gloves were securely in place, and then bent down and pulled it open. He stood up again, his heart beating wildly. Metcalfe's eyes were blazing with excitement. Struggling to remain calm, Collison dialled again. "DC Willis, incident room, please," he said. "This is Superintendent Collison calling." Metcalfe watched him exultantly, listening to Collison's side of the conversation.

"Karen? I need you to get SOCO back over to Clarke's flat...yes, right now...Tell them we've found something in the loft...a cardboard box...yes, a hammer and five items of female underwear."

Chapter Ten

For the next few weeks the skeleton team at Hampstead worked hard to bring the mass of information collected during the investigation into a thorough and comprehensible paper chain for the forthcoming court case. A young man from the DPP was nominally in charge of this process but both Collison and Metcalfe knew that the standard of their staff was notoriously low, with many prosecutions having to be abandoned due to procedural errors or lost evidence. Nor did this particular individual, a man who wore earphones permanently around the office and who clearly suffered from what was either a worrying skin condition or an appalling shaving rash, inspire confidence.

"Try to ignore him, Bob," Collison advised quietly. "Do what he says but make sure the filing system is our own, and wherever possible keep at least one back-up of everything."

"You don't trust him, then?" Metcalfe asked with a smile.

"In a word, no. Not his competence, anyway. From the few chats I've had with him he doesn't appear to have any legal knowledge at all. Is he actually a solicitor, I wonder? We could check I suppose. But even if he is, God only knows where he got his degree. I mentioned similar fact evidence the other day and he didn't seem to have any idea what I was on about."

"I'll be careful. By the way, there's something I should tell you. I've had Tom Allen on the phone. He's convinced we've got the wrong man."

"Really? Well, we should take that seriously; he's a good copper. What's he spotted that we've missed?"

"Nothing specific. Just his copper's instinct, he says. Personally, I think it may just be sour grapes that we caught Clarke after he couldn't. Bit embarrassing really."

"I'd be sad if that were the case," Collison said quietly. "I was hoping Tom wouldn't take any of this personally, though I suppose that was too much to hope for, human nature being what it is. Well, ring him back and ask if he has any fresh evidence. If so, we'd be happy to receive it. If not, just pass on my best wishes."

"Sure. I'll do that, and don't worry about the bundles. I'll do them myself with Karen."

Metcalfe was as good as his word. In the space of less than three weeks the incident room, which had seemed strangely devoid of people in the days since Clarke's arrest, was filled steadily with boxes of files, numbered and referenced in a master ledger, with each individual document within each file further sub-referenced. Metcalfe, Willis and Desai toiled over their detailed report for the prosecution. It was grinding, tedious stuff, which every so often sent them out onto Hampstead High Street in search of strong coffee, but it was thoroughness in this—the essential and unglamorous side of real life police work—that was valued by fellow professionals.

A report on the death of each victim highlighted the relevant forensic evidence, stressing the identical MO of each killing. A separate schedule showed that on each such occasion Clarke had no alibi, and furthermore that the only alibi he *had* advanced had been shown to be a lie. A copy of Susan McCormick's statement was referenced at this point.

A separate scientific report dealt with the fish food that had been found on Kathy Barker's body, and identified it as the same type as had been found in Clarke's flat. Details were also provided of Clarke's NSU treatment, though Collison doubted whether the judge would allow this to be introduced; it was circumstantial at best.

The clinching pieces of evidence, though, were the witness statements of Collison and Metcalfe, who described how they had found the box in the loft above Clarke's flat and identified its contents. A further forensic report confirmed that the DNA recovered from each piece of underwear matched that of one of the victims.

In short, the DPP's work had been done for them, Collison reflected, and very well done into the bargain. All the DPP's office now had to do was to turn the police report into a brief to counsel, and surely they could be trusted at least to get that right.

A call to Alistair Partington brought some reassurance. Though the august personage of a QC would probably lead the proceedings in court, Alistair would be preparing the prosecution case. He was already deeply into Metcalfe's report and supporting documents, and liked what he saw. He was confident that once Clarke's lawyers recognised the strength of the case against him, they would recommend a guilty plea. In any case, matters would not long be delayed; with the prosecution able to certify that their case was complete, a start date for the trial had been fixed just two weeks ahead.

Collison dropped into the incident room to break the good news. The atmosphere felt almost more unreal than before; even the boxes had disappeared. Priya Desai was absent, taking some time off to be with her father who was sick. Perhaps a theatre felt like this, he mused, once the sets had been taken down after the last night of a production.

Bob Metcalfe and Karen Willis were standing by the window drinking coffee, watching a couple of technicians disconnect the last few computers. They looked as they felt: purposeless and a little dazed. For weeks after the arrest had been made, they had been hard at work on preparing the case. Now the sense of anti-climax was palpable. There was something else as well though, he reflected. There was the sense of a bond having grown between them during the last stages. Standing close together, it was almost as if they had the look of a couple. He wondered if he had missed anything, something he should have noticed but hadn't, or whether this was something that had just evolved gradually from long hours of working together. There again, perhaps he was completely mistaken. He had learned the hard way that intuition was not his strong suit.

They turned towards him as he approached and, in the process, seemed to move a little further apart.

"Nothing left to do?" Collison asked.

"Don't think so, sir," Metcalfe replied, a trifle uncertainly. Had he overlooked something?

"Good. Then take the rest of the day off, both of you. You've more than earned it these last few weeks."

They both looked uncertainly at their watches. It was only just after twelve.

"Go for a long lunch somewhere," he suggested. "Relax. A bottle of wine, that sort of thing."

Karen Willis turned to Metcalfe and smiled. He felt something perform a somersault inside him.

"Why not?" she said.

It was one of those days that cannot decide whether it wants to be summer or winter, and Hampstead was canopied by a Turneresque purple clouded sky, in which the sun every so often ripped a savage gash and broke through to bathe the streets in sudden blinding light. Even as fashionable shoppers shaded their eyes or reached for their sunglasses, it would disappear again, gleaming briefly through the sombre clouds on its way.

With the threat of rain ever present, it was not the sort of day to be eating outside. A small French restaurant at the bottom of Flask Walk beckoned. Sitting in the window and looking out, it was a strangely silent environment. Few vehicles ventured along the back streets in the village. Occasional Asian tourists walked past uncertainly, keeping to the narrow, elevated pavement. Women of a certain age with dogs of a certain type moved more purposefully, often in the middle of the road.

The menu was not a large one, the choice of a main course revolving largely around whether one was in the mood for fish or meat.

"A Sancerre perhaps?" Metcalfe ventured uncertainly, looking up from the wine list.

"An excellent choice," his companion concurred approvingly.

"You know about wine?"

"A bit," she admitted. "My father was a great wine enthusiast, and so is Peter. In fact, he reminds me of my father in many ways."

"They do say," Metcalfe said before he could stop himself, "that women often look for the qualities of their father in men they find attractive."

"And similarly men with their mothers when it comes to girlfriends," she countered.

"True," he replied awkwardly. "I suppose."

"You suppose?"

"Well, I mean, I haven't had a girlfriend for a while now— the job gets in the way, I find—and I can't say that she was particularly like my mother apart from the fact they both had dark hair. But I'm aware of the principle."

The waiter arrived and they ordered.

"I can't really put it to the test for myself, either," Karen said. "I do have a boyfriend, as you know, but I never knew my father, my real father that is. I was brought up by a really nice couple, but neither of them was a biological parent. I was adopted when I was little, and I can't remember either of my real parents."

"Really? So was I."

"Well, that *is* a coincidence. What are the odds, I wonder?"

"Not very high," he replied firmly. "Only about five thousand kids get adopted in the UK every year."

"Really? How do you know that?"

"I looked it up. I was curious."

"So that's..." She struggled with the maths and gave up. "What, one percent or something?"

"No, much less. About one in ten thousand, I think."

The Sancerre arrived and Metcalfe waved for Karen to try it, which she did with every appearance of knowing what she was doing, and pronounced it excellent.

"Do you ever think of trying to trace your real mother?" she asked, as they replaced their glasses on the table.

"From time to time," he admitted. "I once got as far as finding out that she lived in Peterborough, but I decided not to follow it through."

"Another coincidence," she said with a smile. "So did I. Mine lives here in London. I even got her name. It's Susan Weedon. I used to carry it round with me for a while, her name and address, trying to decide whether to contact her or not."

"You obviously decided not to."

She nodded.

"Any particular reason?"

"Not really. I just reckoned she must have had good reasons to need to get rid of me, and that whatever they were I should respect them. I was very happy with my adopted parents, so it's not like I feel any great emotional need to find her—although some people do, I'm sure. With me, it's just curiosity. What's she like, why did she do it, that sort of thing."

"I know what you mean," he acknowledged. "It's pretty much the same with me, though sadly my adopted parents split up when I was fourteen."

"How was that?"

"It was OK actually. It was just a hassle from an administrative point of view. The adoption people had to come back and assess my mum as a single parent. In the end they decided it would be more disruptive to move me than to leave me where I was, which suited me fine."

"Do you still see her much?"

"Not as much as I should," he admitted guiltily. "It's difficult, because she moved out of London down to Devon, and the job keeps me so busy, but that's no real excuse I know." He took another sip of wine and noticed the first few drops of rain beginning to speckle the window pane.

"I wonder if that's why we find it so easy to be friends," Karen mused. "As you say, it's a highly unlikely thing to have in common."

"Perhaps, yes," he replied.

He felt a sudden inner certainty that a defining moment had arrived, a split second in which a certain thing could be said, or at least hinted at. A moment which, if allowed to pass, might never recur.

"Actually..." he began uncertainly, feeling his chest tighten.

"Please don't," she said quietly.

His gaze was more eloquent than anything he could have said.

She shook her head silently, gazing intently into her wine glass and twirling her fingers around the stem. Finally, she spoke. "We can't have this conversation, at least not now. I'm not free and it wouldn't be fair to Peter to pretend that I am, or even that I might be. It's my problem and I need to resolve it. I need to work out what I want."

"I'm shocked," he said, though quite unnecessarily. "I thought you were happy with him. I mean, when I see you both together it feels like there's a real bond between you."

"Oh, there is. I've never respected anyone as much as I respect Peter. He's hugely intelligent, he has more integrity than anyone I've ever met, and he's a thoroughly nice person."

"That's the way he strikes me too," Metcalfe was forced to admit. "But of course, there's his...well, I mean he can be a bit..."

"The word you're looking for is 'strange,' I think," she said with a sad little smile. "Don't worry, it's what a lot of people think. And if you mean 'not normal' or 'not like other people,' you'd be right."

"I'm not sure I meant it quite like that," he said uncomfortably. "What is 'normal' anyway? Maybe 'eccentric' might be a better word, or 'individual' perhaps."

"A good one certainly—'eccentric,' I mean. I used to think he was just genuinely eccentric in the fine old English tradition, pretending that the second half of the twentieth century had never really happened, affecting the dress and mannerisms of the 1920s, all that sort of thing. Then I realised that it wasn't like that at all." She took a drink of wine and he waited for her to go on.

"It's more than that for him, and more serious too. It's a defence mechanism. He finds real life challenging, particularly when it places him under any sort of pressure. He's a very gentle soul really, brilliant but fragile, rather like a beautiful vase. When it all gets too much he retreats into all this period tomfoolery, but for him it's deadly serious. He's using it to run away from something he finds overwhelming, the way a kid might hide behind the sofa if something frightens him on television."

"Where does he get it from?" Metcalfe asked hesitantly. "I can't help feeling there's a book in there somewhere, or perhaps a whole series of them. Is it Jeeves and Wooster?"

"Not really. It's actually Lord Peter Wimsey. He's completely obsessed with him—always has been since he was young. He grew up in a house without television and his mother had the complete set of Dorothy L. Sayers in her bookcase—you know, the originals in the yellow covers. He claims she even named him after Wimsey."

"I don't know," he said ruefully, "about the covers, I mean. I tried them in paperback, well, one or two anyway, but to be honest I don't think I ever managed to finish one."

"Then I think you're the poorer for it," she said judiciously. "I'm not sure they're particularly great detective stories, and I agree they can drag terribly from time to time, but they're very well written, and Wimsey is one of the great literary creations. If I was a man and I wanted a comforting literary figure to hide in I think I'd probably choose him too. As it is, when he's in that sort of mood I get to play Harriet Vane, and she's not so bad either."

"Did Sayers base Harriet on herself?" he asked, feeling it was a very intelligent query to make.

"Well, sort of. She's more of an idealised version of what Sayers would like to have thought of herself as, just as Wimsey is the idealised man she always wanted to meet and have fall in love with her. Poor woman, apparently she had a very unhappy love life in reality."

The conversation halted while the empty main course plates were collected.

"Is it...well, difficult—the play-acting I mean?" he asked diffidently.

"To be honest, I enjoy it hugely," she said, tossing back her hair with a smile. "I suppose it's a bit like going on holiday. Hartley said the past was a foreign country, didn't he? Well, he's right, and it's fun. You get to wear elegant clothes and be treated like a lady, and everyone has perfect manners. That's why so many people get turned on by it."

"Really? I had no idea."

"Oh yes, it's not just Peter, you know. Why, there must be anything up to a hundred people or more at some of the vintage evenings we go to. Everyone loves dressing up and dancing proper dances, and having someone help you with your coat and open the door for you.

"In fact," she went on, laughing at the thought, "we met Collison and his wife outside one the other week. She looks very nice, by the way."

"Don't tell me they're into that sort of thing?" He gasped.

"Oh, no, they were just looking for somewhere to have dinner. Though I think he'd fit straight in. There's an air of the natural gentleman about him. In fact, before Peter had even met him I told him Collison reminded me a bit of Rory Alleyn, and after he'd had a chance to observe him himself he agreed with me."

"And Rory Alleyn is...who?" He floundered.

"Oh, Bob, he's Ngaio Marsh's detective, silly. Don't you read anything from the Golden Age?"

"A bit of Agatha Christie, from time to time," he answered defensively. "So, tell me," he said, deciding it was high time to move the topic of conversation away from authors with whom he had at best a nodding acquaintance, "if you enjoy all this period stuff so much, why are you thinking of splitting up with Peter?"

"I wasn't thinking of it at all until I met you," she replied simply. "Then almost at once being around you made me feel, well, disturbed I suppose. And that in turn made me start to question what I feel for Peter, though I know very well that the poor lamb is very much in love with me."

Metcalfe felt a spasm of disbelief. Had she really just said what he thought she had just said?

"You mean...?" He floundered for a way of asking what it was he wanted to ask.

"I mean I'm pretty sure I know what you feel and yes, I feel it too. Now please, let's change the subject."

They sat in silence.

"Could I just ask"—he was still in a daze—"I mean, not to put you under any pressure or anything, just for my own peace of mind, when you think you might make a decision?"

"Sooner than you think, perhaps," she said with another quick smile. "Peter and I are going away tomorrow and not coming back until the day before the trial. I cleared it with Collison yesterday. He was concerned about my arrears of leave and was very keen for me to get away somewhere. I think he's going to have the same chat with you, by the way."

"Oh God," he said in dismay, "I hope not. It's not as if I really have anywhere I want to go."

"Devon, perhaps?" she suggested gently.

He flushed. "Yes," he said. "I'm sorry, I shouldn't have said that, should I? Must have sounded very selfish or ungrateful or something."

"Not at all."

She picked up the bottle and showed him that there was still enough left for a glass each. "May I assume that we at least have time to finish the wine?"

To his great disgust he then heard himself say something very corny indeed. "Yes, of course. In fact, I think we may have all the time in the world."

Chapter Eleven

"Bit of a turn up for the books, Simon," Alistair Partington said ruminatively. He and Collison were sitting side by side on one of the benches in the lobby of the Old Bailey. "I thought chummy would plead guilty," he went on, "but it seems from what his silk has just told us that we're going to have a fight on our hands."

"He's going to plead 'not guilty'?" Collison asked in amazement. "But the evidence is overwhelming."

As he spoke, Karen Willis arrived wearing a black skirt suit that momentarily deprived him of the power to think about anything else at all. From the slightly glazed eyes and inane smile on Partington's face as he introduced them, it appeared that his learned friend was similarly affected.

"I'm sure," the barrister went on, trying but failing to keep his eyes away from Karen, "that they're just going to test the evidence. I really don't see what else they can do."

"Will he give evidence, do you think?" Metcalfe asked. He had joined the group unseen.

"Well, we shall see what we shall see," Partington replied. "But personally I wouldn't let chummy anywhere near the witness stand."

They were all in court ten minutes later to hear Gary Clarke say "Not guilty" faintly but defiantly as each of the five charges of murder were put to him.

Patrick Barratt QC rose to his feet with an air of faint ennui. "May it please you, my Lord," he intoned, "I appear for the prosecution with my learned friend Mr Partington. M'learned friend Mr Smithers appears for the defence, with Ms Belinda Jilkes."

The Honourable Judge Brownlow, entitled despite his rank to be addressed as 'my Lord' since he was sitting as a judge in the Central Criminal Court, had all this information in front of him already, but he nodded sagely and pretended to write it down nonetheless. "Yes, Mr Barratt," he said.

"Members of the jury," Barratt began, turning slightly to address them. "As you have just heard from the charges which were put to the accused, this is a most distressing case involving five counts of murder, the violent and gruesome murders of five women to be exact. I regret that some of the evidence which you will have to hear and see you may find disturbing."

A slight frisson ran through the courtroom, as indeed Barratt had intended that it should. He looked down at his notes and then back over the top of his half-moon glasses at the jury, as he began to open his case.

While Barratt outlined the circumstances of each killing, Metcalfe felt his attention wander. For one thing, he knew this particular story all too well. For another, he had not had a chance to speak to Karen since her return from leave. Now here she was sitting next to him and he was all too conscious that their thighs were almost touching but not quite. In an effort to divert himself, he gazed at the junior counsel for the defence but since she was ugly and exuded an air of gratuitous aggressiveness, he found little solace in that direction.

As might be expected of a respected member of the senior bar, Barratt put the case calmly, simply and effectively to the jury. At one point he said, "It is, I believe, common ground, that five items of female underwear were found at the address where the accused was living, and that these each respectively bore the DNA of one of the five victims."

The defence QC half-rose apologetically to ask that his learned friend amend this to 'the common parts of the address where the accused was living,' whereupon the judge murmured something approving and Mr Barratt gestured in a distinguished yet deferential fashion and made the necessary correction. There was however something about his manner as he did so which conveyed to the jury the unmistakeable impression that they were entirely free to treat this intervention as the example of trivial legal pettifogging that it undoubtedly was.

By lunchtime the prosecution had taken the jury through each of the five murders, detailing how each body had been discovered, the findings in each case of the post-mortem examination, and whatever was known about how each victim had come to be in the place where she had been found. Much stress was laid on the common modus operandi in each killing: the use of chloroform to subdue the victim and the subsequent single blow to the head, probably from some sort of hammer.

The police team adjourned to a cafe around the corner. It was not a pleasant experience, being both crowded and noisy, but they found some sandwiches and a corner in which to wedge themselves.

"So, just remind me," Collison said, "how we are going to deal with the evidence." He had been largely out of contact with the case for the last couple of weeks.

"Well, strictly speaking we don't have to ask anyone to give oral evidence," Metcalfe replied, "since the defence agreed all our witness statements at the committal proceedings. Except Susan McCormick's, that is."

"Makes sense." Collison nodded as he swallowed a piece of something which was masquerading as ham. "The only chance they have is to shake her evidence, and they can only do that in cross-examination."

"Quite so," Metcalfe agreed, suddenly realising that he was lapsing into legal patois himself. "Anyway, she's here for when we need her. I checked."

"OK, come on," Collison said as someone pushed clumsily into them from behind, "let's get out of here if you're finished."

"Has anyone noticed if Dr Barker is in court?" Karen Willis asked as they walked back.

"He's not coming," Metcalfe announced. "I went yesterday to make sure he had all the details of which court we were in, but he said he didn't think he could face it."

"Understandable," Collison said briefly.

Towards the end of the afternoon Mr Barratt, by now noticeably a little hoarse, concluded his opening speech to the jury, and turned to address the judge. "May it please the court," he said, "we now come to the question of oral evidence, on which an issue arises which both Mr Smithers and I are agreed might most happily be dealt with by your Lordship in the absence of the jury."

"Yes," said the judge, who had been expecting just such an eventuality ever since he had read his papers the day before. "Members of the jury," he continued, addressing them with what he imagined to be an avuncular smile, "an issue has arisen of a strictly legal nature, which it is right that I should discuss with counsel alone. You should not infer anything at all from the fact that such submissions are being made. Indeed they are quite common in criminal trials. Would you now please go with the usher, who will take you to the jury room. I hope we will not detain you long."

He waited for them to file out of court and then looked down at the two QCs. "Now then, Mr Smithers," he said, reaching for the appropriate folder, "I assume you wish to address me on Ms McCormick's evidence."

"Indeed, my Lord," replied the defence QC, rising to his feet. "Your Lordship will note that, as agreed between the prosecution and the defence, two different versions of the McCormick witness statement have been prepared, one including matters to which the defence objects and the other which does not. According to whatever decision your Lordship reaches on this matter, one can be used and the other discarded.

It was felt by my learned friend and myself that this would be the most convenient way of dealing with the matter."

"Very sensible," the judge commented.

"I'm obliged, my Lord. The issue arises in this way. The defendant, when questioned, put forward alibi evidence for the night of the killing of Katherine Barker, the nature of his alibi being that he spent that night at home with Susan McCormick. When she was asked to confirm this, however, she declined to do so. My Lord, we recognise that this raises an express issue of fact on the evidence and that it is right that she should give her evidence on this and be cross-examined upon it."

"Indeed," the judge acknowledged, "but presumably you seek to exclude the wider evidence which she gave on other matters."

"Your Lordship has the point exactly. Ms McCormick says that she visited the defendant's flat on one occasion only, that she was there only for a short period, that she cut short her visit because she felt him to be behaving strangely towards her, and that after leaving the flat she began to believe that a drink she had been given by the defendant had in fact been drugged."

"And the basis of your submission is...?"

"My Lord, this evidence is hugely prejudicial to the defendant and yet is vague and incapable of independent verification. What sort of behaviour constitutes 'strange' or 'weird,' and to what extent may Ms McCormick's view have been coloured retrospectively by the fact that by the time she was asked these questions it must have been obvious that the defendant was being investigated by the police? As to the allegation of the defendant attempting to drug her, no medical evidence at all of this has been submitted. We do not question Ms McCormick's good faith, but again hindsight may be colouring her views. Suppose she just felt sleepy for perfectly natural and unconnected reasons?"

He watched the judge's pencil and waited for it to stop moving.

"My Lord, this is not similar fact evidence. It is common ground that each of these killings featured the topical application of chloroform, not the ingestion of some sort of sleeping draught. My fear is that if your Lordship should allow this evidence to go before the jury then its prejudicial effect would far outweigh its probative value."

"Thank you, Mr Smithers, that is most helpful. Mr Barratt, what do you say?"

"My Lord, may I say at once that I do not seek to argue that this is similar fact evidence. I hear what my learned friend says on that, and am content not to contest it. However, I do say that as a matter of common sense and practicality, it may prove very difficult to excise it. The accused says the witness spent the night with him. She says she did not. My friend will presumably ask her in cross-examination how she can be so sure about that. Surely any answer she gives is likely to lead us straight into the circumstances of this earlier meeting?"

"I think we can leave it to Mr Smithers how he chooses to put matters in cross-examination, Mr Barratt. This is your witness. The issue is surely what matters you may properly put to her during examination in chief?"

The judge looked over his glasses at the prosecution benches with the air of a man who knows he has just scored a palpable hit.

"My Lord, clearly I do seek to put these matters to the witness."

There was a pause during which the spectre of the Court of Appeal hovered menacingly over the proceedings.

"Then I must give a ruling," the judge said calmly. "I find I am with Mr Smithers on these points. You may ask the witness how many times she visited the defendant's flat and how long any such visit may have lasted. I will exclude any further aspects of the McCormick evidence. Mr Barratt, in case you might at any time wish to raise this point in other proceedings I will happily deal with it fully during my judgment."

"I am obliged, my Lord," Barratt replied, bobbing up and down again languidly with every appearance of indifference.

The jury were now recalled and informed that the prosecution had concluded their opening speech. It was explained that all the evidence in the case had been agreed as just stated by prosecuting counsel save only for the question of a disputed alibi.

"It is of course for his Lordship to direct you," Barratt said with a deferential nod in the direction of the bench, "after both the prosecution and the defence have closed their cases. However, if it assists at this point, the prosecution would willingly concede that if you believe the accused's evidence as to his alleged alibi then clearly you must acquit, since by definition he could not have been at the crime scene at the time when the murder was committed."

"That is indeed helpful, Mr Barratt," the judge said. "Thank you."

"I call Susan McCormick," Barratt said.

The tall figure of Susan McCormick took the stand and recited the oath in a clear, steady voice as she glanced calmly around the courtroom.

"Ms McCormick," Barratt said, "there is only one matter I wish to ask you about. Can I ask you please to look at the witness statement in front of you? My Lord, members of the jury, in the interests of convenience the witness is being shown a photocopy of the document you have beginning at page 14 in bundle number 3."

A rumbling of folders and fluttering of pages now ensued as the jury self-consciously found the right place in the right bundle.

"What you have there, Ms McCormick, is a statement given to the police by the accused after his arrest but before he was charged. Can I take you to the second page? You will see in the second paragraph that he says that he was with you on the night Katherine Barker was killed. In fact, not to put too fine a point on it, he claims that you spent the night with him at his flat. The whole night."

"I see that, yes," she said. "It's not true. I've already told the police that."

"Quite so," Barratt said, "but it is contested by the defence and so I am afraid we have to ask you to tell the jury and his lordship as well. Just to be clear, when you say it's not true, does it contain any truth at all? Did you, for example, spend some part of that night, or even the evening, at his flat?"

"No," she said firmly, glaring at him. "I did not."

"How can you be so sure?"

Smithers jumped to his feet. "Really, my lord," he exclaimed. "Is my friend intending to cross-examine his own witness?"

"Yes, Mr Smithers," the judge acknowledged. "Mr Barratt, I am uncomfortable with giving you too much leeway here, particularly in view of my earlier ruling."

"Then perhaps I could make the question less open-ended," Barratt suggested smoothly. "Ms McCormick, have you ever in fact spent the night at the accused's flat?"

"I will allow that," the judge said, "but after Ms McCormick has answered the question I think we must leave it to Mr Smithers to decide whatever he may or may not wish to raise in cross-examination."

"I am in your Lordship's hands, of course," Barratt said loftily. "Ms McCormick, could you answer my last question, please?"

"I have never spent the night with the accused," came the reply, "whether at his flat or anywhere else. Just to be clear, I have never had any form of sexual contact or physical intimacy with him—of whatever nature. Nor would I ever wish to."

She seemed to shudder at this thought, and an expression of distaste, or even disgust flitted across her face. It was only there for a moment, but Barratt was quick to notice it, and hoped the jury had too.

"Thank you," Barratt said, sitting down. "Could you stay there, please? I think my learned friend may have some questions for you."

Smithers stood up and shuffled his papers. "Ms McCormick," he said finally. "I have to put it to you that what you have just said is not true."

"It most certainly *is* true," she responded very firmly indeed.

"I put it to you," he pressed on, ignoring her reply, "that in fact you did over a period of time have some form of relationship with the defendant, a relationship which perhaps you now regret, particularly in the light of the grave accusations which have been made against him, but a relationship which nonetheless happened?"

"No," she said, "I did not."

"You may wish to reconsider that reply," Smithers said, looking at her gravely. "I know you do not have the full trial bundles in front of you, but let me point out from the forensic reports that when the defendant's flat was examined by Scene of Crime Officers, some DNA was discovered which did not belong to the defendant. It was subsequently identified as being your own, after you gave a saliva swab to the police."

"That's hardly surprising," she riposted with a tight smile. "I didn't say I had never been to the flat. I went there once and once only after he did me a favour by fixing my computer for me. He invited me round for a drink and I felt it would be churlish to refuse."

"Which rooms did you use?" Smithers asked.

"The living room, of course—and the bathroom, I think. Yes, I used the bathroom while I was there, just before I left."

"Not the bedroom then?"

"No, of course not."

"Then can you explain how your DNA came to be found in the bedroom—on the bed itself, in fact?"

A murmur ran through the court. For the first time, Susan McCormick seemed rattled and taken aback. "No," she said uncertainly.

"No further questions, my Lord," Smithers said, sitting down with a sigh of relief.

Barratt had already risen. "Ms McCormick," he said soothingly, "do you remember if you had a coat or a handbag, or both, with you when you visited the accused's flat?"

"A handbag certainly," she said, with a nod. "I'm not sure about a coat, but possibly. In fact, I remember I had some shopping with me as well. I'd just been to the supermarket."

"Do you remember what happened to any of these items when you put them down?"

She wrinkled her face in concentration. "I do have a dim recollection that he took them away from me, because I can remember him going to get them when I left, so I suppose they must have been in a different room."

"Thank you very much," Barratt purred. "No further questions."

Chapter Twelve

After all the legal sparring over Susan McCormick's evidence, the few minutes which it had taken to deliver and test it seemed to pass very quickly.

"That concludes the case for the prosecution, my lord," Barratt said, and sat down with the air of a job well done.

Now it was Smithers's turn to stand up again. "May it please the court, I call the defendant, Mr Clarke."

Collison noted to himself that the defence team would always refer to the accused as "the defendant," as if to blur the line between criminal and civil proceedings, whereas for the prosecution it was always "the accused" or even "the prisoner."

Clarke took the stand looking tense.

"Mr Clarke," Smithers said, "would you please tell the jury where you were on the night of 15th May last? If I may be permitted to lead on this point, just to be clear, that was the night on which it is common ground that Katherine Barker met her death."

"I was at home all night," Clarke replied.

"Alone?"

"No, I was with Susan McCormick, the lady who gave evidence earlier."

"So you heard her say that your claim was untrue?"

"I did, yes."

"But you still say that you were at home that night and that she was with you?"

"Yes, she stayed the night."

"Just to be clear," Smithers said, turning to the jury as if to apologise for trespassing on a sensitive area, "when you say she stayed the night, do you mean that she spent the night with you in your bed?"

"Yes, I do."

Smithers turned again to the jury, before continuing. "Could I now take you to a different point? Much has been made of a box which the police found in the loft area accessed from outside your flat."

"Which they *say* they found there, yes," Clarke replied.

"Well, as to that the jury must of course make up their minds—," Smithers said hurriedly, but Barratt was already on his feet.

"My Lord," he said, looking deeply pained, "could I remind the court that the witness statements of the police officers concerned were agreed by the defence at the committal proceedings. Does my learned friend now seek to re-open these matters? If so, that would of course give rise to various procedural issues..." He let the sentence hang in the air.

The judge was also clearly unhappy. "Quite so, Mr Barratt, quite so," he concurred. He glanced at the clock. "Mr Smithers, since you will undoubtedly wish to take instructions on this point, would that be a convenient moment for me to rise? And will you please inform my clerk as soon as possible what the basis of those instructions might be?"

"Thank you, my Lord," Smithers said. "That would indeed be convenient."

The court rose while the judge gathered his papers and left, having first bowed to the members of the bar, who reciprocated.

The police team gathered once again in the lobby, this time in the august company of both Alistair Partington and Patrick Barratt QC. The latter had pushed his wig towards the back of his head as if to signal that the day's serious business was over.

"Clients who won't follow the script really are a barrister's worst nightmare," he said. "I'm sure he'll have been told that he wasn't allowed to say that."

"Does it matter, do you think?" Collison asked.

"Not a scrap," Barratt said confidently. "The defence will bob up tomorrow, withdraw the remark and ask the judge to ask the jury to disregard it."

"But they've already heard it," Karen Willis pointed out, not unreasonably.

"Yes, but if anything it hurts the defence," Barratt replied. "A defendant casting doubt on the word of two senior police officers with not a shred of supporting evidence? No, I rather think they will take it for what it obviously was: the last throw of a desperate man."

"What about that DNA evidence?" said Metcalfe. "Funny, I don't remember that from the lab reports."

"That one came late, if you remember," Karen explained. "We only just had time to get it into the bundles before they went out."

"I don't think it really adds much, does it?" Partington said sceptically. "We know she was in the flat and if her coat or something was put on the bed that would explain the DNA. It was only a minute amount, after all."

Barratt nodded sagely and gazed meaningfully at his watch. Taking the hint, the party stood up and took their leave, the barristers sauntering off towards the robing room. Collison sensed, with some amusement, that the other two wanted to be on their own and left them with a cheery farewell. Metcalfe looked at Karen.

"Oh Bob. Not here, not now, please."

"I just need to know," he said abjectly, "whether you've made a decision, I mean. I've been on tenterhooks since you went away."

"Yes I have, and yes, it's you," she said. "There, so now you know. But please give me time to do this right, or as right as I can anyway."

"Have you said anything to Peter?"

"No, and that's why I need some time," she said calmly. "We've been together for five years now, and it's not the sort of thing I can just blurt out. I need to choose my moment."

"OK, OK," he said hurriedly, trying to stop himself from beaming. "You must play it exactly how you want. Don't worry. Now I know how you feel I can be as patient as you like."

"Thank you, Bob. I won't be long, I promise."

She leaned towards him and they kissed, awkwardly, for the first time. It was the briefest of kisses, no more than a peck on the lips, but he smelt her perfume and felt giddy with happiness. He gazed at her, unsure of what to say.

"Goodbye, Bob," she said gently. "See you tomorrow."

Little more than an hour later she was home in Hampstead and beginning to prepare dinner when she heard Peter's key in the lock. She called out to him, "I'm in the kitchen!"

He came into the room and, putting his arms around her from behind, kissed her gently on the top of her head. "Evening, old thing," he said. "How did it go?"

She finished chopping some garlic. "Why don't you pour us both a glass of wine?" she suggested. "Then we can sit down properly and I can tell you all about it."

"Good thinking," he replied.

As he judiciously selected a bottle of Meursault and drew the cork, she washed her hands and went to sit down in the living room.

"All right," he said, following her into the room and handing her a glass of wine, "now shoot."

So she did. He listened carefully, nodding now and then, particularly when she told him about the discussion over the McCormick evidence.

"Our 'perp' is still denying it, then?" he commented when she had finished. "That's odd. It worries me a bit, in fact."

"How so?"

"Well, most serial killers deny everything at first, of course. In fact they may be interviewed several times, as the Yorkshire Ripper was. But when they're confronted by hard evidence of their guilt, they usually flip and start bragging about what they've done and trying to explain why."

"Which is never anything to do with them, of course."

"Absolutely not. Either they'll claim to have heard voices telling them what to do or it will be some sort of big grudge against society, usually brought about by their own inadequacies. And yet you say there's no sign of that?"

"None whatsoever."

"And he claims that the police planted the evidence in the loft area outside his flat?"

"Yes," she said with a grim smile. "Big mistake, hopefully. The prosecution evidence was agreed at the committal proceedings so the only way he can challenge it now is for his barrister to ask the judge for a new trial, and there are no real grounds for doing that."

"But the jury have already heard his allegation, haven't they? I mean, it's all very well the judge directing them to disregard it, which is presumably what he will do, but that's easier said than done. Might they not be prejudiced by it? I hate to tell you this, but there are a lot of people out there who believe that the police *do* fabricate evidence, you know."

"And sadly, they've been right on various occasions in the past," Karen acknowledged.

"My point exactly. Aren't the prosecution worried that the jury might feel the defence has raised just enough doubt for them to be unable to convict?"

"They don't seem to be," she said. "Their view is that they're likely to go the other way, taking a dim view of him casting aspersions on the police evidence without being able to make good his claims. At first I thought exactly the same as you, but having had a chance to consider it some more I think I incline the other way."

He was silent for a while. "I'm still troubled by this apparent stalking of the last victim. It really doesn't fit the pattern."

"But *he* does," Karen reminded him. "He fits the profile you gave us exactly. You were brilliant."

"Was I though?" he mused, tugging the lobe of his ear. "Suppose all I did was to create a template and you lot just went off and looked for the first chap who fitted it?"

"But that's what profiling's all about, silly," she said in exasperation. "The profiler limits the search to as narrow parameters as possible so that from then onwards the police are still searching for a needle, but in a much smaller haystack."

"And I suppose the evidence is pretty overwhelming, isn't it?" Peter asked, as if to reassure himself.

"You bet it is. He fits the perpetrator's profile exactly, doesn't have an alibi for a single one of the murder dates, and the murder weapon and trophies taken from the victims were found at his property."

"Yet he claims that he does have an alibi," Peter objected, "and for the most important of the murders in many ways, as it seems to be the only one that might not quite fit the pattern."

"Oh that's stuff and nonsense and you know it. There's ample evidence that the man is a complete fantasist. Look at how he lied about his supposed military service, for example. I've no doubt he's held out Susan McCormick to various people as being his girlfriend and now feels he has to live out the lie regardless, perhaps because reality is now so far away from what he wants for himself, what he wants to be or do."

"Timothy Evans was a fantasist," Peter said mildly, "but he was still innocent, while Christie had a police commendation but was guilty."

"Oh, Peter, you really are quite impossible this evening," she replied. "I'm going to see to the dinner."

The next morning the defence, as anticipated, indicated that they would not be pursuing the point raised by Gary Clarke the previous day and the judge, as anticipated, directed the jury to disregard it.

Having chosen to give evidence in his own defence, Clarke now had to submit to cross-examination by Patrick Barratt who rose to his feet, spent what seemed like a long time studying a note in front of him and then looked up to gaze at the accused in a vaguely absent-minded manner.

"Mr Clarke," he began, "you're asking the jury to believe that Susan McCormick spent the night with you at your flat, whereas you have heard for yourself that she flatly denies that any such thing ever took place."

"Yes," Clarke replied. "I am, because it's true."

"Ah, well, there we may have a bit of a problem. You're not much given to telling the truth, are you? In fact, not to put too fine a point on it, you tell what might fairly be called a pack of lies on a regular basis, don't you?"

"Sit down, Mr Smithers," the judge said as the latter showed signs of intervening. "Mr Barratt, I will grant you some indulgence, but I trust you are going somewhere specific with this line of questioning?"

"Indeed I am, my lord," Barratt replied smoothly. "Mr Clarke, is it not the case that you told various of your work acquaintances on several occasions that you had spent some years in the military, and had in fact served as part of what are generally known as special forces?"

"I don't know," Clarke said uncertainly.

"Allow me to assist you," Barratt said evenly. "The evidence to which I refer is contained in various of the prosecution statements, the contents of which were agreed by your counsel at the committal proceedings. I will ask you the question again: is it true that you have claimed in the past to have served with special forces?"

"I might have done."

"And is it not the case that in fact your only military training was a few weeks with the Territorials, with whom you failed even to complete your basic training?"

"Yes," Clarke admitted reluctantly.

"So those were lies then, the stories which you told."

"If you say so."

"It's not I who say so, Mr Clarke, but you," Barratt explained as though to a backward child. "You made specific statements of truth to various people which you now admit to be untrue." He paused but Clarke made no response.

"You told lies."

Again there was no response.

"Very well," Barratt said, having gazed meaningfully at the jury. "Let us move on."

He picked up a piece of paper and held it out for the clerk. "Would you please look at this, Mr Clarke? Members of the jury, my lord, you will find this behind tab 6 in prosecution bundle 3."

The jury shuffled self-importantly through their binders. Barratt waited for them to find the right place and then went on. "Mr Clarke, do you recognise this document? It is in fact the CV which you submitted when you took up your present employment, isn't it?"

"I think so, yes."

"Right at the top of the document, you list your qualifications: A Levels in Physics and Mathematics, and a Bachelor of Science degree in Information Technology from the University of East Anglia. That is correct, is it not?"

"That's what it says."

"It is indeed what it says, Mr Clarke, and yet it's all untrue, isn't it? The police have ascertained that you never attended the University of East Anglia or indeed, so far as they can tell, any other university."

He waited ostentatiously for a response, but none was forthcoming. "I see that you do not challenge the police evidence on this point."

"I may have made up the degree," Clarke acknowledged, "but the A Levels are real enough. I could have gone to university if I'd wanted to. I just chose not to because I couldn't afford it."

"I see," Barratt replied. "You refer, I assume, to the A Level certificates which the police found at your flat?"

"Yes."

"Also behind tab 6, members of the jury," Barratt said with a smile in their direction. "You will see that they are A Level certificates in Physics and Mathematics issued by the Oxford and Cambridge examination board.

"There is only one problem, Mr Clarke," he went on, turning back to the witness box. "They're fakes, aren't they? The police have checked with the examination board and they have no record of you ever obtaining any A Levels with them. Their opinion is that these are in fact O Level certificates, or GCSEs as we must say these days, which have been altered, possibly having first been scanned into a computer."

Clarke made no reply.

"So it comes to this, then," Barratt continued. "You ask the jury to believe something, a crucial piece of evidence, mind, in spite of the fact that the only person who can confirm your story—a respectable lady with no apparent reason to lie, and someone moreover who is giving evidence on oath in court—flatly denies it."

"I'm on oath too," Clarke pointed out.

"Indeed you are, Mr Clarke, and I ask you to remember the significance of that. Now, let me ask you again, having admitted that you have lied repeatedly in the past, is it not the case that you lied earlier when you told work colleagues that you had a girlfriend, namely Susan McCormick, when in fact you did not? Is it not the case that she was by way of being a fantasy girlfriend and that your relationship with her, beyond a few innocent everyday encounters, existed only in your imagination?"

"No," Clarke said stubbornly, "it's true."

Barratt waited a few moments and then smiled at the judge. "No further questions, my lord," he said, sitting down with another significant glance at the jury.

A few minutes later he was on his feet again, beginning his closing address to the jury. Briefly he rehearsed the details of the first four murders, those of Amy Grant, Jenny Hillyer, Joyce Mteki and Tracy Redman. At the conclusion of each description he stated coldly that Clarke had no alibi for the night of the killing. He described how in each case the victim's underwear had been removed and found later by the police in the loft space outside Clarke's flat. Then he came to the last murder.

In the case of Katherine Barker, he noted, there were two additional factors. On the one hand there was the fish food which, while admittedly circumstantial, could be argued to link Clarke to the killing. On the other hand lay the fact that for the first time Clarke was claiming to have an alibi which, if true, would conclusively show that he could not possibly have committed the murder and thus, by implication, any of the murders.

"You have heard what the accused has to say on the subject," Barratt said, staring hard at the jury, "but against that you have to weigh three things. First there is the evidence of Susan McCormick, a lady who has no reason to lie. Second, you have heard evidence, including from the accused himself, that he has in fact lied regularly about various matters in the past. Third, and I make this point reluctantly but I think it is a necessary one for you to consider, you may look upon both the accused and Ms McCormick, an attractive and intelligent woman, and ask yourselves how likely it might be that such a relationship would appeal to her."

"Frankly, ladies and gentlemen, for all the reasons I have stated, I put it to you that the accused's allegations of an alibi are quite simply incredible, and that you should disregard them. The prosecution's evidence, on the other hand, is overwhelming. There is no reason why the murder weapon and the trophies taken by the murderer from his wretched victims should have been found outside the accused's flat, in an enclosed space not publicly accessible, unless the murderer himself put them there, and the conclusion is inescapable that the murderer and the accused are one and the same man."

Barratt sat down with the air of a job well done, and Smithers rose to reply.

The evidence was entirely circumstantial, he argued. It was not for Clarke to prove that he had not committed the murders, but for the prosecution to prove that he had. Yet all the evidence they had produced simply did not meet the necessary burden of proof. Many people bought the same fish food. Anyone who had at any time had a front door key to Clarke's building would have had access to the loft space.

He moved onto the alleged alibi. Just because Clarke had been untruthful about certain minor events in the past did not mean that he was being untruthful now about a completely different subject and in very different circumstances. The DNA evidence was at the very least consistent with his story, even if it was not conclusive. All that the defence needed to do, he reminded the jury, was to raise reasonable doubt as to the defendant's guilt, and surely the claimed alibi did exactly that?

The judge then summed up for the jury. He urged them to place "whatever weight they felt to be appropriate" on the discoveries in the loft. The fish food was indeed circumstantial but again it was for the jury to decide for themselves how much weight they attached to it; they were the sole arbiters of fact. As to the alibi, there was a straight conflict of evidence. Only one of Susan McCormick and Gary Clarke could be telling the truth. It was for the jury to decide which witness they found the more compelling.

The jury retired to consider their verdict.

"Don't go far," Barratt warned the detectives. "I can't see this taking very long."

His instincts proved accurate. In less than an hour the jury filed back into court and gave a unanimous verdict of guilty on all counts.

Sitting in the public gallery, Metcalfe felt a strange feeling of unreality. The case had consumed his life for so long that it was hard to come to terms with the fact that it was all over. Sitting next to him Collison smiled, shook his hand and then reached across to do the same with Willis. Meanwhile the judge asked Clarke if he had anything to say.

"Yes," Clarke said loudly. "I didn't do it."

Having asked if that was all he had to say, the judge then sentenced him to five terms of life imprisonment, to run concurrently. He was taken down the stairs to the cells while the judge thanked the jury for their efforts.

A few minutes later Collison was facing the inevitable barrier of cameras and microphones outside the Old Bailey. Standing on the steps, he gave a brief statement. "As always," he said clearly, as the journalistic clamour quietened, "the police are delighted that a criminal has been brought to justice, particularly in a case of this nature since it also achieves closure for the victims' families. We'd like to thank them for their patience and support during this enquiry."

"Do you think he may have killed more than five times?" shouted a journalist.

"Did he have an accomplice?" called another.

Collison raised his hand for silence and waited as the hubbub threatened to derail proceedings. Some of the journalists at the front of the crowd turned and shouted "Quiet!" to their colleagues further back.

"I'm just going to say one more thing," Collison said, ignoring the shouted questions, "and it's an important one."

"This has been a long investigation and a thankless and often difficult time for the investigating team, which I joined only recently. I'd like to express my respect and appreciation for the efforts and professionalism of everyone who was involved, particularly my predecessor, Detective Chief Inspector Tom Allen, who led the team for over a year."

More questions rang out but he turned and walked away to where Bob Metcalfe and Karen Willis were waiting a little way off. "A job well done," he commented with a smile, "congratulations, both."

They thanked him awkwardly.

"Not sure what I'm going to do with myself now," Metcalfe said ruefully.

"I know what you mean," Collison replied. "You were on the case from the beginning, weren't you? That's a long time."

"There were times when I wondered if I'd end up spending my whole career on it."

Collison nodded. "I once spoke to someone who worked on the Yorkshire Ripper enquiry from the start. Six years, I think it was. It must have felt like a lifetime."

"That must be really awful," said Willis. "I wonder what happens if it goes on so long that your hope eventually dies, that you stop really believing that you're ever going to catch him."

"It was only by accident when they did," Metcalfe reminded her.

"Fortunately," Collison said briskly, "we shan't have to find out, not on this enquiry anyway. By the way, when I said 'a job well done,' I meant it. I've commended you both to the AC Crime."

Again there were embarrassed thanks.

"How about dinner tomorrow evening?" he suggested. "A restaurant if we can get a table somewhere, our place if not. I'll let you know when and where. Invite Peter of course, Karen, and you feel free to bring someone as well, Bob." He nodded and walked off. His phone rang and as he answered it he passed out of earshot.

Karen knew what Metcalfe was about to ask, and forestalled him.

"I need time, Bob," she implored him quietly. "Please give me time."

Chapter Thirteen

"Did you enjoy dinner last night?" Collison asked his wife.

"Very much," Caroline replied. "Nice people, your colleagues. Interesting too. Shame that Bob Metcalfe doesn't have a girlfriend. It's the job, I suppose. Too many nights and weekends in the incident room."

"I suppose," he answered absently. "Tell me something, darling, did your feminine intuition notice anything odd about the atmosphere?"

She looked puzzled. "No, I don't think so. What do you mean?"

"Oh, I don't know." He put teabags in two mugs and switched on the kettle. "Maybe I'm sticking my nose in where it doesn't belong, but it seems to me that Karen and Bob have become very close."

"Well, that's to be expected isn't it? After all, they've been working on the case together. Or do you mean something more?"

"I wonder, yes."

"Oh dear, that's all going to be a bit complicated isn't it? If you're right, I mean. What about that poor Peter? He's very lovely, but seems totally unsuited to the real world. He'd fall apart without Karen, and that *is* my feminine intuition talking."

"I know," he said moodily. "Let's hope I'm wrong." He poured the tea and added milk.

"Wouldn't it create problems on the force as well? They're different ranks, aren't they?"

"It would," he said heavily. "Strictly speaking you're supposed to register a relationship with a colleague, though the rules do allow quite a bit of discretion about what constitutes a relationship, and when it's deemed to have started."

"One night stands are OK, then?"

"God, yes. If they weren't, half the Met would be in trouble."

"Charming!"

At this juncture the phone rang. He answered it. "Collison here."

"The AC Crime's office, sir. He rang in from home. Have you seen the news this morning?"

"No, I haven't switched it on."

"Gary Clarke was attacked in prison, sir, almost as soon as he was moved across from the remand wing. He's in hospital with serious head injuries. Critical condition."

"Thank you for letting me know," Collison said after a pause.

"There's something else as well, sir. The AC Crime wonders if you could spare him a few minutes at ten o'clock?"

"Of course. You can't give me a clue what it is, I suppose?"

"Sorry, sir. Something the AC Crime wants to discuss with you personally."

"Very well, I'll be there."

He rang off.

"What was that all about?" Caroline asked.

"The AC Crime's office. Wanted to let me know that Clarke was attacked in prison. Sounds like he may not survive."

"Oh, Simon, that's awful."

"It happens," he said shortly. "They don't like SOs—that's what they call the sexual offenders. Strange. They're in there for all sorts of horrible things yet they all take a stand against sex crimes. I don't know whether that's comforting or just down-right hypocritical."

"Dreadful thing to happen, though," she said, looking at him with concern. "You mustn't blame yourself."

"I know, I know," he replied. "It's just my job to find them and put them away, right? What happens thereafter is none of my concern."

"Exactly. And there's no way you could have anticipated anything like this anyway."

"You're right there. Usually it's just scalding with cocoa.

"Damn!" he burst out suddenly. "Why didn't they keep him segregated from the others? At least for a few weeks."

"Overcrowding perhaps?" she suggested gently.

"I suppose so, yes." He sighed and picked up his tea. "And the AC wants to see me, so I'd better get going."

"Well, that's good isn't it?" Caroline asked. "He probably wants to congratulate you on a job well done, and discuss your next career move."

"That's what I was thinking too, but it's not necessarily good. He's already hinted that he wants to take me off operations, and that's what I really want to do."

As it turned out, his thinking was wide of the mark.

"Sit down, Simon," said a strangely distant AC Crime. "Look, I'll come straight to the point. We may have a problem with Clarke."

"Yes, I know, sir. Your office telephoned me earlier."

"No, not that. Well, yes, of course that's bad, but the real issue is this."

He stood up and walked to the window, looking out. "Late last night someone rang the Yard switchboard and asked to speak to someone on the Clarke case," he said without turning round. "Said he had some fresh evidence that should have been considered at the trial. An alibi, in fact, for one of the earlier killings. What do you say to that?"

"I would say," Collison replied evenly, "who is he or she, and why didn't they come forward earlier?"

"His real name is Bob Grant. He's a homeless person who goes by the nickname of Kitbag. He knew Clarke slightly a year or two back and claims that on the night Jenny Hillyer was murdered he and Clarke got drunk together way over in Essex. Clarke was so drunk he could hardly walk and so the hostel in Barking where Kitbag was dossing allowed him to stay the night since they had a spare bed."

Collison felt an iron band clamp itself around his chest. "We asked Clarke several times if he had an alibi for any of the killings, sir, and the only one he ever advanced was for Katherine Barker."

"I'm well aware of that," the ACC said, turning back to face him. "I've been reading the interview notes in the file. The fact remains that this is potentially important new evidence and needs to be investigated."

"Of course, sir. I'll get onto it right away. But I still don't understand why this Kitbag character didn't come forward before. After all, the case has been all over the media."

"Tom Allen says Kitbag doesn't read newspapers or watch TV, and anyway most of the time he's off his head on meth and has little idea of what's going on."

"Tom Allen?"

"Yes. He rang me first thing this morning." The ACC shifted uncomfortably, walked back to his desk and sat down. "It seems," he said heavily, "that Allen has been investigating the case on his own, exactly as you suspected, in fact. He's been digging around among all his snouts and one of them came up with Kitbag. Allen says he only found him yesterday."

Collison tasted something nasty in his mouth, and swallowed to try to get rid of it—without success. As he did so the phone rang. The ACC picked it up, listened, said "Thank you," impassively, and put it down.

"Clarke is dead. Never recovered consciousness apparently. So now we have a fresh murder case on our hands."

There was a long silence.

"Would you like me to take it on, sir?"

"No," the older man said decisively. "Much better if we can show that we've kept them separate. Better too if you stay out of the way on this Kitbag fellow, for the moment anyway. Send Metcalfe over to Barking to check out the hostel, and then you report back to me ASAP. I need to brief the Commissioner."

"Very good, sir."

"Simon," came a voice behind him before he could reach the door. "As I said, I've read the interview notes, albeit briefly. It seems quite clear to me that you did everything you could to get at the truth. If this does turn out badly I want you to remember that it's not your fault."

"Thank you, sir," he said quietly over his shoulder, "but somehow that doesn't seem to matter right now."

"Karen, it's Bob," Metcalfe said on the phone later, as he walked through the rather depressing environs of Barking station. "We've got a problem—with the Clarke case."

"What?"

"The guvnor rang me earlier. Somebody contacted the Yard with apparent alibi evidence that puts Clarke well away from the scene on the Hillyer killing. Said Clarke was staying the night in a hostel in Barking. Well, I've just been there and it checks out. They keep a record of all overnight guests and sure enough his name is in the book."

"That doesn't prove it was him," she pointed out. "He might have got someone to stay there and give his name."

"I agree, but then it doesn't really make sense, does it? Why go to all the trouble of constructing an alibi for yourself and then not raise it in court?"

"Quite right," she said gloomily. "Then it looks like we've goofed, though God knows how or when. I thought the case was so strong. Absolutely everything fell nicely into place."

"I know. I feel really choked. I was convinced we'd got our man. Now it looks as if we'll have to start all over again."

"So what happens now? I suppose Clarke will be released pending an appeal, which we won't contest?"

"Haven't you heard?" Metcalfe said awkwardly. "He's dead. Attacked in prison yesterday. Died in hospital this morning."

"Oh my God..." Her voice trailed away.

"There's more," he said grimly. "The new witness was found by Tom Allen, who has apparently been as good as his word and has been pursuing a parallel investigation on his own."

"Damn the man!"

"I know how you feel. Don't forget he dropped me right in it. But you've got to give credit where it's due. His instinct told him we'd got the wrong man and he worried away at the case until he found something."

"He just wanted to prove us wrong, if you ask me."

"Agreed—but he did."

"Have you told Collison?"

"Yes, just now before I rang you."

"Poor man. How is he?"

"Subdued," said Metcalfe with the air of a man choosing his words with care.

"That," she said, "is nothing to what Peter is going to feel. Oh God—and I have to tell him."

"Collison wants us to reconvene at Hampstead tomorrow. I'm arranging to have all the files brought out of storage. It means setting up the incident room and starting all over again. I think I've managed to grab Priya Desai, but I'm not sure about the others yet."

"OK, I'll see you then."

She rang off and sat down, where she stayed staring blankly out of the window for a long time. Then she took a deep breath and walked into the next room where Peter sat at his desk, taking notes as he read.

"Peter, darling," she said. "There's something I have to tell you."

❧ ❧ ❧

"Well, that is a turn up for the books and no mistake," said Lord Peter Wimsey. "Fancy Charles Parker getting the wrong man convicted. But from what you say it was the fault of that damn fool profiler, or whatever you call him."

"Not entirely," Harriet reminded him. "The profiler only offered a guide as to where the police should look. It was Charles and his men at the Yard who conducted the enquiry. And they did find pretty compelling physical evidence of the man's guilt. Good grief, Peter, surely the victims' underwear would be damning enough for most people?"

"True," Wimsey conceded. "But the fact remains that he must have taken a false turn somewhere, or he wouldn't have ended up at the wrong place. There must be a proverb in there somewhere."

"And it was up to the jury, don't forget. Charles's job is just to find the evidence, not try the case."

"True, oh wise one," Lord Peter said, throwing up his hands in defeat. "I am justly rebuked."

"I say, though," he went on, "what a dreadful thing for old Parker-bird. Particularly this new evidence not coming to light until after the poor blighter had been hanged. I do hope sister Mary is looking after him. Should we invite them here? He must be feeling absolutely wretched."

"We could do that, of course," she said cautiously, "but you may find he'd rather spend some time on his own for a while."

"Quite so," Lord Peter agreed. "Perhaps you should sound Mary out and see how the land lies?"

"Of course I will," she replied.

"I wonder," Wimsey said slowly, "whether Charles would like me to review the evidence for him. Go back to the beginning and start again? Difficult though, what? Wouldn't want the feller to think I was trying to interfere. He's a dear old chap but he can be a bit touchy."

"Well, why don't we take one thing at a time?" she suggested. "Let's see whether he wants to pay us a call and then we can feel out the situation for ourselves."

"Capital idea," he agreed. "Shall we send Bunter round with a note?"

"Bunter is away," she said. "Don't you remember? He's visiting his aunt down on the south coast somewhere."

"Oh, is he?" Wimsey asked vaguely. "I really don't remember."

"Don't worry, Peter," she said with a sad smile. "Leave it to me. I'm used to living without servants, after all."

Collison and Metcalfe stared at her in dismay as she told them the news.

"Oh dear, how dreadful," Collison said at last. "I'm sorry, that seems very inadequate somehow."

"Just when I was thinking that at least things couldn't get any worse," Metcalfe chipped in, "they have."

"But surely he can be made to realise that whatever happened wasn't his fault?" Collison said. "Bob and I found the evidence and made the arrest, and it was the jury that convicted him, and understandably too, on the evidence. Perhaps I should speak to him?"

"It wouldn't do any good, I'm afraid, sir. In fact, according to the therapist I've been speaking to, it might make matters worse. Presenting him with an alternative world view that doesn't fit with the one he's chosen to inhabit for the time being may only add to his problems."

"So what *can* we do?" Metcalfe asked.

"There are apparently three possible courses of action," Karen explained. "First, a hospital could have him heavily tranquilised and let him just sit around and vegetate in the hope that it will pass off naturally, just as it came on in the first place. I'm not keen on that, partly because I don't like the thought of pumping drugs into people, partly because I have a feeling that it won't work, and partly because I couldn't stand just sitting around and doing nothing to help."

"I think I'd be with you on all of that," Collison said. "What about the other two?"

"Second, I could confront him with some sort of shock version of reality as it is," she said. "Apparently what is happening here is an extreme version of something we all do naturally every day, which is slightly to alter our perception of reality to make it more palatable to our belief system of how reality ought to be. That's sort of what being in denial is all about. When the gap between reality and perception becomes too big to bridge we end up having to alter our beliefs, which we do only eventually and reluctantly because we have to. We don't want to because psychologically it's painful."

"But this is much more than that, surely?" Collison asked.

"Yes, and that's why I'd be very reluctant to try shocking him out of it. What we have here is more a sort of trauma. It's much more usual, when confronted by something that is too horrible to come to terms with, either to forget about it altogether, blank it out as it were, or to retreat into yourself, perhaps by becoming unresponsive or even totally mute. What's happened here is that Peter has retreated all right, but into an alternative reality that I suppose he's always had waiting for him should something really awful happen. Like a sort of internal panic room."

"So what's left, then?" said Metcalfe.

"I think I have to get into the room with him and try to show him a way out of it. I've discussed it with the therapist who is dubious. When it's done normally it would be handled by a trained psychiatrist, and it can take years. My idea is that if I try very hard I might be able to do it, but to be honest I just don't know." She broke off and stared at them helplessly.

"How would you go about it?" Collison asked uncertainly. "It doesn't sound the sort of thing one should muck about with without the proper training."

"Damn training!" she exclaimed. "Most so-called counsellors are just quacks anyway. Very few of them are even doctors.

What do they know? I know Peter. I know how he thinks and how he feels. I *know!*" Her eyes were blazing. It was as though a curtain had been ripped aside to reveal a new person, a woman in pain.

Collison and Metcalfe looked at each other awkwardly. Karen sat bolt upright, staring into space. Then she snapped open her handbag, grabbed a handkerchief and crumpled it viciously in her hand. A single tear rolled down her cheek.

"So if you don't want to try shocking him out of it," Collison eventually said, with an air of normality which suddenly sat awkwardly with the tense atmosphere in the room, "the only logical alternative is to go along with his version of events."

"Yes." Her voice was strained and small.

"For how long?"

"For as long as it takes. I know that sounds crazy, I know it makes me sound as though I won't face up to what I don't want to hear, but I honestly think it might work."

"Go on," Metcalfe prompted her.

"Well," she said, still clutching the handkerchief, "if I'm right he's withdrawn into this parallel world of his because reality became too painful to deal with, making the fantasy seem more attractive. But suppose it works the other way round as well? If we can find a way of sustaining the fantasy while feeding in a realisation that the reality may not be as bad as he thought—that he really wasn't to blame, in other words—then why shouldn't the process go into reverse? After all, he often slips in and out of the whole Lord Peter Wimsey persona for a few minutes at a time. This is just a more extreme example. Why shouldn't he slip out of it again just as he always has before?"

It gradually dawned on the two men that she had said "we." Somehow it didn't seem strange.

"It goes without saying, Karen, that we'll back you in whatever you decide to do," Collison said gently.

"Of course," Metcalfe concurred. "Er, what *would* we have to do exactly?"

"We'd have to act out the fantasy, of course," Collison said, "so you'd better do your research on Dorothy L. Sayers PDQ, Bob. Peter seems to think that I'm Parker, so that's all right. I think I can carry that off. Karen is clearly Harriet. Lady Mary I think we'll fudge by saying she's away in America or something, but if necessary I suppose Caroline could be pressed into service. She loves the books anyway."

"What about me?" Metcalfe asked.

"I'm afraid, Bob, that you must be Bunter, Lord Peter's valet."

Metcalfe looked dubious.

"Bunter was Lord Peter's sergeant during the War—that's the First World War of course—and became his manservant afterwards. He's a dab hand at photography and at eliciting information from pretty housemaids, though I doubt we'll have much call for the latter."

"Don't worry," Karen said quickly. "We'll try to keep you out of the way as much as we can. I've told him you're away visiting a relative at the moment."

"How do you want to play this, then?" said Collison.

"Well, I think the best thing is for him to meet Parker and get involved in the investigation," she said slowly, "but the question is how and when? After all, sir, you're going to be busy getting the enquiry re-opened."

"No time like the present," Collison replied. "Give me the address and I'll come round at seven this evening."

Priya Desai walked back into the room. It seemed clear from her demeanour that she had hoped never to see it again.

"Welcome back," Metcalfe said sardonically.

"Delighted," she replied with equally heavy irony.

"Hello, sir," she greeted Collison. "I thought you might like to see the afternoon papers."

"I doubt that," he said, but took them anyway.

The headlines were predictable: "Police Got The Wrong Man" and "Innocent Man Dies In Prison" competed with "Thud And Blunder At The Yard."

"Are you going to have to be interviewed, sir?" Willis asked anxiously.

"No. Not for a while anyway. The ACC has told the press office to deal with it—that's what they're for, after all." He tossed the papers onto the table. Nobody else bothered to pick them up. "The ACC feels," he went on, "that dealing with the press would be a distraction from the task at hand, which I'm sure I don't need to remind you is to catch a serial killer before he strikes again."

"We should be up and running by the morning, anyway," Metcalfe informed him, "though we'll be shorthanded for a while. Most of the team were happy to get off the case and nobody's anxious to be assigned to it now."

"Well, we'll just have to make the most of what we've got," Collison said philosophically. "And after all, we do have a secret weapon. Nobody else at the Yard has the assistance of Lord Peter Wimsey."

Desai stared at him blankly, to which he returned a rather sad smile.

"What time would you like to make a start tomorrow, guv?"

"Team meeting at nine, Bob. Let's get straight back in the saddle. Karen, or should I say Harriet, I'll see you later."

Chapter Fourteen

"Hello Wimsey, old man," Charles Parker said as he came into the book-lined room carrying a bulky folder. "How are you?"

"Tolerably spiffin', I thank you," Wimsey replied, "but let's talk about you, my dear chap. This wrong man stuff don't sound good, do it? Not at all good, in fact."

"I know, it's the devil, isn't it?" Parker agreed as he sat down opposite Lord Peter, the folder dropping to the floor with a dull but substantial thud. "I was rather hoping you might be able to help out a bit."

Harriet placed a glass of whisky before him, and then went and sat on the sofa next to Peter.

"Always delighted to be able to help the Yard, naturally," Wimsey said, "though perhaps it's a shame you didn't call me in earlier."

"Well, it seemed like such an open and shut case," Parker said, with a glance at Harriet that looked very much like a distress call, "that we didn't want to bother you."

"And anyway you were away sorting out that thing for the Foreign Office in Romania," she said. "Surely you remember? You've only just got back."

"Have I?" Wimsey mused vaguely. "Of course, that would explain it."

"So in your absence," Parker explained, "we spoke to this profiler fellow, and do you know, old man, he really did an awfully good job. What happened wasn't his fault, not at all."

Harriet glanced at him and frowned. Clearly things were moving too far too quickly. "Why don't you give Peter the background to the case?" she suggested.

"Exactly what I came to do, of course," Parker said, picking up the file and handing it over. "I've brought you a copy of the barrister's main briefing bundle from the trial. Careful, it's damned heavy."

"Appropriate enough for a serial killer, I suppose," Lord Peter said, "to persist in doing wrong."

"Beg pardon?" Parker looked at Harriet again.

"Thus to persist in doing wrong extenuates not wrong, but makes it much more heavy," Wimsey said, looking hard at him. "Do buck up, Charles, you normally guess Shakespeare straight away, and anyway I may want to use him again this evening. Not one of my better quips though, I must admit."

"You're quite right, I should have caught that," Parker said. "Though I'd rather this particular chap didn't persist in doing any more wrong, whoever he might be."

"Quite so, old man, quite so. Not in the best of taste perhaps. I suppose there's no doubt that it is just one chap we're lookin' for?"

"Well, it's exactly the same MO in each case and all the underwear was found together, so I'd say yes, absolutely," Parker said firmly.

"And that's one aspect of this case which really is puzzlin', old fruit. The blessed underwear." Wimsey cradled the unopened folder on his lap. "If it really did belong to the murdered women, and it seems that it did, then the only person who can have had access to it, at least initially, is the murderer."

"Yes, of course."

"Well, then, how do you explain the fact that it turned up at our man's flat, since we now know the poor blighter was *not* the murderer?"

"Well, we're going to begin a complete review of the case tomorrow..." Parker said defensively, "and I'm sure that will be one of the first things we consider."

"And you need to, Charles old bird, you need to. Bit of a poser, what?"

"Yes," Harriet interjected. "You're onto something there, Peter. Logically it can only have been put there by the murderer, or someone to whom it was given by the murderer."

"Yet it wasn't a public place," Parker pointed out. "So if we draw up a list of everyone who had access to the property then one of those people must be the killer, or at the very least know who he is."

"There's something else you need to consider," Wimsey said. "Was the location of the hiding place random or deliberately chosen?"

"What do you mean exactly, Peter?" Harriet asked.

"Well, I think it makes a difference, don't you know. If it was randomly chosen then it was selected simply because it seemed like a good hiding place and our chap, whoever he may be, had access to it, so it was convenient. If, on the other hand, the evidence was specifically planted there then it looks like someone was deliberately trying to frame the poor devil who lived there—and successfully too."

"In which case," said Parker, catching on, "we also need to consider anyone who may have had a grudge against him. I say, Peter, that's rather good."

"Lulled in the countless chambers of the brain," he replied, "our thoughts are linked by many a hidden chain."

Parker counted the syllables on his fingers and said "Pope" triumphantly.

"Now that's cheating," Harriet said reprovingly.

"Buck up and play the game, old man," Wimsey said. "You know the rules."

"Sorry," he apologised. "It's a bit late in the day to be spotting heroic couplets."

"And anyway," Wimsey continued, "I believe that was a pure guess on your part. It could just as easily have been Dryden."

"Well, it's never too late in the day for iambic pentameters," Harriet said playfully. "Why, I read them in bed."

"True," Wimsey said with mock solemnity, "though not entirely apposite. All heroic couplets are iambic pentameters, but not all iambic pentameters are heroic couplets."

"I know that, silly," she responded. "I did go to Oxford too, you know."

"Then you should know better than to read them in bed," Wimsey said. "They can induce the weirdest dreams."

"Not the Shakespeare sonnets, surely?" interjected Parker, knowing that for once he was on firm ground.

"Oh Lord, I knew we would get back to Shakespeare sooner or later with you around, Charles. I've never been able to work out if it's your reading habits that are deficient, or simply that there is no breadth to your imagination. The former I suspect; all that readin' the *Police Gazette* must be very limitin' for a man."

Parker got up with a laugh. "Well, fortunately, Peter, there seems to be no limit to your imagination. You've given us a couple of good points to follow up."

"Consider it as nothing," Wimsey said, waving languidly. "By the way, how are the little Parker birds? Well, I trust? And Mary?"

"The children are enjoying robust good health," Parker replied, trying to remember how many of them there were. "Mary is up at Duke's Denver visiting His Grace your brother."

"What, Gerry, that old fathead!" Wimsey exclaimed. "Wonder what he wants."

"Nothing in particular, I don't think. Not unless there's some new problem with Gherkins, that is."

Wimsey frowned. Mention of his nephew rarely found him in good humour. "Gerry at least has every excuse for being a fathead," he said with an air of judgment. "He can't help it. His son is another matter. A chap could be forgiven for thinking he's a professional troublemaker whose one objective seems to be to drag the family name through the mud. If there *is* a problem with Gherkins, Mary should feel free to tell Gerry that I would be perfectly happy to step in and deal with him."

"I shall pass that on," Parker said.

"By the way, Harriet," Wimsey said as Parker moved towards the door, "I think we'd better summon Bunter back from wherever he is. Can't investigate a bally murder without him now, can we? Think how miffed he'd be when he found out."

Harriet and Parker exchanged concerned glances.

"Alright, Peter," she said quietly. "I'll see what we can do."

The next morning Metcalfe buttonholed her when she arrived in the incident room.

"Have you said anything yet?" he asked quietly.

"No." She looked at him guiltily. "I'm sorry, Bob, but it's impossible right now while this Wimsey thing is going on."

"Thank God," he said in relief.

She gazed at him quizzically. "I thought you'd be mad at me that I hadn't..."

"No, on the contrary, I was feeling hugely guilty thinking that maybe you had, and that it was that which had brought all this on."

She glanced round to see if anyone was watching and then laid her hand briefly but firmly on his arm. "You're a very fine man," she murmured, looking him straight in the eye for a moment.

"Oh, I don't know about that," he mumbled.

"So you're OK with hanging fire for a bit?"

"Yes, of course. You've got more than enough on your plate right now—I mean the two of you."

"Here's Collison now," she said warningly, looking over his shoulder.

"Morning, guv," he said, turning.

"Morning," Collison said briskly. "How are we fixed, Bob?"

"Incident room's fully operational. We have eight bodies at present, with the promise of two more to come, but only Priya was on the team before. Everyone else has been reassigned to new teams—"

"...and isn't keen on transferring back again," Collison broke in. "Yes, I get the picture. Well, let's get going."

Metcalfe called for silence, but it was hardly necessary. Most of the new team had never met any of the others before, and so had been standing around warily scanning their new colleagues. A hush had fallen as soon as Collison entered the room.

"Morning, everybody," Collison said. "I'm Detective Superintendent Collison and I'm in charge of this investigation. I assume that you've already met DI Metcalfe here." He felt the awkwardness of a room full of individuals not yet ready to merge into a group. It was always like this when a new team was forming. At least he had been spared the experience on this case initially, although taking over Tom Allen's team had posed challenges of its own.

"You all know why we're here," he went on, "so let's make a start. I'm glad to see that DI Metcalfe and DC Willis have reinstated the whiteboard overnight. They were both members of the original investigation team, as was DC Desai over there." He gestured in her direction. "We're also hoping to be able to recall DS Andrews.

"The sequence of events is also set out in the folders which you have in front of you," he went on. "As I'm sure I don't have to report, Gary Clarke was convicted of these murders not long ago, only to be apparently cleared by alibi evidence which was not presented at the trial. This was duly checked out by DI Metcalfe and appears to be kosher, which means that ordinarily we would have been recommending to the Home Office that he be released pending an appeal which the Crown would not oppose.

"Unfortunately," he continued flatly, "Gary Clarke was attacked in prison as soon as he was moved from the remand wing, and later died in hospital."

He felt that nobody in the room wanted to meet anyone else's eyes, least of all his own.

"So where are we going to restart this investigation from?" he asked rhetorically. "Well, we could do a complete cold case review, going through every single interview note and witness statement, but I'm going to suggest a different approach, unless anyone disagrees with that."

Metcalfe smiled wryly. It was unlikely that anyone would take issue with a suggestion made by a Detective Superintendent.

"Something emerged last night in discussion with DC Willis and—and an expert who's been helping us with the case, our profiler Peter Collins. Dr Collins spotted that we now have a key avenue of enquiry to pursue which we did not have available before, and one which should logically lead us straight to our killer, if we can only do it right. I'll ask DC Willis to explain." He nodded to her and moved aside.

"As you can see here," she began, pointing to a photograph of the loft opening which had been affixed to the whiteboard, "damning evidence was found in this loft space outside Clarke's flat by DS Collison and DI Metcalfe, namely the murder weapon and underwear belonging to the victims, which we can only assume was removed and kept as a trophy—quite common behaviour in serial killers.

"In the light of this evidence there seemed little justification for seeking further suspects, particularly as there was strong circumstantial evidence incriminating Clarke. In hindsight, of course, we clearly got it wrong as it transpires that he did have an alibi for one of the killings after all. Perhaps if he had told us about it or if he hadn't been such a fantasist, things might have been different."

"Let's not go there, Karen," Collison said sombrely. "We got it wrong. Simple as that. Now it's up to us to put it right—so far as we can, of course."

"Yes, sir," she replied, flushing a little. "Well, the point is this. We know that only the killer would have had access to those items—initially at least. So whoever put them there must either have obtained them from the killer, or actually be the killer themselves."

Desai put her hand up. "Just thinking aloud," she ventured, "but could our murderer have had an accomplice?"

Willis looked at Collison.

"A sensible point, Priya, which Dr Collins also raised and which we ought to bear in mind," he acknowledged, "though it is unlikely as most serial killers work alone, isn't that right, Karen?"

"Correct," she confirmed. "It would be very unusual but as you say, sir, it's worth bearing in mind."

"So it comes to this, then," Collison said, realising to his horror that he was beginning to talk like Alistair Partington, "if we can identify all the people who could possibly have had access to the common parts of that building, then one of them ought to be our killer."

"DC Gates, sir," said a rather spotty young man, raising his hand. "Even if we can do that, how will we know which is our man?"

"Good old-fashioned police work," Collison answered briskly. "He won't be able to produce an alibi for any of the nights in question. He is also likely to fit—though I don't want to place too much weight on this—the profile provided previously by Dr Collins, which you will find in your folders. But bear in mind that the profile is not evidence, just a guideline which may make our task a little easier."

Metcalfe stepped forward. "The building in question was originally a house which has been converted into four flats: one on each floor and one in the basement. How do we go about identifying all the people we need to speak to?"

He picked up a marker and started writing on the board.

"This being Hampstead, not a single one of the flats is occupied by its actual owner. They're all 'buy to lets,' so for a start we need to identify not just the owners of each flat, but also their tenants. Then of course, the tenants will mostly have cleaners, who may well have keys to the building. Then there may be the freeholder, their managing agents and perhaps a contractor or two retained by the managing agents. Finally, we need to be sure we have accounted for every set of keys, which means not just owners and tenants but also any friends, family members or lodgers. So, not as easy as it sounds. The chances are there may be five or six sets of keys for each flat, each one including a key to the main front door."

"I'm going to ask DI Metcalfe to assign responsibilities in a minute so that we can crack on with all of this straight away," Collison said. "But before we do that, there is one further element to this which we need to explore. Karen, please."

"Another point we need to consider," Willis explained, "is whether the evidence was dumped in the loft space almost at random, simply because the killer had access to it and it was a convenient place to stash stuff, or whether it was chosen deliberately. If it was, then it may have been chosen to incriminate Gary Clarke, in which case we need to investigate if anyone out there bore him a grudge."

Desai put her hand up. "Isn't that a dangerous assumption?" she asked.

Two or three of the new team members looked at her strangely.

"I can see a few of you looking puzzled that a DC should challenge the view of a senior office—me, that is," Collison said with a smile. "There's a reason for that. I believe that the only way we can make real progress is to test all our arguments and assumptions as we come up with them, so please feel free to do exactly that. Having been on the team before, she already knows this. Go on, Priya."

"Well, sir. If anybody in the house had access to the space, then would it necessarily have been Clarke whom someone was looking to implicate? I agree he's the most likely candidate since his door opens directly under the loft, but it could actually have been any one of the four tenants."

"Good point," Collison conceded. "Put it on the board. Anything else, anyone? No? Then carry on please, Bob."

As Metcalfe began to assign responsibilities someone slipped into the room. He waited for him to finish and then approached Collison. "Superintendent Collison, sir? I'm DI Andrew Leach. The AC Crime asked me to join the enquiry."

"That's very kind of the ACC," Collison said, puzzled, "but I already have a DI—Bob Metcalfe over there."

"The ACC is well aware of that, sir, and has every confidence in DI Metcalfe. Indeed, I understand that he has already written something very favourable on his file on your recommendation."

"Well, then?"

Leach looked uncomfortable. "The ACC thought it might be helpful to have a fresh pair of eyes on the case, sir. Someone who wasn't, ah, involved in the initial enquiry. I'm just here as an observer, but please feel free to make use of me in any way you wish if you think I can be of help."

"I see," Collison replied. "Bob, are you free for a moment?"

Metcalfe came over.

"Bob, this is DI Andrew Leach. The ACC has asked him to sit in as an observer."

"Very good, sir," Metcalfe responded woodenly.

"I'm just wondering if there's any aspect of this enquiry that he could take charge of?"

"Well, there's the freeholder angle, sir. I was wondering how we were going to take care of that, to be honest. I need four bodies for the four flats, eight really if we're to do it justice, and then there's the possible grudge angle to look into..."

"That sounds like a good idea," Collison concurred. "But presumably you'll need time to read yourself into the case, Andrew?"

"Not necessary, thank you, sir," Leach replied. "I've already read the files. I did have a question before we start, though."

"Go ahead."

"I'm not entirely clear about how the profiler came to be

involved, nor about exactly how his profile was used. Did it lead you to Clarke?"

"Technically, it did," Collison said, sitting down on one of the desks. "But only in the sense that it narrowed down our field of search. It suggested, for example, that our killer lived in the area, and might have received treatment at some time for a sexually transmitted disease. That he would probably be socially inept, inadequate and a fantasist. Clarke fitted the profile like a glove."

"Yet he was innocent," Leach pointed out.

Silence greeted his words.

"I'm sorry, sir," Leach said. "I didn't mean to imply any criticism. Having read the files, I agree that the case against Clarke seemed obvious and overwhelming. I was just wondering exactly what part the profiler played and how he reached his conclusions. Might it be possible for me to meet with him?"

"No!" Willis broke in before she could stop herself.

"What DC Willis means," Collison said smoothly, "is that sadly Dr Collins is most unwell at the moment. He can't see anyone."

"Oh dear," Leach replied. "When will he be able to speak to me, do you think?"

"Not for quite a while," Collison said. "DC Willis and I saw him last night and he really is quite sick."

"But I thought you said, sir," Leach persisted, "that he wasn't able to see anyone? If he's well enough to see two members of the team then surely another one wouldn't make that much difference?"

Collison sighed heavily. Karen and Bob looked at each other.

"DC Willis saw him because she does every day; she lives with him," he said flatly. "I saw him at her request because she thought it might help with his recovery. As to that, it's too early to say."

Leach looked at him expectantly, as though assuming that this was only the beginning of an explanation.

"If you must know," Willis burst out, "Peter has had some sort of breakdown. He blames himself for Clarke's conviction and so also for his death. It's nonsense, of course. He was convicted by the jury on the evidence presented in court and nobody ever mentioned the profile, but that's the way it is. He won't be able to have a sensible conversation with anyone for quite some time."

"Oh dear," Leach said again, and then, "I'm sorry; that must sound very insensitive and inadequate—I didn't mean it to. I am genuinely very sorry to hear that. It's awkward, though. The ACC specifically wanted me to look into the whole issue of the profile."

"Well," Metcalfe interjected decisively, "the ACC will just have to wait, I'm afraid."

"So it would seem," Leach murmured.

Chapter Fifteen

"I hope you've done your homework, Bob?" Collison asked as they stood outside the door.

"I think so, sir," he replied. "There hasn't been time to go back and read the books, but I've been all over the internet looking at Peter Wimsey sites, so I think I've got most of the background."

"Good man," Collison said approvingly as he rang the bell. "Don't worry, Karen and I will help you through anything that crops up. The main thing to remember is that you're his valet and that at the time Sayers was writing all this class stuff was really important. So make sure you call Peter and Karen 'my lord' and 'my lady' respectively."

"And you, guv?"

"Difficult to be sure, since I don't quite know what stage my career is supposed to have reached yet. I think I start out as a sergeant and end up as a Commander, no less. I'm also Wimsey's brother-in-law, by the way. I'm married to his sister, Lady Mary. You'd better play safe and just call me 'Mr Parker.' Oh, hello, Karen."

Metcalfe gasped involuntarily as she opened the door. She was dressed in a figure-hugging woollen suit, stockings and black high heels. She was fully made up, with a lipstick that was so brilliantly red that on anyone else it would have looked faintly ridiculous. On her it seemed perfect. Hell, it *was* perfect. The suit clung to her hips as she shifted her weight from one foot to the other. A low moan started from somewhere deep inside him. Fortunately, while it was still at the back of his throat she spoke.

"Good evening, Charles," Harriet said loudly. "Oh, and I see Bunter has come back with you. Good, Peter will be pleased."

"Good evening, my lady," Bunter said self-consciously. "How is his lordship?"

"Tolerably well, Bunter, I thank you," Wimsey cut in, putting his head round the door of the living room. Evenin', Charles. Do come in, all."

Peter, Harriet and Charles sat down. Bunter hovered uncertainly.

"How about a cocktail, Charles?" Wimsey suggested. "It is that time of day, after all. The hour when a swift shot of somethin' stimulatin' can lift the human spirit."

Noticing Bunter stare in some alarm at the array of bottles nestling around the cocktail shaker on the sideboard, Parker demurred. "If it's all the same to you, old man, I'd just as soon have a sherry. Your sister has been somewhat displeased of late about the amount of hard liquor I drink."

"Good God," Wimsey ejaculated, clearly shocked. "Mary? Lecturing about the perils of the demon drink? Some mistake, surely?"

"Your sister is a reformed character, Peter, as well you know," Harriet said firmly. "And since dear Charles here is largely responsible for the transformation I think we should defer to his wishes. Sherry for everyone, please, Bunter. Oh, I may have moved the bottle while you were away. It's to the right of the cocktail shaker now."

"Very good, my lady," Bunter acknowledged.

"Pour one for yourself, Bunter, and then sit down and talk with us. Chief Inspector Parker has some detecting to discuss."

"If it's all the same to you, my lord, I'd rather stand," Bunter said at once, drawing an admiring glance from Harriet.

"There he goes again," Wimsey said with a sigh, "reminding me not to forget my place. Very well, Bunter, perhaps you could perch on the bally sideboard or something."

"I think I may have moved the silver tray as well, Bunter," Harriet informed him as he began to walk across the room holding a glass of sherry in each hand. "You should find it on that table over there."

"Thank you, my lady," he said, veering towards it, "I was wondering where it had got to."

"Well, Parker, old bird," Wimsey cajoled him once they all had drinks. "Tell all. How goes the investigation?"

"We've been following up on your ideas," Parker responded. "We're looking at the whole range of people who might have had access to the common parts, but it's turning out to be more complicated than we anticipated. All the flats are tenanted so there are multiple sets of keys in circulation for each—never less than four, since most of the tenants have a cleaner who comes in while they're at work, and in one case as many as seven."

He took a sip of sherry, and went on. "Then there's a managing agent employed by the freeholder, and of course they have two sets of keys to the front door only, but that's enough to get access to the loft space. And just to make things even more complicated, two contractors recently did work in the building—one doing some fire and safety work, and one decorator painting the common parts. They were given keys, which they duly returned, but of course there's nothing to stop them from having had copies cut."

"Come to think of it," Wimsey cut in after an approving sip of his sherry, "there's nothin' to stop *any* of the bally keyholders from having had copies cut. There could be an infinite number of possibilities."

"Not infinite, no," Parker reassured him with a smile. "Less than thirty sets of keys in all, we believe, and we're putting the whole team onto identifying and interviewing the holders of each. Sooner or later if you're right—and I'm sure you must be—we'll come to someone with no alibi for any of the murder dates."

"But that won't be easy, will it?" Wimsey mused. "Contractors employ casual staff, somebody may have worked short-term at the managing agent, and one or more of the flats may have been sold or had new tenants during the period in question."

"All true, I'm afraid," Parker acknowledged with a wry smile, "but don't worry, it's just a matter of good, old-fashioned police work. Sooner or later we'll exhaust all the possibilities. I just wish we had a few more bodies to throw at the problem."

"Oh, then why don't you borrow Bunter and me?" Harriet said at once. "Peter wouldn't mind, would you, Peter? Charles can give us things to do and we can come back in the evening and tell you how things are going."

"I suppose so," Wimsey said vaguely, "and I could stay here and do some research." He gestured at the bulky case folder and then at the books which lined the room. Parker got up and casually strolled over to the section of bookshelves which he had indicated. "But these are just detective books, old man," he said, puzzled.

Harriet shot him a hard stare.

"Ah, I think I can see where you're coming from," he said hastily. "You're working on the assumption that there's nothing new in crime and thus at one time or other, someone must have written about exactly such a situation."

"Spot on, Charles." Wimsey beamed. "Yes, and worked out how to solve it as well."

"Capital, Peter," Parker said warmly. "You do that while we get on with the boring stuff and Harriet and Bunter can keep you abreast of what's going on. Now, I really must be going. I promised Mary I wouldn't be late."

"Why don't you take Bunter with you?" Harriet suggested. "He can give you a lift home in Mrs Merdle."

"Good idea," Parker agreed and then, as Bunter hesitated, "grab the keys to Mrs Merdle, then, Bunter, and we'll get her out of the garage in the mews."

"Thank you, Bob," Karen said the next morning as she handed him a coffee, "you were great."

"Oh, I don't know about that"—he flushed—"but thanks anyway. Obviously I didn't do my homework well enough. Mrs Merdle threw me. The name's familiar, but I've never heard a car called that before."

"Wimsey called all his cars Mrs Merdle, for some reason," she replied. "Not quite sure why. She's a fairly minor character in *Little Dorrit* who's married to a swindler."

"Curious choice."

"Exactly. Can't think what Sayers was thinking of. I would have thought someone like Guinevere would have been more in Wimsey's line, but there we are."

Metcalfe sipped his coffee then wished he hadn't, as it was scalding hot. "Do you really think this is working—this whole Peter Wimsey business, I mean?"

Karen shook her head. "I really don't know. The therapist is still dubious, and mutters about it being unethical to encourage someone in a delusion, but I still feel it's the right thing to do."

"You don't think there could be something in the idea of trying to talk him out of it, make him face up to what is real?"

"Yes I do," she agreed. "Of course I do, but I just think that the time is not yet. The only person who really knows Peter is me, because we've been together for so long, and he's a very fragile character at the best of times. I'm frightened that if I or anyone else tries to shake him out of it now it could do something terrible to him. By going along with my plan I think we're almost putting him into a protective coma. It may not do any good by itself, but at least it gives him a private place in which to recover."

"And how will that happen? The recovery, I mean?"

"I don't know, Bob. I'm flying blind here. The therapist has made it clear that she's washed her hands of the whole exercise. God, if only I didn't feel so totally alone." She started to cry and then stopped, brushing angrily at her tears.

"You're not alone," Bob said quietly but urgently, looking around the incident room. He wished he could take her in his arms. "I'm here for you and I always will be—whatever happens."

"I'm sorry, Bob," she said, composing herself. "That was thoughtless. Of course I'm grateful for your support, but I hope you can understand we can't be together, not yet anyway. If Peter were to have any inkling right now that there was anything wrong between us then that really could be the final straw."

"Here's the guvnor," Priya said suddenly from behind them. Metcalfe wondered how much she had heard.

"Morning, everyone," Collison said briskly. "OK, Bob, what have we got?"

"Making progress on eliminating the keyholders, guv," Metcalfe began. "We've identified twenty-seven possibilities, and have so far managed to interview fourteen, all of whom claim an alibi for at least one of the dates, mostly for Katherine Barker, since we start there and work backwards. We're checking out those alibis right now."

"Very good," Collison said. "But I hate to break it to you, people, that we may need to cast our net a little wider. As a result of some discussions yesterday, it's been suggested that we also need to check out former employees of the managing agents, as well as former tenants, and possibly owners, of the flats."

"Over what period, guv?" Priya asked.

"Since they last had the locks changed," Collison said grimly. "Bob, we need to find out when that was."

Metcalfe dolefully wrote on the board.

"Anything else to report?" Collison asked.

"I've been looking at the possible grudge angle, sir," Leach volunteered.

"Good—any progress?"

"Afraid not," Leach replied ruefully. "I've been to Clarke's former employer and managed to interview a few people he worked with, but it seems he was pretty nondescript and nobody really took much notice of him—except to register that he told a lot of tall stories. They find the idea of someone wanting to frame him for murder quite amusing, actually."

"Amusing or not," Collison said noncommittally, "it's a valid line of enquiry, and we need to pursue it until we're sure we've exhausted all its possibilities. What about his personal life?"

"Next thing on my list, sir. I thought I'd start with Susan McCormick."

"Not sure about that," Collison said thoughtfully. "I think she's been through enough for a while, and we have a full statement from her on file."

"I agree, guv," Metcalfe interjected, staring hard at Leach.

"But this is a whole new angle, sir..." Leach allowed the suggestion to hang in the air.

"*Possibly* a new angle," Collison corrected him. "Possibly, Andrew. Start with anyone else you can find and if you do identify anything worth re-examining with her then we'll go back to Ms McCormick, but check with me first, please. I'm conscious that we've already put her through an ordeal in the witness box to no good purpose."

"Anything else, anyone?" Metcalfe asked.

It seemed there was not.

"Very well, carry on," Collison called out. "I know this all seems tedious but remember that we're onto something real here. Only the murderer or someone close to him could have put those items in the loft. We need to keep on eliminating people and sooner or later we'll find our man."

"Excuse me, sir," Leach said, approaching Collison as the others drifted away to their tasks, "but these discussions last night. Would they have involved Dr Collins at all?"

"Why do you need to know?" Collison asked, knowing the answer.

"This is very difficult, sir, and I've no wish to place anyone in an awkward position, but I do have specific orders from the AC Crime that I'm to speak to Dr Collins as soon as possible and get his version of what happened with Clarke."

"I'm afraid that won't be possible for a while. He's not well enough to see anyone he doesn't already know."

"Perhaps I could see him jointly with you, or one of the others, sir?" Leach suggested. "You know the AC Crime as well as I do and he's being very insistent on this point."

Collison sighed. "I know, I know. It's not your fault, Andrew, and I don't blame you. It's just that there are—well, some sensitivities around Peter Collins's situation at the moment and I'd rather they didn't get flushed out into the light of day until they absolutely have to be. Could you find some way of stalling the AC for a couple of days to give us a chance to resolve them—why, by then we might have caught our murderer too."

"I don't think I could do that, sir," Leach said carefully. "And in order even to consider it, I'd need to know more about what these sensitivities might be."

"Oh, very well," Collison said wearily, "I need a break anyway. Let's go out for a coffee and I'll tell you about it."

They walked downstairs, out of the main entrance, and began climbing the steep hill up toward Hampstead station. It was a grey day and as they dodged the inevitable baby buggies determinedly wheeled towards them by grim-faced women they felt a few light spots of rain.

"Have you noticed how much bigger pushchairs seem to have got over the years?" Collison said, making conversation. "Or is it just me getting old?"

"They *have* got bigger," Leach agreed cautiously. "Though I think their owners' behaviour is that much more aggressive than it used to be, particularly in certain parts of London. A sort of pavement rage, you might say. Your average pedestrian is just expected to get out of the way or be run down. Same in shops and even pubs, God help us."

They moved to the other side of the road via the zebra crossing at the community centre and walked on, uphill all the way. Just past the King William IV pub was a small cafe and they stopped.

"Let's sit outside and take a chance on the rain," Collison suggested.

Leach adopted the expression of a Detective Inspector accepting a Detective Superintendent's proposal even though it might be the stupidest idea he had ever heard, and they sat down, Leach ostentatiously brushing a few specks of rain from his chair with an abandoned napkin. Within seconds, it seemed, a waitress was clearing the table and taking their order.

"Now then," Collison said, gazing not at Leach but vacantly across the road in the general direction of Barclay's Bank, "I think the fairest thing for everybody is if I tell you the full story and then leave it to your discretion what you need to relay to the ACC, and when."

So he did. It was a fairly lengthy exposition during which their coffees arrived and started to grow cold, for it was not a warm day. Eventually Collison finished his narrative and took a long mouthful of cappuccino. Leach, whose expression had grown more disbelieving as the tale had unfolded, did likewise.

"Who is this Lord Peter Wimsey?" he asked at length, rather faintly.

"He's a fictional detective from what they call the Golden Age," Collison explained. "Three of the main writers, all women, were Agatha Christie, Margery Allingham and Ngaio Marsh, who created the characters of Poirot, Campion and Alleyn respectively. But for many people Dorothy L. Sayers was perhaps the best writer of the lot, and her Lord Peter Wimsey the best detective.

"You need a bit of stamina, though," he concluded as he finished his coffee, "since her books tend to be quite a bit longer than the others'."

"I see," Leach said. "And so you're all pretending to be characters from the book in order to keep Peter Collins involved in the investigation?" His blank tone failed to disguise his incredulity.

"Well, not really. At least, that wasn't the intention. The plan was to provide him with a kind of comfort blanket that would allow him to emerge from this altered state as gently and harmlessly as possible. It just so happened that on our last visit he made some good observations, so we are acting upon them."

"Forgive me, sir," Leach said, preparing to step over the mark, "but these are observations made by a madman, someone who is clearly living out some sort of deluded fantasy. Is it really sensible for a DS to give them so much weight?"

"You have to be very careful with words like 'mad,'" Collison chided him gently. "What is 'mad'? People like Laing and Foucault said that we live in constant states of 'fantasy' as you put it, using perception to filter out a reality which we might otherwise find too upsetting. If that's true—and it seems to me that this is exactly what Peter is doing—then you could argue that what you might call madness is simply a sane reaction to an insane world."

"Foucault?" Leach echoed, staring blankly at Collison. "Didn't he invent the pendulum or something?"

Collison sighed. "You don't read much, do you, Andrew?"

"You mean books? No, not really. Who does these days?"

"So how many books do you think you read every year? I'm asking just out of interest, you understand."

"Well, I take one on holiday with me, and say two or three others."

"I see," Collison said thoughtfully as he paid the bill. "So how do you learn things, then?"

"Isn't that what the internet's for, sir? Anytime you want to know something, you just look it up."

"But doesn't that presuppose," Collison replied as they started strolling back down the hill towards the police station, "that you know what it is that you're looking for in the first place?"

"How do you mean, sir?"

"Well, clearly the internet is a fantastic information source but reading is different. With books you learn things, random things, whatever the author might be talking to you about, and you sort of soak them up like a sponge over the years. They are stored away in some dim recess of the unconscious mind until one day some equally random stimulus sparks a connection, and you find that you've combined different items of memory and perception into a completely new insight."

"Even detective stories?" Leach countered.

"Ah," Collison said ruefully. "Yes, there you have me I'm afraid. I must admit that I read those purely for pleasure."

Chapter Sixteen

"So let me see if I've got this right," the AC Crime said in a measured tone. "You bring a psychologist who has no previous relevant experience, and no formal police accreditation, into the team as a profiler…"

"You approved his appointment, sir," Collison interjected.

"At your recommendation, Simon," his superior replied smoothly. "When a talented officer with a previously outstanding record makes a suggestion, naturally I back his judgment."

Collison noted the 'previously.' The ACC waited to see if any response would be forthcoming and, when it was not, pressed on. "He then comes up with a profile which sounds fine enough, but which we have no real means of checking. On the back of this profile you arrest someone who turns out to have been an innocent man all along with, as things turn out, tragic consequences."

"I made the arrest, sir, based on evidence which at the time seemed overwhelming. I agree that the profile guided our efforts, but it's common ground that the items found in Clarke's loft were indeed genuine articles either used or taken during the commission of our murders."

"But without the profile you might not have been looking in Clarke's loft in the first place. Or, should I say, a loft to which Clarke had access along with various other people."

"With respect, sir, I think that's unfair. Whether the profile was accurate or not we won't know until we catch our killer and see if he fits the picture. We aren't using it as a basis for our enquiries, as you know, only to narrow the search. And whatever the circumstances, we *did* find the evidence. It's just that we now know—which we couldn't possibly have known at the time—that it wasn't pointing us in what seemed like the obvious direction, but somewhere else entirely."

Across the desk, the other man looked unconvinced.

"Furthermore, sir, Peter Collins specifically questioned whether Gary Clarke was our man. There was evidence that he might have stalked Katherine Barker, and Peter said that didn't fit the pattern. It was me who decided to proceed, notwithstanding his reservations."

"That's all very well, Simon," the ACC said, with a wave of his hand, "but I need to get at the facts here before the newspapers do. I don't need your damn public school instincts kicking in and making you do something noble by carrying the can for other people."

"That's not how it is at all, sir," Collison averred doggedly. "Dr Collins expressed reservations and I pressed on anyway because I felt the strength of the available evidence was overwhelming. That's how it was."

"Without doubting your word, Simon, I need to investigate this for myself. Furthermore I need to be *seen* to investigate it myself. Imagine my irritation, therefore, when the officer I appoint to make some enquiries for me reports back that Dr Collins has had some sort of nervous breakdown and is in no fit state to be interviewed."

"That is the case, sir."

The ACC fiddled with a pencil on his desk, and then continued as though he could hardly believe what he was saying. "I now understand that Dr Collins has in fact completely lost his grasp on reality to the extent that he believes himself to be a famous fictional detective...?"

"Put like that it sounds rather bleak, sir," Collison said, trying to find the right tone. "What seems to have happened is that he blames himself—wrongly, as I have just shown—for Clarke's death, and has adopted this particular harmless little fantasy as a defence mechanism to shield himself from what he believes to be the awful reality while he comes to terms with it."

"I don't call it a harmless fantasy, Simon, when a key member of a murder enquiry team loses the ability even to know who he is."

"Like I said, sir, it's a defence mechanism. We don't anticipate it will be permanent, or even prolonged. And anyway, Dr Collins is no longer part of the enquiry." Collison bit his tongue as he realised what must come next.

"Is that so?" the ACC asked ominously, putting down the pencil on the desk with a distinct crack. "Then perhaps you can explain why members of the team are being asked to pursue lines of enquiry which he is suggesting—in, let us not forget, the persona of Lord Peter Wimsey, a fictional character?

"Perhaps you could also explain," he went on before Collison had a chance to find an answer, "why you and some of your colleagues are spending time in conversation with Dr Collins when at the same time you told my representative that he was in fact too ill to see anybody?"

"To see anybody other than us, sir, yes. It would be too great a strain for him."

"Is that what his doctor says, or psychiatrist, or whatever he is?"

"It's a therapist, sir."

"Very well, then, therapist. What does he think about all of this?"

"To be completely honest, sir, *she* disagrees with our approach. In her opinion Peter needs to be jolted out of his state but DC Willis—who is Dr Collins's partner—disagrees. So we've sort of agreed to differ for the time being. We trust

Karen's judgment and we're supporting her in trying to ensure he recovers as gently as possible."

"Your approach being what?"

Collison swallowed hard. "We're going along with the... well, the pretence I suppose you could call it. In order to do that, we're assuming the roles of different characters from the books. I'm Charles Parker, the police detective his sister marries. DC Willis is Harriet Vane, and so on."

The AC squeezed the sides of his nose between his forefingers and stared deeply at the top of his desk.

"Simon," he said at length, "do you have even the faintest idea of how this would all look if the media got hold of it? First we take on a profiler who was clearly of an unreliable state of mind to start with. Then we use his profile to catch a 'serial killer' who turns out to be innocent, and who is murdered in prison before we can get him released. Then the profiler goes completely off his trolley—and don't start, because that's exactly how the tabloids will describe it—and rather than having nothing further to do with him, senior detectives visit him and play bit parts in his deluded little fantasy.

"And then, God help us," he continued after a moment's thought, "suggestions which he makes while believing himself to be a fictional detective get taken seriously and acted upon by the real life investigating team."

"They were things we would have done anyway, sir," Collison protested. "It's just that he got there first. He's got a very quick mind—regardless of who he thinks he is."

"Simon, I thought you were a modern police office. I thought you understood the importance of the press."

"So I do, sir."

"No, I don't think you do at all," the AC said heavily. "The press can be a great help to your career by raising your profile, but they can also destroy it anytime they like with something like this. Can't you just imagine how a maliciously intentioned tabloid could present it? Next thing you know they'd have you listening to fairy voices at the bottom of the garden, or throwing stones like in *Twin Peaks*. Can't you see how vulnerable you are at the moment, what with this whole Clarke business?"

"I'm willing to take that risk, sir," Collison said stubbornly. "I'm supporting a friend at a difficult time, a friend for whose condition I feel partly responsible. If I'd listened to his doubts at the time perhaps this might never have happened."

"There you are, you see," said the AC in exasperation. "I knew we'd get to this bloody public school nonsense sooner or later. Snap out of it, Simon, for heaven's sake."

He waited for a response, but none came.

"I have to tell you that I'm very close to taking you off the case, Simon. I'm not going to, at least not yet and subject to one condition, because I want you and your team to have a chance to redeem yourselves, but don't push me."

"Thank you for your support, sir," Collison said calmly, "but what is the condition?"

"The condition," the ACC said, "is that you and your team have nothing further to do with Peter Collins, or to make it more specific since Willis lives with him, Peter Collins is to have no further involvement with this case. I wish him a speedy recovery—God knows this whole wretched business is a dreadful thing to happen—but I will not have the image of the Met tarnished by you and your colleagues' playacting. You may be prepared to take that risk but I am not, so if you will not or cannot accept my condition then you must be prepared to step aside. Now, what is it to be?"

Collison thought for a moment. "I understand your position, sir, and I appreciate your continued support. I will accept your condition, but I ask to be allowed to see him one last time to try to find some way of breaking the news to him as gently as possible."

"Granted," the ACC replied, "but how will you do that? If he's completely lost touch with reality, how will you...reach him, as it were?"

"I don't know, sir, but I know that I need to try."

❀ ❀ ❀

"So, Charles, old man, how goes it?" Wimsey asked later that evening. "Come and tell all to your Uncle Peter."

"Hello, Peter," Parker said as he followed Harriet into the room. "Not too well, I'm afraid."

Wimsey rose and, as they shook hands, gestured to an empty armchair.

"Ah, and here's Bunter too," Wimsey said happily. "How is Mrs Merdle, Bunter?"

"Going tolerably well, thank you, my lord," Bunter replied. "I have had the tappets adjusted and that seems to have resulted in a distinct improvement." He glanced at Harriet, who smiled approvingly.

"The tappets, eh?" Wimsey marvelled. "Who would have thought it? And where have you been, old sergeant of yore? I haven't seen you beetlin' around the place for quite some time."

"Duke's Denver, my lord. His Grace your brother sends his regards. Lady Mary is remaining with him for a few days more, I believe."

"Dashed bad form, Charles, for your wife to leave you all alone in London, what?" Wimsey commented, turning to Parker. "Mice will play and all that, don't you know?"

"This particular mouse is in the middle of a murder investigation," Parker reminded him, "and thus has not the time to play even if he had the inclination."

"I stand justly rebuked," Wimsey said with every appearance of being chastened. "Or sit justly rebuked, anyway. Now tell all, do."

"Sadly, there's not much *to* tell," Parker said as he took a glass of sherry from the silver tray proffered by Bunter.

"Trackin' down the keyholders, weren't you? How is the trackin' business by the way? Thriving, I trust?"

"Not as well as I would have hoped," Parker said with a worried air. "We're up to twenty-eight now, all of whom we've interviewed, in person where possible and by telephone where not, and all of them have been able to produce an alibi for at least one of the murders."

"Eliminate the impossible, old chap, and what remains must be the bally truth, no matter how improbable it may seem. I learned that from Sherlock Holmes when I was hardly off the mater's knee. Ergo, there must still be at least one keyholder whom your chaps have not yet identified."

"I know, I know," Parker concurred, "but it's the very devil tracking them down, Peter. The main lock hasn't been changed for at least seven years, so technically anybody who lived there, or had any business there during that period is a suspect until eliminated."

"Yes, it's much more difficult than we imagined, Peter," Harriet chipped in. "What worries me is that there may be someone who slips through the net and who we never even find out about. For example, tenants might have had lodgers or even just friends or family staying with them, and given them copies of the key which then were forgotten about, or discarded and picked up by other people."

"There's also the possibility, my lord," Bunter interjected respectfully from his post by the sideboard, "that someone may have borrowed a key and had it cut without the keyholder even knowing about it."

"True, oh trusted family retainer," Wimsey acknowledged. "Truth be in the field. Let her and falsehood grapple. Oh, the deuce, Charles. I had no idea it would be so difficult."

"We'll continue with the enquiries, of course," Parker assured him, "but it may be worth thinking about whether there may be other lines we could pursue as well. Apart from anything else, it may be difficult to keep up the troops' morale much longer. Rightly or wrongly we were all expecting a quick result."

"There's always the grudge angle," Wimsey reminded him. "Why did those particular items end up in that particular loft space? Were they dumped there randomly, in which case we are looking for a keyholder for whom it was just a convenient place to which they had access, or were they put there specifically?"

"And if specifically," Harriet said, taking up the thread, "then for a specific purpose, which could only have been to throw suspicion on Clarke."

Bunter caught a meaningful glance being thrown at him by Parker. "Excuse me, my lady," he interjected, "but we may have overlooked something."

"Go on, Bunter," Parker urged him, glad that he had remembered his lines.

"Suppose it wasn't Clarke on whom the murderer or his accomplice wanted to throw suspicion, sir, but someone else? After all, everyone in the house had access to that space, at least theoretically. It wasn't locked, just a simple catch, that's all."

No-one spoke for a while and then Parker said "Damn" in a most credible fashion.

"Damn it is," Wimsey agreed. "Bunter, perhaps it might have been better if you had stayed the night at Duke's Denver."

"Don't be so disagreeable, Peter," Harriet chided him. "Bunter has spotted something which should have occurred to all of us, that's all. Well done, Bunter."

"Thank you, my lady," Bunter said calmly. "Though it does throw an unwelcome light on the matter."

"Unwelcome indeed," Wimsey replied. "It means that I may have made a complete ass of myself. My theory about someone indulging themselves in a grudge against Clarke may have been purest hogwash."

"If so," Parker said, "then no more of an ass than I made of myself by focusing on Clarke to the exclusion of other possibilities.

"After all," he went on with a glance at Harriet, "that profiler chap said it couldn't be Clarke. He was right and I should have listened to him."

He and Harriet stared briefly at Wimsey to see what effect this sally might have, but none was evident. The great detective was staring rather crossly at the case papers on the table. "Hang on," he said suddenly, and crossed the room. He flicked through the papers, stared intently at a few pages, and then returned to his chair. The others watched in silence as he steepled his fingers and stared evenly at Parker. "Charles," he said at length, "tell me everything you can remember about discovering the evidence in the loft. Every little detail, no matter how unimportant it may seem."

"If only you knew how many times I'd asked people that," Parker replied with a rueful chuckle. He looked across with a smile, but Wimsey was still gazing at him impassively. "Well," Parker began, "we'd been for a con with that pompous ass Alistair Partington and he said we'd no real evidence against Clarke other than the purely circumstantial, so Bob and I—that is to say my inspector and I went back to his flat and had a root around. We found nothing of course. It was really just a last desperate attempt, because we knew that the forensic chaps had already been over it with a fine-tooth comb."

"Go on," Wimsey said.

"We were just leaving," Parker said, concentrating hard on remembering things exactly as they had occurred, "when we noticed the loft door over our heads on the landing. We wondered about how to get up there and then I remembered having seen a ladder, well, more just a set of steps really, so we went back and got them and then my inspector climbed up into the loft. He couldn't find a light switch—"

"Hold your horses, old bird," Wimsey cut in. "Not so fast. Tell me exactly how he got up into the loft."

"He pulled himself up, I think," Parker responded, with a glance at Bunter, who nodded.

"He pulled himself up?" Wimsey repeated. "So he couldn't just reach up through the door or lean forward from the top of the ladder?"

"No, as I said, the ladder was quite short, just the sort of thing you have at home for changing a light bulb or reaching into the top of a wardrobe."

"How tall is your inspector?"

"About six foot, I'd say," Parker said with another glance at Bunter, who nodded again.

"Oh dear, oh dear," Wimsey murmured, shaking his head. He realised that everyone in the room was looking at him. "Gary Clarke was five feet eight inches," he said sadly. "I've just looked it up. And I daresay he was a lot less athletic than your colleague, Charles. So it was most unlikely to have been him who put those things in the loft. He wouldn't have been able to reach."

"Perhaps he had a longer ladder somewhere," Harriet said helplessly. "Oh dear, no, that won't do. I'm clutching at straws, aren't I?"

"Positively graspin'," Wimsey agreed. "Though I suppose it's theoretically possible. Was there any sign of another ladder anywhere in the building, Charles?"

"No, there wasn't," Parker said with a frown, "but I'll have the whole place checked again tomorrow."

"Well, assuming that no long ladder suddenly hoves into view," Wimsey mused, "we have at least learned something useful this evening. It seems likely that whoever placed those objects in the loft—and let's assume for the sake of argument that this person and our murderer are one and the same—must be at least six feet tall. That might narrow things down a bit, what?"

"Yes, it might," Parker replied thoughtfully. "And I'll tell you something else, Peter. It might also modify our conjecture that someone could have been trying to incriminate Clarke. After all, they would presumably have assumed that we would be intelligent in our approach, in which case we would have come to our present conclusion sooner rather than later."

"Only if they knew that Clarke didn't have access to a long ladder, sir," Bunter pointed out. "In which case it would have to be someone who didn't know him very well, certainly someone who had never been inside his flat."

"Or someone who wasn't bright enough to put two and two together, or who simply didn't care," Harriet interjected.

"If it was someone who didn't know him very well, what possible motive would they have for trying to incriminate him?" Parker asked.

"Oh dear." Wimsey sighed. "Perhaps we're not making as much progress as we thought." He drank the last of his whisky and gazed reflectively into the glass. "Maybe I should come and visit you at the Yard tomorrow? Listen in to your morning briefin', talk to the troops, that sort of thing?"

Harriet and Bunter both turned to Parker in sudden alarm.

"Actually, Peter, there's something I need to tell you," he began awkwardly. Unable to continue for the moment, he got up and paced towards the bookshelves. "Incidentally," he said, glad to change the subject even if only temporarily, "I forgot to ask how you were getting on with your own research."

"Slowly," Wimsey said, looking somehow like a confused child. "I did make a start, but…" He gestured rather helplessly towards the stacked bookshelves.

"What an amazing collection," Parker said as he ran his fingers lightly over the spines. "Why you must have just about every detective story ever written."

"He has," Harriet confirmed.

"I see you have the Martin Beck series," Parker said. "That's impressive. Not many people have even heard of them." His fingers travelled over the books. Suddenly they stopped and went back in the opposite direction, coming to rest ruminatively on the fourth book in the series. "Oh, dear God," he said quietly. "How stupid of me not to have thought of that."

Harriet and Bunter looked at him questioningly but he did not elaborate.

"Peter, you old dog," he said suddenly, "your research was much more advanced than you led me to believe. Why, I think this may be the breakthrough we've been looking for."

"It is?" Wimsey asked, looking a little bewildered. "Jolly good."

"I have something to ask you, though," Parker said, "something which I am sure you will recognise as necessary from a police procedure point of view."

"Ask away, old fruit," Wimsey invited him vaguely.

"You have given us a lead which may well result in the case being solved. I can't tell you how grateful I am, but I have to ask that you have no further contact with the case. Tiresome, I know, but the Yard's getting rather hot on procedure these days. That extends to discussing it with us or indeed anyone else who is involved with the investigation. Your job is done now, and jolly well done too. You can leave the rest to us."

"Right-oh, then," Wimsey agreed readily.

"Just as well really, Peter," Harriet said comfortingly. "I think the Foreign Office has another little job for you coming up in the Balkans."

Chapter Seventeen

"Come on, guv," Metcalfe urged. "What's up? I've hardly been able to sleep all night wondering what you suddenly thought of."

The three of them were sitting outside a small cafe in one of the little pedestrian alleys that run off Hampstead High Street, home to costume jewellery sellers and coffee shops.

"I've hardly been able to sleep either," Collison confessed. "On one level it seems obvious, yet on another I can't help worrying that I'm over-complicating things."

"Over-complicating *what*?" Willis asked, with a certain measure of exasperation evident in her voice.

"Martin Beck," Collison began, "was a fictional detective created by a husband and wife team called Maj Sjöwall and Per Wahlöö, though I'm not sure I've pronounced either of those names properly—they're Swedish, and they both have those funny umlauty things or whatever you call them. Anyway, they wrote ten books together featuring this chap, Beck. The books are supposed to portray the decay of Swedish society from a socialist point of view, though I can't say that I see that myself."

He took a sip of coffee.

"I've always enjoyed the books and I was impressed when I saw them on Peter's shelves because not many people outside Sweden have heard of them, let alone own them. As I was looking at them I was recalling the stories and when I got to *The Laughing Policeman* something suddenly hit me."

Willis, who had read the books, puckered her eyes in concentration, but it was no good; she couldn't remember.

"In that book," Collison continued, "somebody gets on a bus and machine-guns the interior, killing several people. The police are baffled as to why this psychopath chose to slaughter so many innocent victims in this way for apparently no reason at all. But they're looking in the wrong place. It turns out that the killer only wanted to murder one particular passenger but killed the others precisely so that the police would go off down the wrong track, looking for a psychopathic mass murderer."

"Oh," Metcalfe said slowly.

"Oh indeed," Collison echoed grimly. "We've been looking for a psychopathic serial killer, someone who's dangerously disturbed, despite potentially appearing normal. We asked Peter to profile a serial killer based on the available evidence. We allowed that profile to point us in a particular direction and it led us to Gary Clarke, who was tried and convicted as a serial killer but turned out not to be either. What if all the time our perpetrator wasn't a psychopathic serial killer but rather a very dangerous and determined individual who wanted to eliminate one particular person, and was prepared to go to any lengths to throw us off the scent?"

"But how likely is that?" Willis asked dubiously. "We've found one example in fiction, but has it ever happened in real life that we know of? I don't think so. Surely it's much more likely that our perpetrator really *is* a serial killer, isn't it?"

"I know, I know," Collison said helplessly. "It's ironic, isn't it? Here I am, drafted into the enquiry to replace Tom Allen, a good old-fashioned copper who believes in gut instincts, and I'm falling prey to exactly the same thing."

"Tom calls it his copper's nose," said Metcalfe. "I can think of a couple of occasions when he just said something out of the blue, and when I asked him how he knew he said 'I just do.' Problem is, he was usually right."

"Well, he was right about Clarke, anyway," Willis agreed reluctantly. "Though God knows how he knew."

"But that's it, isn't it?" Collison replied. "He had an instinct and he was prepared to back it, even to the extent of doing an enormous amount of work in his own time until he finally had the evidence to prove that what he believed was true. I always thought that was the difference between him and me, yet here I am suggesting we do exactly the same thing."

"*Are* we going to do the same thing?" Willis asked forthrightly. "After all, we may still turn something up with our keyholder enquiries."

"That's what's tormenting me, to be honest," Collison said candidly. "On the one hand I now have Tom's copper's nose nagging away at me. On the other, it would mean completely derailing the investigation and turning it in a different direction, and you can imagine how *that* might go down with the ACC."

"How are things with the ACC?" Metcalfe asked cautiously.

Collison reflected on this, searching for the right answer. "A trifle tense," he admitted finally. "He was less than impressed with our amateur dramatics. The worst part of it is that in his place I would feel exactly the same. In strict confidence, if I hadn't agreed to have nothing further to do with Peter he would have taken me off the case. Thank God this *Laughing Policeman* idea came up literally at the last minute so I could exclude him from things without upsetting him. How is he, by the way, Karen?"

"Difficult to say. We're in uncharted waters here. He seemed very quiet and thoughtful this morning. I think what you said about the profiler got through to him."

"Well, let's just hope that something comes of it," Collison said.

"So what *are* we going to do?" Metcalfe asked persistently.

"*Mais revenons à nos moutons*," Collison said and then, with a start, "Christ, I'm starting to talk like Lord Peter..."

Metcalfe looked puzzled, though he tried not to.

"I'm really not sure," Collison continued. "I think we have to find some way of testing this theory, but I'll just have to try to fudge things a little in the hope that Andrew Leach won't go running off to the ACC with evidence of fresh insanity on my part."

"I never did like a sneak," Willis said determinedly.

"He's acting under orders," Collison reminded her. "If anything I think we should feel sorry for him. It can't be very pleasant having to act as a spy in the cab on one's colleagues."

"I wonder," she said slowly, "whether you might be able to slant this in a direction he might be inclined for us to take it anyway, sir?"

"I'm open to suggestions. What do you have in mind?"

"Well, wasn't it him who was keen to follow the idea of someone having had a grudge against Clarke? Couldn't you present this new line of enquiry as a sub-set of that?"

Collison pondered for a moment. "Good thinking in principle, but I'd discounted that possibility. It seems so unlikely."

"Agreed. So suppose instead of having a grudge against Clarke, someone simply offered him up as a convenient scapegoat? Someone, for example, who might be prepared to murder a whole batch of people just to throw us off the scent of the one person he really wanted dead?"

"It might work," Collison said, nodding. "It would explain why the knickers were hidden outside Clarke's flat."

"But who would have been able to predict that we would find them there?" Metcalfe objected. "After all, we nearly didn't. They might have lain undiscovered for ever."

There was a silence.

"Maybe they really were just hidden there at random," Willis said in the end, though without much conviction.

"Synchronicity, you mean?" asked Metcalfe, recalling an earlier conversation. "Extreme coincidence. Someone just happens to dump some murder evidence right outside the flat of a man who is a tailor-made suspect?"

There was another silence, longer this time. Metcalfe stared moodily into his cup.

"I'll tell you what might be an explanation to fit the facts," Collison said suddenly. "It's just come to me, and a very nasty thought it is too."

They both looked at him.

"Suppose somebody has been manipulating events all along. Suppose somebody created a set of facts which they knew would lead to a particular profile, and that this particular profile would lead us to Clarke?"

"Oh, come on, guv," Metcalfe protested, "that's pretty fantastic, don't you think? For a start, how would anyone know in advance that we would bring in a profiler? It never occurred to Tom Allen when he was leading the investigation."

"Maybe you're right, Bob. I certainly want to believe that you're right."

"That's surely a step too far, sir," Willis said firmly. "Bad enough to know that we may have been hoodwinked by a deception plan without thinking that we've been manipulated into the bargain."

"Time we were off, anyway," Collison said, looking at his watch. "We've got to brief the troops."

An air of frustration was beginning to pervade the incident room. A few days ago they had believed they had the means to crack the case quickly and simply, but the slow process of tracking down and eliminating potential suspects was not only tedious work, but didn't seem to be leading to results.

"Well, folks, we're going to try a difference of emphasis," Collison said, deliberately breezy. "We'll keep some bodies on tracking down the remaining keyholders and I'd like to keep open DI Leach's line of enquiry as to whether anyone might have had a grudge against Clarke, but there's something else I'd like to consider as well, potentially related to that latter point."

He perched on a table. "Up to now this enquiry has focused on investigating this series of killings on the assumption that they are linked; that we are hunting a serial killer."

"You mean they're not linked, sir?" Desai asked, struggling to keep the incredulity out of her voice. "That they're the same, but not connected?"

"Of course they're linked in the sense that the same person committed them all. I'm not trying to deny that. No, it's that I think we should consider the possibility, no matter how unlikely it may seem, that the murders may not be the random acts of a serial killer but instead have a different purpose behind them; namely to camouflage the fact that the killer may have had a motive for committing one of these killings, but has deliberately laid a false trail for us to follow to hide that fact."

"Is this your own theory, sir?" Leach asked innocently.

"Yes, entirely my own," Collison responded briskly and decisively. "It's something that came to me overnight."

"It's a very bold theory, sir," he observed.

"Bold in what sense?"

"Well, in two senses really," Leach said slowly. "Firstly, there's no evidence at all to support it. Secondly it might mean re-opening the whole investigation from the very beginning."

An audible moan of protest ran round the room.

"Perhaps there's no evidence to support it because nobody has ever looked for it," Collison pointed out mildly. "In any event, let's ask DC Willis to review the individual victims just to see if the idea might have some validity."

He moved aside and Willis stepped forward to take his place.

"Victim number one was Amy Grant, a student. We never found out exactly what she was doing that weekend in London. If we are going to re-open the investigation then we could try once again. She seems to have disappeared completely after she got the train from Birmingham. There's no trace of her having stayed anywhere and she didn't have family down here—she was from Darlington."

"I suppose the most likely explanation is that she was staying with a man somewhere," Metcalfe interjected.

"Maybe, maybe not," Willis commented. "There were suggestions by a few of her university friends that she might have been gay, though nobody was really sure. She was apparently a quiet person who kept herself to herself. No-one really seems to have known her at all."

"Sad," Collison said quietly. "But given someone would have to be very determined indeed to murder not just her but several other women to cover it up, she seems an unlikely candidate."

"May I make a suggestion, sir?" Leach asked.

"With pleasure," Collison replied.

"Well, if this theory is to have any validity, our murderer must be a very obvious suspect for one of the killings. Otherwise why go to all this trouble?"

"A good point," Collison acknowledged. "I should have thought of that. Thank you, Andrew. Yes, it would have to be someone who would normally be our first port of call: husband, boyfriend, something like that."

"So far as we know, Amy Grant was single," Metcalfe said. "So I agree that she seems an unlikely candidate for our 'real' victim."

"So does Tracy Redman," Collison observed. "As a prostitute she would have had a higher than usual chance of being killed by a deranged client, but there's no way it would be the sort of killer we are talking about now."

"And I think we can rule out Joyce Mteki as well, guv," Desai proffered. "She worked as a nurse, lived alone and was a born-again Christian. Again, she seems an unlikely candidate to attract this sort of killer."

"Jenny Hillyer was an office worker who lived as a single girl in a flatshare," Metcalfe said, consulting his notes. "She did have a boyfriend but he had an alibi which we were able to vet carefully as we were pretty confident about the time of death in her case. I interviewed him myself and frankly he didn't seem the type to kill anyone, let alone pull a stunt like this."

"There was also evidence from her flatmates that she and her boyfriend were on very good terms," Desai interjected. "They were planning to move in together."

"So that leaves Katherine Barker," Collison concluded.

"Who had a pretty ropey relationship with her husband, featuring frequent shouting matches, according to the neighbours," Willis pointed out.

"A husband who is on our list of potential keyholders," Metcalfe said, half-lifting his copy of the list from the table, "and thus had access to the loft space."

"And who owned the flat where Clarke lived and had no real alibi for the night his wife was killed," Desai added, staring hard at Collison.

"And who is someone who might have had possible cause to have a grudge against Clarke," Leach said with sudden excitement. "There was some talk of him having stalked Katherine Barker, wasn't there?"

"And might it be significant"—Willis was thinking out loud now—"that the killings seem to have stopped with Katherine Barker? Perhaps that meant our murderer's task was now complete."

The tension within the room was palpable.

"I suppose," Collison said, striving to keep calm, "that we never really checked out his alibis for the other murders because we 'knew' that we were looking for a serial killer, whereas he was simply the bereaved husband of one of our deranged killer's victims."

"Correct," Metcalfe confirmed. "Just as we reckoned that it wasn't overly suspicious that he didn't have a provable alibi for his wife's killing because we 'knew' that she had been murdered by the same man who killed the others, and Barker had absolutely no motive to kill four unknown women."

"We need," Collison said with understated determination, "to re-interview the good doctor. But let's get as much background on him as we can. Karen and Priya, drop in on the neighbours again and see if they having anything new to add.

Andrew, look into his professional life; see if there are any skeletons in the closet there. Bob, you organise the financial checks. The rest of you, carry on with eliminating the keyholders."

"Excuse me, sir," Willis said, "but couldn't we use the keyholder enquiries as an excuse to re-interview Dr Barker?"

"My thoughts exactly," Collison replied. "That way we shan't arouse any suspicions. But let's get as much as we can through other channels first. OK, people, thank you. Let's get to work."

"Charles seemed dashed excited last night," Wimsey said later.

"So he should have been, Peter," Harriet responded. "You gave him a really good idea for the investigation, don't you remember?"

"Did I?" He seemed distracted.

"Yes, don't you remember? It's taken the enquiry down a whole new path. We now think that Katherine Barker's husband may have done it."

"What, all of them?"

"Yes, Peter, just like you found in one of your books, to conceal his wife's murder as part of a serial killer's rampage."

"Well, it's a viable theory, I suppose," Wimsey said, shaking his head a little, "but a wee thing prosaic, don't you think? The husband? Oh dear, that makes it just a simple crime of passion after all. How dashed boring."

"Don't start thinking about it all over again, there's a dear. Charles specifically told you that you couldn't have anything more to do with the case, don't you remember?"

"I think so, and I'm sure there must have been a good reason but I can't quite remember it. I say, Harriet, what's wrong with me? Why am I having such trouble remembering things? Have I been ill?"

"I'm afraid your nerves have been bad again, Peter. I have some pills from the doctor if you'd like to take them."

"Oh God, not the shell shock again? I do hope I haven't made a bally nuisance of myself."

"Of course you haven't," Harriet said warmly. "Anyway, we all just want to see you well again."

"Well, that might explain it, I suppose," he said, rather vacantly. "Being ill, I mean..."

Harriet knelt, took his hand and kissed it. "Don't worry, Peter," she assured him, "you're going to get well, and soon."

He smiled weakly at her.

"You know," he said after a while, "I've been thinking about what old Parker bird said about that profiler fellow. About how he told the police that he didn't think they'd got the right man, and how they ignored him."

"That's quite right," Harriet confirmed, staring at him intently. "The evidence seemed so strong, you see."

"I'm sure Charles did nothing wrong, he's a good man," Wimsey said.

"A pity you couldn't have been there, though, darling. I'm sure you would have sided with the profiler and put things right."

"I don't know about that," he protested. "As you say, the evidence was overwhelming."

"The important thing to remember," she said, weighing her words carefully and trying to see what effect they might have, "is that the profiler did nothing wrong. On the contrary, he was right. Had the police listened to him then, Gary Clarke would be alive today."

"It does look rather like that," he mused.

There was a long silence during which the clock of Christchurch could be heard striking eight.

"Would you like something to eat?" she asked eventually. "Bunter's not here but I could rustle something up."

"I think perhaps I would," he replied. "Though I'm so tired, Harriet. I feel as if I haven't slept for months."

"Well," she said, getting up from the floor, "after dinner why don't you have one of the doctor's pills. It'll help you sleep."

"A gentle thing, beloved from pole to pole," he murmured.

"Wordsworth?" she hazarded.

"No, some other cove," he said. "Coleridge, I think."

"Nature's soft nurse," she said gently.

"Oh, not Shakespeare, Harriet, surely?" He groaned. "Why, you're becoming almost as predictable as poor old Charles."

Chapter Eighteen

"You're going to re-investigate the husband?" the ACC asked.

"Not really a re-investigation, sir," Collison demurred. "At the time we were confident that we were only looking for a serial killer and so once we had established that Kathy Barker's murder fitted the pattern we ruled out the husband as a possible suspect."

"But you *are* looking for a serial killer, aren't you?" the ACC said pedantically. "You're surely not suggesting that some of these crimes were committed by different people?"

"Not at all, sir, there's no doubt they are all the work of one murderer, but it's the motive that's key. I'd say we might now be looking for a multiple killer rather than a serial killer. A small difference but a significant one."

The ACC made a noise that sounded suspiciously close to "Harrumph."

"So what I'm proposing is really a proper investigation *ab initio*, as you might say."

"I hope you're not using Latin phrases down at Hampstead nick. We don't want to alienate the troops more than is absolutely necessary."

"It means 'from the beginning,' sir."

"I know what it means," the ACC retorted. "Just tell me what you have in mind. Are you going to bring him in?"

"Not until absolutely necessary, sir," Collison said warily. "I'd like to get as much background as possible first. I have people re-interviewing the neighbours and checking out his professional and financial circumstances—discreetly of course. To that end, sir, I'd like to apply for a court order to examine his bank account."

"Hardly necessary, is it? Even if he did murder his wife it doesn't seem likely his motive was financial."

"Even so, sir. I'd like to do it. I'm very conscious that we've got it wrong once already and I don't want to be left wondering whether there's anything I should have looked at that I didn't."

"Hm," said the ACC, and then, "Oh, all right. But be careful, Simon. If it turns out you're wrong about this, the press will have a field day accusing us of harassing the bereaved husband of a sex killer's victim."

"I'm aware of the sensitivities, sir."

"I'm sure that you are but I'm the one who's going to have to face the Commissioner and explain the media coverage if anything goes wrong. In fact, I think on reflection that you need to report back to me before any attempt is made to re-interview the husband. Informally or otherwise. Is that clear?"

"Perfectly, sir," Collison said primly.

"Now I wanted to ask you something," the ACC went on in a different tone of voice. "I've made Tom Allen senior investigating officer on the Clarke prison murder. What do you think of that?"

"It's not for me to advise you, sir, but it sounds like a good call. Allen needs to get back to work, and mounting an enquiry within a prison calls for a good, hard copper, which is exactly what he is."

"You don't have a problem with him, then?"

"No, on the contrary, sir, we're friends and I have a lot of respect for him."

"I'm glad you said that. I'm going to put him and his team into Hampstead nick alongside you. It's a question of resources. It's not practical to base the enquiry at the prison and there's plenty of space at Hampstead. We've been trying to close the place for years, as you know."

"Oh," said Collison, and then stopped.

"Oh, what?"

"Well, there's the enquiry into the leaks, sir, if you recall? Might it not be a bit of a conflict to have Tom working in the very police station that is being accused of leaking inside information to him?"

"Oh, that," said the ACC dismissively. "Yes, I didn't have a chance to tell you. I've had the initial report from Internal Affairs. In their view identifying the culprit will prove extremely difficult and would not be a good use of resources. So I've recommended to the Commissioner that we drop the whole thing. I'm sure he'll agree."

"Oh," Collison said again, struggling to keep the surprise out of his voice. "Well, then I suppose it doesn't really matter."

"Exactly," the ACC said airily. "All water under the bridge. Glad you see it that way. You were quite right to bring it to my attention, though. Well, off you go but keep me posted. And remember, no move is to be made to approach Dr Barker without my express authorisation."

"I understand, sir," said Collison.

"How is Peter?" Metcalfe asked as they walked up Hampstead High Street. "Any change?"

"I'm not sure," Willis replied. "He seemed to be groping towards some sort of reality last night. I think Collison's comments about 'the profiler' may have got through to him on some level. I managed to get him to take one of the tranquilisers the doctor prescribed; he went to bed early and he was still asleep when I left this morning."

"Where shall we go?" Metcalfe asked as they reached the end of Flask Walk. "The Flask? The Wells?"

"What about the Holly Bush?" she suggested. "I haven't been there for ages."

"OK," he agreed. "Less likely to run into anyone from the nick there anyway. They're too lazy to climb the steps."

Shortly after they crossed the road by Hampstead station they began the ascent themselves. Conversation ceased as they laboured up the steep flights of steps which led up to Holly Mount. At the top, it felt as though they were looking out from the top of a cliff over the sights of London laid out for their delectation. They turned right and picked their way with care over the cobblestones to the pub on the corner. An eighteenth-century house with leaded windows, exposed beams and low ceilings, it was like walking onto the set of a Dickensian costume drama.

They each ordered a soft drink from the bar and then found a pew-like seat for two in the small room at the front. It was almost empty apart from a middle-aged man on his own with a pint of London Pride and what looked like chicken pie. He gazed at Karen in frank admiration. Almost certainly a writer, she thought as she sized him up.

"So I guess it's still way too early for us to break cover, then?" Metcalfe asked awkwardly.

"Oh," she said, glancing quickly around the room to see if there was anyone she recognised, "I'm so sorry. Yes, it is. I still can't even begin to imagine what the news might do to him right now. I really *am* sorry, Bob. This is all my fault."

"Don't be silly," he said quickly. "Of course it's not your fault. It's nobody's fault. It's just life, that's all, the way things work out. As long as you haven't changed your mind or anything, I can wait for as long as it takes."

"I haven't," she said, taking his hand and squeezing it. "We just have to be strong and patient. One day, somehow, this will all come out alright."

He lifted her hand, which was still wrapped around his, and kissed it. "OK, as long as we're on the same page."

"We are, I promise."

"OK then."

There was one of those long, smiley silences, which couples experience as tender moments of intimacy and onlookers find either charming or nauseating, depending on their disposition and the current state of their own love lives. The middle-aged man looked across the room at them as though he fell into the latter category.

"So what do you reckon to the guvnor's new idea?" Metcalfe asked finally, releasing his grip on her hand. She let it rest casually on his knee, which he found unexpectedly comforting.

"I'm really not sure," she answered after a moment's thought. "It's all very clever, but is it really plausible that somebody would plan the murder of various innocent people just to cover up a future murder of their own? I know it happened in a book but that's fiction, isn't it?"

"I know, I've been thinking about that myself. But I think at the very least it would be wrong to rule Barker out as a suspect at this stage just because we don't have him marked as a multiple murderer."

"Perhaps I'm just being naïve. I think maybe I have problems coming to terms with the idea that anyone could go out into the night to kill those poor women for no apparent reason, yet rationally I know that people do go out and do precisely that all the time, all over the world."

"In a warped sort of way it almost feels logical to me," he mused. "I mean, if you imagine yourself inside the mind of a psychopath, that is. Someone who feels no sense of right and wrong."

"There's a bit more to being a psychopath than that but yes, I see what you mean."

"Isn't that right, then?" he asked in surprise. "I thought the whole point about being a psychopath was precisely that—it's as if someone has taken out their conscience chip."

"Psychopathology is complex. For example there are different types of psychopaths, only some of whom are likely to commit violent criminal acts. I agree that a lack of sense of right and wrong is what it usually looks like, but you have to get behind that and see what is actually producing that effect."

"Which is?"

"It's often a combination of a lack of empathy and a lack of inhibition. Without empathy they lack the basic ability to imagine the suffering of others, and can therefore be indifferent to whether they inflict such suffering or not. With the rest of us, the reason we don't go around hitting people in the head with hammers is not just because we know it's wrong, but because we can imagine what it would be like to have our skulls smashed in and so would never dream of inflicting that sort of pain and damage on other people."

"And inhibition?"

"Psychology talks about its opposite: disinhibition. It embraces not only a basic lack of behavioural control but also an unusually high desire for immediate gratification, which in turn tends to lead a psychopath to think only of the moment, and ignore the long-term implications of their acts. You often see fraudsters and embezzlers stealing money when they must know on any rational level that there is no way of concealing their crime for long, yet they do it anyway, not thinking about the consequences of getting caught. There was a well-documented case of a prisoner who was transferred to an open prison to serve the last few weeks of his sentence, and simply jumped out of an open window and ran away. 'Pointless' you might say, and you'd be right, but their brains don't work in the same way."

"I see," Metcalfe said, "or rather, I think I do."

"I'm only scratching the surface," she said sheepishly. "Peter's the real expert. I could listen to him talk about it for hours."

With this sudden mention of Peter, it was as if a spell had been broken, dissolving to reveal two people sitting slightly awkwardly together in a Hampstead pub.

"Come on," Metcalfe said. "Time to get back."

❀ ❀ ❀

They were astonished to be confronted on their return with the figure of Tom Allen, standing beside Collison in the incident room.

"Hello Bob, hello Karen," he said as if nothing in the world had occurred to disrupt their relationship since last they had met.

Metcalfe said "Hello, guv" in a rather strained sort of way and looked at Collison, trying to work out what on earth this could mean.

"Tom has been appointed as senior investigating officer on the Gary Clarke murder," Collison said quickly, trying to defuse an awkward moment. "He's setting up an incident room upstairs but popped in to say hello."

"And to set up some lines of communication, sir," Allen reminded him, with a slight emphasis on the 'sir.' "After all, the two enquiries are related."

"To an extent," Collison demurred, "but only a small one. I presume your investigation will focus almost entirely on what happened to Clarke in prison."

"You mean after he was convicted?" Allen said innocently, letting the question hang in the air.

"Exactly," Collison replied. "Whereas the ACC was at pains to make it clear that those events should form no part of *our* investigation."

There was silence while everyone wondered who was going to speak next, and what they would say.

"So please feel free to drop in from time to time, Tom," Collison said, "but right now you'll have to excuse us, I'm afraid. We have a catch-up scheduled."

"What's the latest theory, then?" Allen asked, unabashed.

"I'm sure you're aware, Tom," Collison said smoothly, "that it is strictly forbidden to talk about an ongoing enquiry with anyone who is not a member of the team. Why, I've had occasion to stress this point formally with my team on a number of occasions. I'm sure you wouldn't want to put any colleague in a difficult position by asking them to give you information which they are not at liberty to divulge."

Willis imagined Lord Peter Wimsey murmuring, "A palpable hit, old boy."

"It was only a friendly enquiry," Allen responded. "Just trying to show an interest."

"Very nice of you, Tom," Collison replied, "but like I said, you'll have to excuse us now."

"Just before I go, I was wondering if I could borrow Bob here."

"Borrow? What do you mean?"

"Well, I've managed to have Ken Andrews posted back to me, but I'm short a DI. Since Bob and I have worked together for a long time, he seems an obvious choice."

"I'm sorry, Tom," Collison said after an astonished pause, "but I couldn't possibly agree to Bob being moved in the middle of an active enquiry. Why, he's the only one who knows where all the records are, for a start. No, it's simply out of the question."

"It has been a very long enquiry, though, hasn't it?" Allen persisted. "I thought you told me that it was now common practice to rotate senior members of a team in the case of such long investigations? New approach, fresh pair of eyes, stop people going stale, that sort of thing? I seem to remember there's been some research on this in America, isn't that right?"

Metcalfe gazed at Collison imploringly. His boss, however, seemed unfazed. "You do rate a DI of course, Tom," Collison said, affecting to ignore Allen's last contribution to the conversation, "and fortunately you're in luck. I have an excellent one you can have. Andrew Leach over there. To tell the truth, he's a bit surplus to requirements anyway."

Allen put his hands in his pockets and stared at Leach quizzically, as if evaluating a racehorse. Leach noticed him staring and looked back awkwardly, unsure for what reason he was being singled out for special attention.

"It is usual, of course, in these situations," Allen said gravely, "to try to palm some poor chump off with a colleague who is, let us say, one of the less effective members of a team."

"Not the case here at all," Collison said briskly. "Absolutely not. In fact Andrew has made a very significant contribution to our efforts since he's arrived. You'll like him, Tom, trust me. He's a solid traditional copper."

"He looks to me"—Allen turned away from gazing at Leach—"like a blot on the landscape."

"Oh gosh, Tom," Collison said anxiously. "I wouldn't let him hear you say that if I were you."

"Why not?"

"Because he's great friends with the ACC. Why, they speak daily on the phone, I believe. That's why he'll be such a valuable member of your team. You'll have a direct line to the top anytime you need it."

Allen, aghast, looked from Collison to Leach and back again.

"Or even when you don't," Metcalfe interjected innocently.

Allen muttered something that might have been "Thank you so much for your generous cooperation," but probably wasn't, as he strode from the room with what dignity he could muster.

A tangible sense of relief swept through the three people whom he left in his wake.

"Bob," Collison said with a smile, "would you ask Andrew to come over here for a minute so we can break the happy news about his new responsibilities?"

"With pleasure, sir."

Chapter Nineteen

"Now then," Collison said as the slightly delayed update meeting began minus DI Leach, "what do we have on Dr Barker?"

"I've re-interviewed the neighbours," Desai said. "There have been some developments. They've seen a young woman coming and going from the flat on a regular basis. In fact she may even be living there. She looks Chinese, apparently, but beyond that nobody knows anything. Oh, and unlike with Kathy Barker, there have been no noisy scenes."

"Interesting," Collison commented, "but hardly conclusive. Anything else?"

"I've interviewed his colleagues at the practice," Willis reported, "discreetly of course. Nothing much to report. He took a couple of weeks off after his wife was killed but then returned to work and appeared as right as rain. In fact when I pressed the receptionist there she remarked that he seemed happy nowadays, which she says he certainly hadn't been before."

"And I suppose you pressed her on that too?"

"I certainly did, but then she got a bit evasive. So I spoke to one of his partners there. He eventually admitted that they had been so concerned about his heavy drinking before Kathy's death that they had convened a formal practice meeting and threatened to suspend and report him if he didn't do something about it."

"I wonder if that 'something' was killing his wife," Desai interjected grimly.

"Let's not get ahead of ourselves," Collison counselled. "The ACC wants something very cogent indeed if he's going to allow us to re-interview Barker, and I understand his point of view. This could rebound on us very badly indeed if we pull him in only to find that we can't make anything stick."

"Well, this might make a difference," Metcalfe reported smugly. "I spoke to the solicitor who's handling Kathy Barker's estate, on the pretext that we needed to tie up a few loose ends procedurally. I asked what the details of her will had been but apparently she never made one so all her assets pass automatically to the husband."

"How much are we talking?"

"Very little, so at first it didn't seem like there was anything there by way of a motive, but then he let slip that the amount of her estate didn't really matter because of the life insurance."

"Life insurance?"

"Naturally I pricked my ears up then and asked him for the details. He suddenly got all coy and wondered whether he ought to have mentioned it. I told him that we absolutely had to have anything relevant to her estate for our files, but he muttered something about privilege."

"Privilege? But Kathy's dead," Willis pointed out.

"Yes but her husband isn't, and he's also a client," Metcalfe explained. "So I asked if he could confirm that he was prevented from answering my question because of legal privilege owed to Dr Barker and he thought a bit and then said yes."

"So…" Collison said slowly.

"So the husband was the beneficiary under an insurance policy on her life, which gives him a motive," Desai cut in excitedly.

"It certainly sounds like that," Collison admitted, "otherwise I don't see why the solicitor should have felt unable to answer the question."

"Then he actually has not one possible motive but two," Willis pointed out. "Desire to get rid of an unwanted wife and the ability to benefit financially from her death."

"And we know he doesn't have an alibi for the night of his wife's murder," Desai continued, "and it would have been the easiest thing in the world for him to have been waiting for her at her sister's flat. After all, he knew exactly where she would be going."

"This is good stuff," said Collison, "but it's all still circumstantial. If only we could link him directly to even one of the killings…"

"He is one of the relatively few people who could have put the evidence in the loft space," Metcalfe pointed out. "In fact he's the only keyholder we've been able to identify so far who has any connection with Kathy Barker other than Gary Clarke, and we know now that he wasn't our man."

"You say relatively few," Collison said quietly. "How few exactly?"

"We may never know for certain," Metcalfe conceded reluctantly. "There are just too many moving parts and uncertainties—agents, contractors, previous tenants and so on—but so far we've identified only about thirty specific individuals."

"What are the odds," said Willis, "that more than one of thirty people who could have planted evidence taken from a murdered woman also has a clear motive for killing her and no alibi for the night of her murder?"

"There's one other thing," Desai volunteered before anyone could answer. "I had a thought about your new theory of the earlier killings being a blind to draw us away from Barker. That would mean that he would have had to be planning all this before the first murder took place."

"Agreed." Collison nodded.

"So when I re-interviewed the neighbours I asked them to try to focus on exactly when it was that all the shouting and screaming started from the Barkers' flat. They agreed pretty much. It turns out that it was about six weeks before the date of our first murder." She looked around the room with an air of quiet triumph.

❀ ❀ ❀

"So you definitely want to re-interview the husband?" the ACC said. "You do remember what I said, Simon, about the need for compelling evidence before you do?"

"Indeed I do, sir. It's all in the report I sent in."

"Yes." He stared at the report sitting on his desk.

"I think I would regard that as 'compelling,' sir," Collison ventured when the other man said nothing.

"It certainly seems strong, but allow me to remind you that you thought we had an even more compelling case against Clarke and we now know it wasn't so."

"All the facts seemed to fit the theory, sir."

"Yes," the ACC said, gazing hard at him. "And maybe that's where we went wrong, Simon. Detective work is about making the theory fit the facts. Perhaps we were drawn into doing things the wrong way round. The tail wagging the dog, as it were."

"I hadn't thought about it that way, sir," Collison replied thoughtfully, "but perhaps there's something to it. We had our nice new shiny profile and it seduced us into not looking too far outside it, even when the profiler himself expressed doubts as to our conclusions."

"Are you sure you're not making the same mistake twice? Once again you seem to have formed some airy fairy theory— this time based on a work of detective fiction if I understand correctly—and the known facts all seem to point conveniently in the right direction."

"Again," Collison conceded, "maybe there's something to that, but we won't know that without speaking again to Barker."

"You're an intelligent man, Simon," the ACC said slowly. "Your academic record shows that. But have you ever considered that perhaps you may be approaching this *too* intelligently?"

"I'm not sure I understand you, sir. How can a police officer, or indeed anyone, be too intelligent?"

"Perhaps I'm expressing myself badly," the ACC said, fiddling with his reading glasses. "'Intelligent' may be the wrong word. 'Rational' might be better." He broke off and put the glasses down on his desk on top of the report. "The best detectives I've worked with in my career were bright too, even though they didn't have your sort of formal education. But they had something else; they had instinct, some sort of subjective awareness that came to them, apparently from nowhere."

"Copper's nose, sir?"

"Yes," the ACC said flatly. "Let me give you an example, an extreme one certainly, but one that demonstrates what I mean. Someone I worked with early in my career was on the West Yorkshire force in 1976 when the Yorkshire Ripper's first victim was found. Apparently the SIO stood beside the body for a while, looked around the surrounding area and then said 'I think we're looking for a lorry driver.' Sadly he died shortly afterwards and other people took over the investigation. Suppose he hadn't? A lot of innocent lives might have been saved."

"It's an interesting example, sir, but with respect I hardly think you can base a whole murder enquiry on intuition."

"Maybe not," the ACC replied, "and that's not what I'm suggesting. Perhaps I'm just not expressing myself well. God knows, inquiries fail for all sorts of reasons."

He got up and walked over to the window.

"What does *your* instinct tell you about this case, Simon? Anything at all?"

Collison hesitated. "To be totally honest, sir, my instinct still tells me that we had the right man in Clarke, though I know that can't be true so I'd rather not trust it again. But for what it's worth, I feel that Dr Barker is somehow intimately connected with all of this."

"Hm," said the ACC.

"What about you, sir? What does your copper's nose tell you?"

"It's not my case," he said briskly, "it's yours. And it's not my job to find the killer, it's yours. My job is to decide whether or not to back your judgment and allow you to re-interview Dr Barker. And I do, so go ahead. You may also apply, if you wish, for an order to inspect his bank accounts."

"Thank you, sir. I appreciate the vote of confidence."

"Understand this, Simon," the ACC said as Collison rose to leave. "Of course a major part of my concern here is for the reputation of the Met. We've already been pilloried for getting the wrong man convicted. If we charge Dr Barker with his wife's murder and then can't make it stick, I can't even begin to imagine what might happen."

"I understand, sir."

"I'm not sure you do. Another part of my concern is for you personally. You're a fine officer and you've risen quickly, but if this goes wrong then those people within the Met who feel threatened by fast-tracked graduates will point the finger and say you've risen *too* quickly; there will be snide remarks that you'd have been better off learning about basic police work. I don't want to see your career destroyed, nor do I want to damage the prospects of the other bright young officers who are following in your wake—DC Willis, for example."

Collison stood in silence in the middle of the room.

"Believe me, sir," he said at length. "Everything you've just said had already occurred to me. But I do think we—I, rather—have to approach this investigation in what seems the most logical way, and without having undue regard to my own personal interests."

The ACC sighed. "In that case, Simon, be careful. Bloody careful."

Karen closed the front door behind her and stood, listening. There was nothing to be heard. She put down her bags, walked past the living room—noting that it was empty—and came to the door of the main bedroom, which was ajar. Inside it was dark. She pushed the door open as quietly as she could and peeped in. The curtains were still closed. As her eyes became more accustomed to what was left of the evening sun being filtered through the curtains, she saw Peter stirring in bed.

"Hello," she said gently, coming in and sitting down on the edge of the bed, "how are you feeling?"

"Damn tired," came the reply. "How long have I been asleep?"

"Well," she said, "you went to bed about nine last night and now it's seven-thirty the following evening. Have you been asleep all this time, Peter?"

"I got up to go to the loo a couple of times," he replied hoarsely, "but other than that, yes."

"Well, I suppose it's good for you, but I think you ought to get up now and have something to eat. Why don't you let me draw the curtains?"

"Alright."

As she opened them, the room filled with dim daylight, and she looked back at the man in bed. He was gaunt and unshaven, and seemed troubled by something. His hands were plucking nervously at the sheets.

"Why don't you get up and have a shower and a shave?" she suggested gently. "I'll go and make a start on dinner."

"Alright," he said again, but without looking at her. Something halfway up the bedroom wall seemed to have his full attention.

She went back into the hall to retrieve her bags and began unpacking the shopping. In the background she heard the shower running. She checked the fridge for wine and took out an unopened bottle of Trebbiano. She had almost finished cooking the pasta by the time he came into the room, dressed in slippers, trousers and an open-necked shirt. She poured him a glass of wine and kissed him gently on the cheek.

"Hello again," she said. "You must feel better for that."

He nodded and sat down on one of the kitchen chairs. He seemed distracted still. She stared at him while trying not to appear to. What was he thinking about? Who was he?

She found herself wishing that Bob was there for support, but dismissed the thought.

"What's for dinner?" he asked suddenly.

"Bolognese. Is that OK?"

"Yes, of course," he said quickly. "Lovely."

He took a sip of his wine, moving it reflectively around his mouth. He seemed to find this a comfort and promptly repeated the process a few more times.

"Nice wine."

"Mmm," she agreed, taking a mouthful herself. "Would you like to hear about the case?" she asked him.

"Yes, why not?" he answered, looking a little vague.

"We're going to bring the last victim's husband in again and re-interview him," she said.

"Oh good," he replied, and then added, "why?"

"Well, if you remember, we're now working on a theory that one of the murders was not motiveless at all, and the others were intended as camouflage. For all sorts of reasons the last one, the Barker murder, seems the most likely."

She took the pasta off the hob and strained it, then added the Bolognese from the other saucepan.

"Whose theory is that?" he asked.

She was about to say "Collison's" but stopped herself. She busied herself with serving the meal and applying black pepper and Parmesan.

"Well," she said as she put a plate in front of him, "it was yours really, if you remember."

He frowned deeply as he ate his first mouthful. She noticed that he had finished his glass of wine, and refilled it for him. Suddenly his face cleared and he started chuckling.

"*The Laughing Policeman*," he said. "Oh dear, in the midst of life we are in fiction."

"Just because someone used it in a book doesn't mean it can't happen in real life," she pointed out.

He nodded and took another mouthful of food. "Particularly if they've read the same book, of course," he said after swallowing, laughing once more. He tried drinking some wine while he was still chuckling. This proved a mistake and he started coughing.

"Oh, Peter," she said, feeling tears welling in her eyes, "it is so good to see you well again."

"Yes, I've been a little under the weather, haven't I?" he said, looking worried again. "Strange, I can't quite remember."

"You just haven't been yourself, that's all." This was true after all, she reflected.

"But why can't I remember?" he persisted. "I recall dreaming about a Peter Wimsey story—one I'd never read, but was sort of making up as I went along. You were in it too. It all seemed very real at the time, but now I'm not sure. What's been happening to me, Karen?"

"You've had a fever, Peter, for quite a few days. Probably just very bad flu. That can make your dreams seem very vivid."

"Yes, I suppose so." He sounded unconvinced. "God knows, I'm tired enough."

"Hungry, too," she noted as she spooned the last of the pasta onto his plate.

"I am, aren't I? I suppose that's a good sign."

"Of course it is. The fever's broken and you're on the mend."

"What would be Dr Barker's motivation for wanting to kill his wife?" he asked, switching the subject abruptly.

"We know that they were having dreadful rows, so perhaps he was having second thoughts about their marriage. He now has a new woman in his life, by the way."

"But why murder? It's a pretty extreme solution. What's wrong with divorce?"

"Well, he'd already been divorced once, so maybe he didn't fancy going through it again. Few men would happily pay maintenance to not one but two women. There again, maybe he felt let down. Perhaps he thought she had enticed him into marriage and then not delivered on what he'd thought was going to be on offer."

"All good conjecture," he commented, twirling the wine in his glass, "but I'd say that it takes a little more than mere everyday factors, no matter how upsetting, to turn a man into a killer."

"There may be a financial motive as well," she said. "We're waiting for the details of his bank account, but it seems that he took out quite a big life insurance policy on his wife shortly before she died. That seems to fit the theory quite neatly. As soon as that news became known he'd be an obvious suspect for his wife's murder."

"True." He nodded. "Of course I've never met the man so I can't really comment, but it still seems a bit of a stretch to move from wanting to be rid of your wife to planning a whole string of murders. Possible, though, don't get me wrong. Dear me, did I really come up with this idea? If so, it must have been while I was delirious."

"To be honest, it was Collison actually," she admitted.

"Well, he's an intelligent man," Peter opined, "so we should take his ideas seriously. And he's an experienced police officer..."

"Not that experienced actually. Remember, he's been fast-tracked. That's the problem too, or at least the potential problem. If he gets this wrong there'll be lots of old-style coppers only too eager to put the boot in and say that this is what happens when college boys start trying to do men's work."

"I see," he said slowly. "Well, then we must hope that he's not wrong."

Chapter Twenty

"OK, people," Collison called out the next morning. "Quieten down and let's get started. I'm going to ask DI Metcalfe to report whatever we may have found out about Dr Barker's financial background. Bob...?"

The hum of conversation died away and everyone looked expectantly at Metcalfe.

"Interesting stuff, sir. The good doctor was struggling to make ends meet. He was paying pretty stiff maintenance payments under his divorce settlement, and he'd taken out a large mortgage to buy the flat in Lyndhurst Avenue. The ex-wife got the marital home as well as regular payouts. Barker's solicitor ran the usual professional privilege stunt but I pulled the financial order from the court records."

"So he needed to buy a new place but the only way he could do that was with a mortgage, and the available income to do that was limited?" Collison asked, making a note.

"Exactly."

"He could have rented somewhere," Desai pointed out.

Metcalfe shrugged. "He could, of course, but maybe the new Mrs Barker wanted to live in style *and* in a place she actually owned. Who knows?"

"What about his income from the practice?" Collison asked.

"Barely adequate. After both the maintenance and the mortgage payments he was only clearing about a thousand a month, and that's *before* things like council tax and utilities. It's clear from his bank statement that he couldn't manage. He was hard up against the stops on his overdraft."

"And just remind me: his wife's life was insured for how much?"

"Two hundred grand."

The team exchanged meaningful glances.

"That would cover an awful lot of maintenance payments," Willis said unnecessarily.

"You say he *was* hard up against the stops, Bob," Collison said. "Has that changed?"

"It certainly has. He received the insurance payout a week or two back. Once Clarke was charged with the murder they must have assumed that Barker wasn't a suspect, since they paid out in full. They didn't actually ask us, of course."

"Well, if they had done, we'd only have given them the assurance they needed anyway," Collison said simply. "After all, he *wasn't* a suspect then."

"But he is now, sir, isn't he?" Desai asked hesitantly. "Just for the record."

"He most certainly is. The question is, what's the best way to play this? It seems to me that we are back in the same situation we were in with Clarke. Strong suspicion but only circumstantial evidence."

They looked hard at one another, without speaking.

"We now know he had a motive for his wife's murder," Metcalfe ventured.

"At least one." Collison nodded. "But we can't place him at the scene. Or indeed, at the scene where any of the other bodies were found."

"We know that he didn't have an alibi for her death," persisted Metcalfe, "so at least in theory he had opportunity.

And wait, there's something else we haven't considered before: he's a doctor so presumably he has access to chloroform. You can't just pick it up in the supermarket. So, he had motive, opportunity and means."

"Damn!" Collison said. "Why didn't we think of that before? Of course the chloroform opens up a whole new line of enquiry. Well done, Bob."

"We haven't fully checked his alibis for the other murders, sir," Willis offered, "because of course at the time there was no reason to."

"Hang on, Karen, let's take one thing at a time. The question is, do we think the case Bob has just outlined is strong enough for us to re-interview Barker?"

"Yes," chorused the team.

"I tend to agree. But what do we do if he flatly denies everything?" He looked around the room, but nobody seemed to have an answer. "If there was something we could do to strengthen the case it might be different..."

"Wait!" Willis said. "The chloroform!"

"What about it?" Collison asked.

"Well, if we're right and it was Barker who had it and used it, he must have got it from somewhere. Logically that would be the practice where he works, unless perhaps he could get it on prescription from a local chemist."

"Excellent! Well, since you and Priya seem to have established good relations there, find out as discreetly as you can if they've had any chloroform go missing recently. Bob, why don't you detail some folks to check out local chemists? I can't believe people come in for chloroform very often, so if they have then someone is bound to remember."

Metcalfe jotted a note on his pad. "Right you are, sir. When would you like to reconvene?"

"Tomorrow morning," Collison said decisively. "I can't see why any of this should take more than twenty-four hours. Thank you, everyone. I have a good feeling about this. Let's hope this time it's really the break we're looking for."

Dr Ian Partridge had just finished his morning surgery when the receptionist buzzed through to ask if he would take a call from Detective Constable Willis.

"Yes, I suppose so," he replied, "put him through."

"It's not a him," the receptionist informed him primly. "It's a her. They do have women in the police force, you know."

He sighed. "Then put *her* through please, Mary."

"Dr Partridge, it's Karen Willis from Hampstead CID. I'm sorry to trouble you again, I know you spoke earlier to my colleague Priya Desai, but I wanted to ask you about some chloroform. In particular, has anybody at the practice noticed any going missing over the course of the last year or so?"

"Chloroform?" he said blankly. "No, I shouldn't think so. I can't think of any good reason why we should have chloroform here in the first place. You're welcome to come and look through our stock records if you like; it's only our patient files which are confidential."

"You're very kind, but I'd rather not come to the practice. We're trying to be as discreet as possible."

"I understand," Partridge said. "Look, I'm off this afternoon. If you like I'll make some discreet enquiries here before I leave and perhaps we could meet somewhere—say at three?"

"That would be extremely kind of you, Doctor. Where would you like to meet?"

"Let's see…do you know the Chamomile Café in England's Lane?"

"I do indeed. I'll see you there at three."

"Hang on, how will I recognise you?" Partridge asked.

"Good point," she said. "I've got your email address. I'll send you a photo."

When the photo arrived a few minutes later any resentment that Dr Partridge might have been feeling about giving up his free afternoon promptly vanished.

The picture was only a head and shoulders shot and had not prepared the doctor for the effect of Karen Willis in person, which not only temporarily deprived him of the power of intelligible speech but also brought the bright chatter inside the cafe to a halt as male customers stared unashamedly, and female customers glared at their male companions.

Somehow he managed to order coffee without making too obvious a fool of himself. She asked for Earl Grey.

"So," she said with a smile, "the chloroform?"

"Well," he replied, glad of a chance to impress, "yes. Let me tell you what I found out but first let me put it in context, because I think this may be of interest to your investigation."

"Gladly," she said, opening her notebook.

"The first thing to understand is that chloroform really has no valid medical use these days. It's still used in a few cough syrups, I think, but the EU is trying to phase that out. There would certainly be no earthly reason for having any at a doctors' surgery."

"Oh dear," she said flatly. "What a disappointment."

"Perhaps not," he responded with what he hoped was a winning smile. "You see, oddly enough some chloroform *did* arrive a while back. We returned it—or thought we had—because it had obviously been sent in error, and asked for a credit note. Our receptionist remembers it distinctly because it ended up causing quite a lot of bother. First the supplier swore blind that it *had* been ordered by someone at the practice over the telephone. Then they claimed never to have received it back from us. After a lot of to-ing and fro-ing we gave up as the whole thing was taking up so much time."

"And where is it now?" Willis asked urgently.

"Buggered if I know, pardon my French," Partridge answered resignedly. "It's certainly not in the stock locker, I checked it myself. For all intents and purposes it might just as well have vanished into thin air."

They broke off as their tea and coffee arrived.

"So let me get this straight," Willis said carefully, looking at her notebook. "Chloroform would not normally be present in a medical practice today. Notwithstanding that, chloroform was in fact delivered to your surgery but may subsequently have gone missing."

"Correct on all counts, Officer," he replied with a grin.

She smiled and tasted her tea.

"Actually," he continued eagerly, "I was wondering if I could talk to you briefly about chloroform. If you'd be interested, that is. If you think it would be proper."

"Proper? What do you mean?"

"Well," he said awkwardly, "I'm not sure to what extent we're allowed to discuss your investigation but there's something which you may or may not have taken fully into account."

She thought for a moment. "I can't divulge any details of our enquiries to you," she said carefully, "but if there's anything you think it would be helpful for the police to know, then please tell me."

"OK," he said. "I was hoping you'd say that. I understand from the press reports of the court proceedings that chloroform was used to subdue the women before they were raped and killed. By the way, that may sound a bit morbid but because Colin's wife was one of the victims, everyone at the practice naturally took a close interest in what was being reported."

"Go on."

"Well, that struck me as very strange."

"How so?"

"I know you always see people being knocked out with a chloroform pad in films but in real life it really doesn't work like that. It can take up to four or five minutes for unconsciousness to occur, and that's an awfully long time to hold it over someone's nose and mouth while they're doubtless struggling like hell."

She stared at him. "What are you saying?" she asked stupidly. "That it's not possible to knock someone out that way?"

"Not impossible," he said, "but pretty impractical certainly. Unless perhaps the victim was old or infirm or there was more than one attacker—but then why use chloroform in the first place?"

"Why indeed?" she echoed.

"Of course, I'm not a forensic expert," he went on, warming to his theme, "but you might want to check how many murder cases you have in your records which have involved the use of chloroform. I'd be surprised if it's that many—certainly in recent times. It hasn't been used in medicine for years and years."

"I will," she said warmly. "Thank you, Doctor, thank you very much indeed."

"You're very welcome," he replied. "Now let me get the bill."

"Oh no," she protested. "Let me; I can claim it back."

He waved his hand expansively. "I insist."

"In that case, thank you again."

"I say," he said hopefully, "I don't suppose I could have your card, could I? Just in case I remember anything else that might be useful?"

"And did you check?" Collison asked her the next morning as she finished briefing the team.

"Yes, guv. The doctor was quite right. There were a few high profile cases a hundred years or more ago—including the millionaire William Rice in the US, incidentally—but we've nothing on record for murder here in the UK at all. There was a case in America in 1991, but that involved a victim who was asleep at the time."

"So we have a puzzle on our hands," Collison said. "Why use chloroform to knock out a victim when it's a very inefficient way of doing it? Why not just hit them over the head with a hammer straightaway and be done with it? Frankly, I'm baffled."

"And how would they get their hands on it anyway?" Metcalfe asked. "What did the supplier tell us, Karen?"

"It's good," she said happily. "In fact, I think it's what we're looking for. Basically chloroform is supplied to two main types of customers these days. There are industrial customers who buy it in large quantities to make chemicals, and science labs who buy it in small quantities as a reagent for chemistry research."

"You mean…?" Metcalfe prompted her.

"I mean," she said triumphantly, "that Colin Barker's medical practice is the *only* surgery in the country to whom they have *ever* supplied chloroform. There are other suppliers of course, but that's still pretty significant."

"I agree," said Collison. "I think it's time we had Dr Barker in for a chat."

"On what basis though, guv?" Metcalfe said warily.

"What do you mean, Bob?"

"Well, it seems to me we have two decisions to make about how we play this."

"Which are?"

"First, if we're going to interview him this time as a suspect rather than as a witness, we need to make that clear to him. That almost certainly means that we'll have to interview him under caution and *that* means he'll almost certainly ask for a lawyer."

"Agreed." Collison nodded. "Unfortunate but it can't be helped."

"The second decision may be a bit trickier, though, guv," Metcalfe went on. "If we ask him about the other killings and then release him on bail, he may be able to find someone—a woman perhaps, or a family member—who's prepared to perjure themselves by giving him an alibi. An alibi for one of them might be all that it would take to persuade a jury to acquit. After all, we'd be asking them to believe that Barker planned and executed a whole string of murders to cover up the one he really cared about. They might take some persuading, especially if he presents well."

This was slowly digested.

"So if we bring him in we may do better to go the whole hog," Collison said. "Caution him, charge him, and persuade the magistrate to remand him in custody."

"That makes it all or nothing," Willis said hesitantly. "Once we charge him we're more or less committed to bringing him to trial. If we don't, we'll look pretty silly."

"And the ACC..." said Desai.

"Quite," Collison acknowledged.

"Can I make a suggestion?" Metcalfe said slowly.

"Please do, Bob."

"How about referring the file to the DPP? If we want to charge him we need their sign-off anyway."

"The phrase 'passing the buck' comes to mind but yes, good suggestion, Bob. Send everything we've got to the DPP's office. Oh dear, I feel that another conference with Alistair Partington beckons."

"OK, people." He raised his voice. "I think we're done for today. Let's reconvene tomorrow. Take the rest of the day off, what's left of it. Bob, Karen, can you stay, please?"

As the room cleared slowly, the three of them drew away towards the corner furthest from the door.

"Karen," Collison said, "I haven't had a chance to ask how Peter is doing."

"He's much better—I think. At least he's dropped the Lord Peter Wimsey persona. I'm just trying to decide whether to get him back with the therapist and if so, how and when."

"I know this is a lot to ask," he ventured, "but is there any chance he might be well enough to discuss the case? I'd be very interested to hear his take on the latest developments."

"I'm sorry, sir," she said decidedly, "but I really don't think he is. He's still fragile and I'm frightened that the slightest little thing might push him back over the edge. Right now he's sleeping a lot, which is probably the best thing for him."

"That's fine," he said quickly. "I'm sorry I asked. You must be the best judge of his condition, of course."

"Anyway, sir," she said with a sudden grin, "I thought you were under orders from the ACC not to involve him anymore."

"That's true. My interaction with him would have had to be necessarily, ah, informal, shall we say?"

"Well, I'll happily keep you informed of his condition," she said briskly, "but I really don't think he'll be strong enough for a while yet."

"Good. Now then, Bob, I know you're going to be busy putting the papers together for the DPP but there's something I'd like you to do for me..."

Chapter Twenty-One

In the event it took two days for the DPP's office to arrange the conference and from the strained tone of voice and pinched expression of the man from the DPP, even this was to be regarded as a major concession on their part to the pressing nature of the situation. Thus it was that two days later Collison and Metcalfe found themselves once more in the august presence of the fustian Alistair Partington.

"Oh," he said, clearly disappointed, as they came into the room. "I was rather hoping you might bring that nice DC Willis with you, Simon."

"Sorry about that, Alistair. We weren't sure she'd be able to cope with the excitement of a meeting with you, so we left her behind."

The ferret-faced man from the DPP looked disapprovingly from one to another as they sat down, clearly of the opinion that such levity was out of place.

"Well now," Partington said, pushing various bundles wrapped in red tape to each side and pulling the DPP's file to the centre of his desk. "I see we have an alternative villain in the frame?"

"Yes, the husband," Collison said matter-of-factly. "He had motive, means and opportunity. He doesn't have an alibi for the time of his wife's murder nor, so far as we are aware, for any of the others. We appreciate that once again the evidence is almost entirely circumstantial, but we're confident nonetheless that it's very strong."

"Let me get this straight from the outset, Simon," Partington said, "just so we're clear. Are you now saying that Dr Barker murdered all these other women masquerading as a serial killer just so that when he murdered his wife nobody would suspect him?"

"Yes, Alistair, that's exactly what we're saying."

Partington gazed at him magisterially. "I'm sure you think you can make your theory good, Simon, or we wouldn't be here in the first place, but I have to say that in my view a jury would find such an idea rather far-fetched, to say the least. Why, it's almost like something out of detective fiction."

"It is, actually," came unexpectedly from the man from the DPP. He rustled his papers to find the reference to *The Laughing Policeman* and gazed at Collison in a vaguely hostile manner.

"Ah," Partington said, glancing in some confusion from one to another, "really? I see."

"Let's park the literary references for the moment, shall we?" Collison suggested levelly. "You've had a chance to read the papers, Alistair. What do you think?"

Partington paused reflectively, though whether he was genuinely choosing his words with care or simply adding extra emphasis when he did finally utter them was a matter for conjecture. "I think it's a good case," he pronounced finally. "Good enough to put to a jury, subject always to my original caveat that they may find it hard to believe."

"But Mr Partington," the man from the DPP piped up, "surely it's wholly circumstantial?"

"It *is* circumstantial," that worthy acknowledged, "but it's strong. We can't actually put our man at the scene of any of the crimes, but we can do just about everything else."

He began to count points off on his fingers as he continued. "Our man had at least one strong motive for killing his wife. He was in deep financial trouble and had recently taken out an insurance policy on her life. Neighbours agree that his relationship with the murdered woman, for which presumably high hopes had been entertained, was experiencing grave problems which manifested themselves in angry shouting matches and the wife storming out of the house late at night on a regular basis—and we know that these scenes began about six weeks before the date of the first murder, which would be consistent with Barker having hatched exactly the plan which DS Collison now alleges.

"We know that chloroform, for which there is no normal requirement in medical practices, was delivered to his surgery and soon afterwards went missing. He knew where his wife was going on the night of the murder and could easily have left immediately after she did to follow her there, or even lie in wait for her. So he had motive, means and opportunity.

"Further," he intoned, moving to quell signs of incipient rebellion from the DPP's office, "we know that the items found in the loft space came from the various murder scenes, and he is the only person we have yet been able to identify who both had access by key to the relevant building, and any possible grounds for suspecting to be the murderer. So far as I can see, and so far as the extensive police enquiries have been able to establish, that is the only possible explanation which can be established for how those items came to be there."

He stopped. The man from the DPP looked mutinous but held his tongue.

"So the issue we now face is this, as I see it," Partington went on. "We need to establish whether chummy has an alibi for any one of the other murders. I say 'any one' because I am sure DS Collison would agree that his theory requires Barker to have committed all the murders. So if he could prove himself innocent of one, we would have to accept that he was innocent of all of them."

He looked quizzically at Collison, who nodded readily in acquiescence.

"In order to do this, he will of course need to be re-interviewed," Partington carried on, "and this is where our possible difficulties would begin, for in my view, given the evidence already available to the police, they would have to make it clear to him that he was being interviewed as a possible suspect, and do so under caution."

He took his glasses off and gazed mildly up at the light fitting, clearly thinking the while. Then he looked back across the table. "The police can of course normally only hold him for twenty-four hours without charge. They feel that it is unlikely they would be able to establish the lack or presence of any relevant alibi within this period, and I agree that this seems a reasonable assumption. They also feel that if he were then to be released he might, now alerted to their suspicions, seek to tamper with the proceedings by manufacturing an alibi with the help of a third party. I cannot comment on how likely this might be to happen, but it must be a possibility.

"In order to forestall this, the police seek to arrest him, charge him and apply to the magistrates to hold him in custody. As I say, it is not for me to advise on police tactics. I am not competent to comment on which is the better course of action to adopt. I would say only that DS Collison is a senior and experienced police officer, and that I am sure the DPP would respect his views."

Everyone naturally looked at the man from the DPP, who squirmed visibly.

"What I *can* advise on," Partington said, with the air of a man concluding a lengthy summation to the jury, "is whether the evidence is strong enough to support the proposed course of action, and in my view it is more than adequate. It is my opinion that if Barker was charged and taken before the magistrates, he would almost certainly be remanded in custody. He would, after all, be facing multiple charges of murder."

"Write that down," Collison said, turning to the man from the DPP.

"But are you saying, Mr Partington," he persisted, ignoring Collison, "that there is enough evidence to charge Dr Barker with all these murders?"

"That is a matter for the police and the DPP," Partington replied blandly. "The test is whether there is a case to answer, and in my view there is. I am confident that, were a magistrate to be presented with this evidence at a committal hearing, he would conclude that the case was more than good enough to go to trial."

"But would we win at trial? I'm sure you can appreciate that the Home Office is very concerned about the publicity which this case has already attracted."

Partington smiled the condescending smile of a man whose opponent has just taken a fatal step too far. "Naturally that is a question which no counsel could answer, or indeed should answer. Juries are gullible, fallible human beings. What I can say is that if I were DS Collison I believe I would be seeking to proceed in exactly the way he is proposing."

"Write that down," Collison said again.

"I never realised that about chloroform," Peter Collins said thoughtfully. He looked pale and thin, but less strained than before.

"Now you're not to start worrying about it, Peter," Karen pleaded. "I don't want you to tire yourself out. It's important that you rest and get well."

"I'm fine," he reassured her. "It gives me something to do. What *does* it mean, do you think? Why use a means of killing that is apparently notoriously difficult when there are other much simpler and more efficient alternatives available?"

"I really don't know," she admitted. "Could it have some symbolic significance?"

"It's a good starting theory"—he nodded—"but what? And why?"

She shrugged helplessly and poured him a fresh glass of wine. "Does it affect the profile at all?"

"I'm not sure. My original idea was based on the assumption that chloroforming was an effective and viable means of subduing someone quickly and cleanly, from which I drew the image of a killer who is weak and inadequate, someone who wants to subdue a victim quickly so they can exercise control over them. The urge to be in control is often fundamental to this type of person. They feel unable to determine the outcome of their everyday existence, perhaps because their work is monotonous or lowly, or they have an overbearing partner, say, and over-compensate by seeking excessive control over other people. All control freaks are essentially inadequate people trying to pretend they're not."

"And now?"

"And now I'm not so sure. Something feels wrong; it doesn't fit. Why try to chloroform someone if it's unlikely to work and in doing so you risk warning them that you're trying to kill them into the bargain?"

"But you always say that there is a pattern to human behaviour, no matter how weird or warped, and that it's only a matter of working out what it might be."

"Do I really? Oh dear, how pompous I must sound," he said with a smile.

"Pompous or not," she replied as she got up to check the saucepan bubbling away on the stove, "I think you're right. Logically there must be an explanation. It's just that it's not obvious yet."

Satisfied that the potatoes were cooked, she drained them and began to mash.

"Here," he said, standing up, "let me do that. You see to the chicken."

"If you're sure you're up to it," she responded anxiously.

"I'm ill, not senile," he said severely, "and actually I'm not sure I'm even that ill. I don't feel as confused as I did a few days ago, though I do still seem to have some gaps in my memory."

He added milk, butter and white pepper and began to mash in a contemplative sort of way. "Perhaps where we're going wrong is to view things objectively rather than subjectively," he said, looking dubiously into the saucepan. "Rather than considering the situation from the outside, we need to get inside the killer's head. What he is doing does not seem rational. Therefore it must be driven, not by reason, but either by some direct emotional driver or an aspect of the killer's personality."

"Perhaps it's obsessive?" she suggested as she served the chicken. "Perhaps he has a need always to do exactly the same thing in exactly the same way. You know, one of those men who arranges everything in the cupboards with all the labels facing outwards or who hangs up his clothes in the same order every day as soon as he takes them off, perhaps graded by colour."

"Well, I do that," Peter said peevishly. "The last bit, anyway. And that doesn't make me a serial killer, does it?"

"True," she conceded.

"Anyway, doesn't everyone?" he asked defensively. "How else are you able to find what you're looking for? You're hardly going to scatter your clothes around the room, are you, or drop them on the floor?"

"I really don't know, Peter," she said with a smile as she put the plates on the table, "but perhaps not all men are quite as tidy as you."

"Well," he said, slightly mollified, "the more fool they, or rather the more fool those who live with them. Imagine having to go to bed amidst clothes strewn around the room. I mean, really!"

He ate silently for a while.

"I think you may be onto something," he said slowly, "but there's another possibility. Suppose that Collison's theory is correct. Isn't it possible that our murderer was as ignorant about chloroform as we were? That he used it the first time because he thought it was going to be effective, but that when it wasn't he was stuck with it? He needs each murder to look the same, to leave no doubt that they really were the work of a serial killer. So he carries on using it not because it was useful for his purposes, but simply because it was necessary to create chloroform burns on subsequent victims to match those on the first one."

"Peter, that's brilliant. If Collison's theory *is* correct, that is."

"You have your doubts?"

"In a word, yes. You'd have to be very desperate and very evil to want to do away with several innocent women just to be able to murder your wife and get away with it. But this damn case is so confusing, and has been going on for so long, that I really don't know what to think anymore. It's got me wondering if the more ridiculous something is, the more likely it is to be the right answer. We've followed all the obvious lines of enquiry and they've all led absolutely nowhere. We thought we'd got Clarke bang to rights and then he turns out to have been innocent all along; just a victim of circumstantial evidence and of our confidence in our own infallibility. Poor sod."

"I don't think you should beat yourself up about that," Peter said uncomfortably. "The evidence was strong, and it did all seem to point in the right direction. Everything the jury was told was true, and they came to their own decision on the facts."

"Well, what do you think about this *Laughing Policeman* idea?" she demanded.

"I must admit that initially I was sceptical," he admitted. "Storylines from fiction always seem inherently improbable to occur in real life, yet when we read them we are happy to suspend our disbelief, which may simply suggest that in our everyday lives we have an irrational craving for certainty and probability."

He took a mouthful of wine and then continued. "Three things now incline me to believe that the idea may have some mileage in it. The first is this new chloroform consideration. Either, as you suggested, our killer is likely to suffer from obsessive-compulsive disorder, or, as I have suggested, it may speak to a desire to make all the killings look the same."

"Go on."

"The second thing is that there was an important way in which the Barker murder was different from all the others. In all the other cases, so far as we know, the victim was killed somewhere else and then the body was moved and dumped after death. Kathy Barker was left and found where she was killed. That also suggests to me that, while she was killed in a public place, the others were not. It seems more likely they were killed in an enclosed, private space, or at the very least somewhere quiet and secluded."

"And what does that mean?"

"I'm not sure, but it *is* an unexplained difference. It could indicate that while the other victims may have been selected at random, perhaps not on the basis of who they were but rather that they were in situations where they could be taken and killed without attracting too much attention, Kathy Barker was targeted specifically—the killer had to take the opportunity when it presented itself, despite the risk of being seen, interrupted or even apprehended."

She put down her knife and fork and stared at him. "Oh God, that really *is* brilliant. Why didn't we think of that before?"

"Well," he said modestly, "it's hardly conclusive by itself, of course. But then there's the third thing."

"Which is?"

"Since the Barker murder there haven't been any others, at least so far as we know—and it's pretty difficult to hide a body in London. It's bound to be discovered sooner or later, and probably sooner rather than later. Yet we know that serial killers don't generally just stop killing. On the contrary, they typically speed up as the thrill becomes less and less satisfying. In cases where the killings do stop it's usually because the killer has moved out of the area, died, or gone to prison for some other offence."

"You mean...?"

"I mean that since our killer has not murdered again then it could suggest that he feels his mission to be complete—that's not consistent with the mind of a serial killer by the way—

which could in turn suggest that his mission was to murder Kathy Barker."

"Of course, of course. When you explain it like that, it seems so obvious." She got up from the table.

"Where are you going?" he asked uncertainly.

"To phone Collison."

Chapter Twenty-Two

"So you want to go the whole hog, then?" the ACC asked, looking up from the papers on his desk and peering at Collison over his reading glasses. "Are you absolutely sure, Simon? The DPP is dubious, you know."

"I can't understand why, sir," Collison replied innocently. "One of his staff was at our con with counsel yesterday and heard the same advice as we did: namely that there is ample evidence to charge Barker and a good chance of being able to persuade a magistrate to remand him in custody."

"That's true, strictly speaking, but it's not really the issue, is it?"

"No, sir?"

"Of course it's not. The issue is whether we are likely to get a conviction if we take Barker to court and charge him with a string of murders, most of which he has no obvious connection to at all."

"I think we can show plenty of connection, sir. He was the only keyholder we can identify, apart from Clarke himself, who had any connection to any of the murdered women. He was one of the very few GPs in the country to have access to chloroform, which, incidentally, has subsequently gone missing from his own practice. According to his neighbours, his problems with his wife started a few weeks before the first murder, which was also when the mystery chloroform consignment vanished without trace."

"All true," the ACC said, holding his glasses pensively to his lips, "but all circumstantial."

There was a pause.

"I suppose," he said tentatively, "there's no way we could simply charge him with his wife's murder? At least there we can show motive, means and opportunity."

Collison shook his head regretfully. "Won't wash, I'm afraid, sir. The Barker murder is obviously one of a series. If we don't charge him with all of them, his defence counsel will have a field day. Either he did them all, or none of them. That's why we have to argue that the others were deliberately intended to provide a smokescreen. After all, what are the odds that a man who wants to dispose of his wife just happens also to be a serial killer?"

"Christie was," the ACC reminded him.

"He was, sir, but there was a suggestion that it was because during an argument she threatened to expose him for the Evans murders. Anyway, whatever the case, the odds against it would be phenomenal."

"Are we sure that the Barker murder really *is* part of a series?" the ACC asked. "Isn't it possible that our man decided to kill his wife and simply made it look like one of a series of murders he had read about in the press so as to throw us off the scent?"

"A very good question, sir. I considered that possibility myself early on, because the Barker murder does stand out a bit, but the answer is no. We deliberately never disclosed the fact that the victims had been raped by a man wearing a condom. The first time that information was made public was during Clarke's trial, which was of course well after the Barker murder. No, whichever way you look at it, I think it has to be the same man in each case."

"When you say the Barker murder stands out, what do you mean?"

"It was the only one in which the victim was left to be found where she was killed, rather than being moved and dumped after death. That suggests either a random encounter or the very opposite: that the killer wanted her and nobody else, and had to take her when and where he found her."

"Couldn't it have been exactly that, though? A random encounter?"

"I don't think so, sir. The FBI studies in America suggest that serial killers are either organised or disorganised. The fact that our suspect had all his necessary equipment with him each time, and exactly the same each time, suggests an organised killer. So does the fact that he was apparently able to kill all the other victims somewhere secluded, at his leisure and without fear of discovery. So, as I say, this one stands out. Why would he suddenly break his pattern? Serial killers don't."

"Hardly something you can put to a jury," said the ACC gruffly.

"Well, how about this, sir? Why have the killings simply stopped after Kathy Barker's death? Serial killers don't just stop. In fact they usually speed up. That suggests that our killer views his task as now having been completed. Which in turn suggests that his mission was to eliminate Mrs Barker, and the only person whom we know had a motive to do that was her husband."

The ACC reflected on this and then sighed. "Simon, are you absolutely sure that you want to nail your colours to this particular mast? Fantastic theories are all very well if they work out: you'll look like a hero. But what if it doesn't work out? Suppose this is just all too difficult for the jury to swallow and they acquit? Coming on top of the wrongful conviction of Gary Clarke, it's almost impossible to imagine what would happen in the press, not to mention the Home Office. You realise the Commissioner would almost certainly feel obliged to resign?"

"It wouldn't only be the Commissioner who would feel obliged to resign, sir," Collison replied evenly. "Coming on top of the Clarke mess, I would obviously offer my own resignation too."

There was a knock at the door and the ACC shouted, "Come in." He sat back in his chair. "Well, if you really have thought this through then do whatever you need to do and I will back you, but by God you'd better be right."

"Excuse me, sir," said the uniformed sergeant who had just come into the room, "but the Commissioner heard that DS Collison was with you this morning and thought you might both like to see the midday edition of the *Standard*."

He put the newspaper down in front of the ACC, who replaced his reading glasses and scanned the front page. Without a word he tossed it across the desk to Collison.

"New Arrest Imminent in Serial Killings" ran the headline. Underneath, the newspaper reported that the husband of the last victim, a Dr Colin Barker from Hampstead, was about to be arrested by the police and charged, not only with the murder of his wife, Katherine, but also with all the previous victims. It was rumoured that the move to arrest the doctor had been sparked by a tip-off from a member of the public about his whereabouts on the night of the murder of Tracy Redman.

Collison felt a wave of nausea rise in his throat. "Oh no," he said weakly. "Not now. Not now."

The ACC stared at him in consternation. "Do you know something about this?" he demanded.

"Yes, sir," he replied flatly. "I'm afraid I do."

"I'm listening," the ACC said.

"It's Ken Andrews, sir. If you remember, he served on the original enquiry team as a Detective Sergeant. He's now back with Tom Allen working on the Clarke prison murder case."

"I don't understand," the ACC said with a puzzled air. "If he's no longer on the team, how would he have had access to this information? And how can you be sure that he's responsible anyway?"

"Because I set a trap for him, and he's fallen into it, only he's been way, way more irresponsible than I could ever have believed."

"You had better tell me all about this," the ACC said grimly, "and then I can decide what action to take."

"Well, I asked Bob Metcalfe to let slip, accidentally as it were, to Ken the next time he ran into him, that we were about to arrest Barker, and to mention that nonsense about the tip-off concerning the Redman death. I thought that once Barker *was* arrested he would sell his information to the papers and because he was the only one to have been in possession of that particular piece of news we would know for sure that he was our man. I never thought for a moment that he would risk jeopardising an ongoing investigation by releasing the story *before* our suspect was arrested."

"Stop," said the ACC, holding up both hands. "Stop right there. First up, why didn't you just accept the result of the Internal Affairs investigation? They cleared everyone concerned."

"No, sir," Collison corrected him. "They said something like it wasn't possible to identify anyone in particular. I wasn't satisfied with that. Someone was compromising my enquiry, I thought I knew who it was, and I was determined to prove it. We all know that the papers have been paying off bent coppers for years to leak details of active cases, and it's something we have to stamp out."

"But how could you be so sure it was Andrews?"

"I couldn't be sure, sir; it was a gut instinct, and a strong one. Call it copper's nose if you like. Whoever it was who was leaking to the papers was also leaking to Tom Allen. Andrews has been close to Allen for years."

"So has Metcalfe," the ACC pointed out.

"Yes, but I was convinced it wasn't him. He's a new-style career copper who's going to go far. Andrews is never going to progress beyond DS and he knows it. Anyway, on the one occasion that Allen tried to persuade Metcalfe to give him confidential information, he came to me to report it, having lost sleep over it all weekend first. I put it in my diary and asked him to do the same. Andrews was always the most likely candidate."

The ACC gazed at him levelly. "It seems to me, Superintendent, that if anyone has compromised this enquiry it's you. Totally without authority you released confidential information to someone who was not a member of the team; exactly the same offence of which you suspect Andrews and, by implication, DCI Allen. Further, you released deliberately misleading disinformation which you intended to be published, or at the least you were reckless as to whether it was published or not."

"I was intending it to be published *after* the arrest, sir. It would have been a simple matter then to deny the tip-off allegation. It would simply have made the newspaper look silly, as well as identifying our culprit."

"The timing is irrelevant," the ACC replied crisply. "As soon as you released the information outside the team you had no control over what happened to it thereafter. It seems to me that the risk of compromising a multiple murder investigation is out of all proportion to the possibility of identifying an internal press source. Surely any responsible senior officer could see that."

"I saw it as a calculated risk, sir," Collison responded, reddening.

"It wasn't your risk to take. It was mine, if anyone's, and had you asked me I would have consulted the Commissioner before making a decision. For the record, I would have recommended that he say no."

"Then I can only apologise, sir, if I have been guilty of an error of judgment. If you think it appropriate, I will submit my resignation. I have no wish to cause any undue embarrassment."

The ACC considered for a moment. "I do think it would be appropriate for you to let me have a letter of resignation, yes. The only reason I am not suspending you on the spot is that someone has to go back to Hampstead and hold the fort while we try to sort this mess out, and you're the only possible candidate. Metcalfe doesn't have the seniority and Allen isn't up-to-date on the case."

"And Andrews, sir?" Collison asked. He felt as he did so that he was pushing his luck, but what the hell. If he was going to be fired over this then he at least wanted to succeed in one aspect of what he had set out to do.

"Do nothing," the ACC said curtly. "I will decide what to do about Andrews once I have spoken to the Commissioner. Go back to Hampstead and babysit the case until I can find a new SIO to take over."

Collison took the tube back to Hampstead in a daze. The sick feeling in the pit of his stomach refused to go away. As he walked down Rosslyn Hill from the station, the air of unreality deepened; passers-by might have been in a parallel universe. The pavement outside the front door of the police station was thronged with reporters and photographers. He spotted at least one television camera and ducked round the corner to enter the building through the side entrance, which led through the old magistrates' court.

The desk sergeant gave him a strange look as he passed and seemed about to say something, but Collison pressed on upstairs to the incident room. The atmosphere there was as if someone had just had a heart attack in the middle of a briefing. Metcalfe looked stricken. Willis had clearly been crying. Collison forced himself to say something before the silence grew oppressive.

"A bad business, Bob."

"Worse than you might think, guv," Metcalfe said quietly. "Dr Barker is downstairs in the waiting room with his solicitor. They're asking for a meeting."

"Christ." Collison sat down heavily. He stared blankly at the whiteboard covered with notes and photos, unable to think.

"Excuse me, sir," Willis said, tear-stained but resolute, "but since he's here anyway, couldn't we just go ahead exactly as we'd planned? Charge him and put him up before the magistrates?"

She and Metcalfe looked at him expectantly.

"We could, yes," Collison said heavily. "The difference is that over the last hour or two since the story came out he's had a chance to arrange an alibi for himself. The whole point was to take him by surprise."

"We either have to see him or send him away," Metcalfe said as the ensuing silence became oppressive. "Do we really lose anything by putting our various points to him? After all, we were going to caution him anyway and as soon as we'd done that he would have asked for a lawyer—he'd be a fool not to. So apart from having lost the element of surprise, we're right where we wanted to be."

Everyone in the room was looking at Collison. He knew this but he felt unable to respond, to give them the lead they were looking for.

"Would you like me to take the meeting, sir?" Metcalfe asked, sensing his indecision.

"No." Collison attempted to drag himself out of the stupor that had suddenly descended on him. "No, I'll take the interview but you sit in with me, Bob. Let's do this by the book." He thought for a moment. "We'll interview him under caution, explain why he's a suspect and see what he comes back with. Then we can decide whether to charge him or not. Since he's already had a chance to concoct a story we've got nothing to lose by letting him go home again if we want to."

"Fine."

"We've already prepared an interview pack, haven't we?"

"Yes, I did it yesterday."

"OK, bring it with you and let's go and see what Dr Barker has to say."

The two of them headed downstairs to the waiting room.

"Dr Barker," Collison said, "I don't think we've met, but I hope you remember my colleague, Detective Inspector Metcalfe."

"I think so," Barker said, clearly nervous.

"I'm Stephen Cohen," the other man said. "Dr Barker's solicitor."

"Pleased to meet you," Collison replied, "and thank you for volunteering to come in like this."

"My client would have been happy to do so at any time," Cohen responded pointedly. "He had no idea that he was being treated as a suspect and so was naturally surprised to read in the newspapers today that he was about to be arrested."

"I can't be responsible for what appears in the papers, I'm afraid," Collison said.

"But the story must have originated somewhere within the police," Cohen persisted, "and you're the senior investigating officer, so you must be able to confirm whether it's accurate."

"The story did not emanate from the enquiry team, nor from the Metropolitan Police press office," Collison said carefully. "So, as I say, we cannot comment on anything they may have said or not said."

"Excuse me, Mr Cohen," Metcalfe said innocently, "but are you Dr Barker's regular solicitor? I'm sure I've seen you before—in court, I think, and I'm not aware of him having been charged with any criminal offences in the past."

"I am often in court, yes," Cohen said. "In view of the nature of the charges which were apparently imminently to be brought against my client, he decided, not unreasonably, to ask his regular solicitor to refer him to a criminal specialist."

"Well," said Collison, "now that we've dealt with the preliminaries, why don't we go through to the interview room?"

"Just so we're clear from the outset, Detective Superintendent," Cohen said primly, "could you please confirm whether you are proposing to interview my client as a witness or as a suspect? It may affect how I choose to advise him."

"We will be interviewing your client as a suspect for the murder of his wife, Katherine, and possibly for what we believe to be the related murders of four other women."

Dr Barker paled visibly. Collison saw that his hands were trembling.

"In that case, would you please caution him?" Cohen requested.

"Of course," Collison said again. "Bob, do the honours, will you?"

"Dr Barker," Metcalfe intoned, "you are about to be interviewed as a suspect in connection with the murder of your wife, Katherine. Do you wish to say anything at this stage? You do not have to say anything, but it may harm your defence if you do not mention when questioned something which you later rely on in court. Anything you do say may be given in evidence."

"OK," Collison said briskly. "Let's go."

Chapter Twenty-Three

"Now then, Dr Barker," Collison said once the tape recorder had been switched on and the preliminary announcements had been made, "I'd like to ask you a few questions relating to the death of your wife, Katherine."

"My client is eager to co-operate," Cohen interjected.

"I'm glad to hear it," Collison replied. "In that case, perhaps we can start with your client's financial affairs. Dr Barker, is it the case that in the months leading up to your wife's death you were in financial difficulties?"

"No, I wouldn't put it exactly like that," Barker protested.

"Then how would you put it, Doctor?"

"Well, it would have been nice to have more money of course, but then when wouldn't it? Kathy enjoyed going out to restaurants and she liked buying clothes. I used to joke that she was a high maintenance woman, but I wouldn't say that I was in difficulties exactly."

"For the tape," Metcalfe said as Collison nodded to him, "I'm showing Dr Barker copies of his bank and credit card statements for the period in question."

"If you examine them, Doctor," Collison said, "you will see that you were only just able to cover your monthly outgoings such as the mortgage, and even then only by running your credit cards right up to their limits."

"OK, I was a bit stretched from time to time, yes."

"More than a bit stretched, and not just from time to time," Collison said, running his finger down one of the bank statements. "Month after month your outgoings were exceeding your income: credit cards, utilities, mortgage payments, divorce maintenance…"

"OK, like I said, I was struggling to keep my head above water. Getting divorced isn't cheap, you know."

"Struggling is the word, Doctor. In fact you were slowly and steadily drowning, weren't you?"

There was no answer to this. Collison tried a new tack. "Did you and your wife argue about money, Doctor? Is that what the rows were about? You asked her to rein in her spending, or maybe get a job? And she told you to get lost? How did that make you feel? Angry?"

Barker looked angry. "No," he said abruptly. "It wasn't like that at all."

"Really? Your finances were going down the drain largely because of your wife's spending habits and yet you never argued with her about money?"

"Sometimes, yes, I suppose," Barker admitted grudgingly. "Yes, I did ask her to get a job and yes, she refused. She said she'd got married to get away from that sort of thing." He grimaced.

"What is your point here exactly, Superintendent?" Cohen cut in. "What can my client's financial situation possibly have to do with the death of his wife?"

"I'm glad you asked that," Collison replied. "If you turn over a few pages you will see that the situation was dramatically transformed after Mrs Barker's death by a substantial inflow of funds."

Cohen looked blankly at the later statement.

"Isn't it the case, Doctor," Collison asked, "that this payment was in fact the proceeds of a life insurance policy which you took out on your wife shortly before she was murdered?"

"Yes, it is," Barker said nervously. His pallor had not improved.

"And does that not provide you with a solid motive for your wife's death?"

"That's not for my client to say," Cohen interjected.

"True," Collison conceded. "It's for a jury to say, but I'm sure they'd be interested to hear anything your client has to say which might have a bearing on the subject."

He looked quizzically at Barker. Barker glanced at his solicitor. Barker's solicitor gave a barely perceptible shake of the head.

"No comment," Barker said faintly.

"Very well, let's move on," Collison said. "I wonder if you could enlighten me, Doctor, as to the present day medical uses of chloroform, particularly within a GP's practice?"

Barker shrugged. "I can't think of any offhand."

"None at all?"

"No, it hasn't been used for years."

"Then can you explain," Collison asked, staring at him intently, "why chloroform was ordered by someone at your practice?"

"No I can't," Barker said with a dark glance across the table, "and if you're referring to the mix-up we had with one of our suppliers a while back then in my view it was just that—a mix-up."

"Yet when it was time for the chloroform to be returned it had gone missing, hadn't it, Doctor? Would you like to tell us anything about that?"

"Once again," Cohen cut in, "you're asking my client to answer questions which require supposition on his part."

"No, I'm not," Collison corrected him mildly. "I'm asking him if he has any personal knowledge of how the chloroform came to go missing."

"I don't," Barker said quickly.

"Nor of how it came to be ordered in the first place?"

"No."

"Nor of why anyone should want to order it in the first place?"

"I think my client has already answered that," Cohen objected, ostentatiously turning back a page in his notebook. "My recollection is that he freely admitted that he could not think of any valid reason why it should have been needed within a GP's practice."

"Very well," Collison acknowledged calmly. "Then perhaps we could turn to the night of Katherine Barker's murder. You told my colleague, DCI Allen, that after your wife left your flat in a distressed condition you made no attempt to follow her?"

"I wouldn't say 'distressed,' strictly speaking," Barker objected. "That makes it sound as if she was just unhappy about something. In fact she was drunk and hysterical, which she often was."

"Thank you for making that clear, Doctor," Collison said quietly, "but the crux of my question was that you made no attempt to follow her: that is right, isn't it?"

"Yes, it is right. I assumed that she'd hail a passing taxi once she got onto Haverstock Hill, and anyway, I knew where she was going."

"You knew where she was going?" Collison asked innocently. "How? Did she tell you?"

"This is all in my original statement," Barker pointed out in exasperation.

"Please answer the question. I wasn't there when you were first interviewed."

"I knew she was going to her sister's because that's where she always went. I followed her a few times when first she started running off like that, and that's always where she went."

"You followed her a few times?" Collison echoed, opening his eyes wide. "But there's no mention of that in your original statement, Dr Barker."

"I didn't think to mention it," Barker said sullenly. "Is it important?"

"I suggest that it is, yes, very important," Collison replied. "If you had followed her before you would not only know where she was likely to be going, as you say, but also exactly how she was likely to get there, and how long it was likely to take. In other words, you might have been close on her heels, or even managed to circle round ahead of her, especially if you were determined enough to risk driving your car even though you'd been drinking."

Barker clasped his hands tightly in front of him but said nothing.

"There is no evidence of that at all, Superintendent," Cohen objected. "This is pure conjecture on your part."

"Yes it is," Collison admitted. "But if you take it together with the conjecture that it was Dr Barker who was responsible for obtaining and removing the chloroform for his own uses, and the fact—not conjecture, fact—that he stood to gain financially from his wife's death, then that would give him opportunity, means and motive."

He glanced at Barker, who looked sunk within himself.

"And I note for the record that I have just given Dr Barker an opportunity to deny having used his car that night, or having gone out at all, and that he has declined to do so."

"That is not true," Cohen corrected him. "You made an observation on which my client did not comment. You did not put it to him as a question, and were you to do so I would say that you have already asked him to confirm that he did not follow his wife after she left, and that he has done so. The point is also, I believe, fully covered in the statement which he gave to DCI Allen."

"Thank you for your clarification," Collison said drily.

"As you know, my client absolutely denies any involvement in his wife's death," Cohen stated emphatically. "And it would seem obvious to my untrained eye, Superintendent, that Katherine Barker was murdered by the same maniac who had already killed four other women in identical circumstances. Are you seriously suggesting that my client was responsible for all those other crimes as well?"

"Since you mention that…" Collison motioned to Metcalfe.

"For the tape," said Metcalfe, "I am passing to Mr Cohen a list of the dates of each of the previous murders."

At this point there was a knock on the door and Willis came in with a note.

"DC Willis has entered the room," Metcalfe informed the tape recorder.

Collison nodded and she handed him a note, then turned and departed.

"DC Willis has left the room," Metcalfe said automatically as Collison pushed the note across to him. It read "Susan McCormick is asking to see you."

Collison pointed to the list of dates, which was still sitting on the table. "Perhaps you and your client could look at this at your convenience and let us know his whereabouts on each of those days, and whether anyone else can vouch for them."

"We will of course," Cohen said evenly, slipping it into his attaché case. "Is that all?"

"Not quite," Collison replied. "Dr Barker, am I right in thinking that you have a key to the front door of the house in which Gary Clarke was renting his flat?"

"Of course," Barker said, staring at him in surprise. "It was my flat. I bought it as a buy-to-let many years back. It was about the only asset I was able to save when I got divorced. Not that it ever made any money for me; I had a couple of long periods with no tenant and I got stuck with a high fixed interest rate from the bank."

"So you had a key?"

"My wife did, yes. She used to go there to show prospective tenants around, and she dealt with any problems that arose. I think I have a spare somewhere but I'm not sure where it is, right now."

"And do you have any knowledge of how various items from the murder scenes came to be secreted in the loft?"

"No, I don't."

"Have you ever had reason to enter the loft there, or even to open the hatch and look inside?"

"No, I don't think so."

"Not even when you originally viewed the flat with a view to purchasing it?"

"I suppose I might have done then, but I don't remember. I think I had a survey done, so I didn't need to make a detailed inspection myself. After all, I was never planning to live there."

"And when was the last time that you visited the property?"

"I don't know. Not for at least a year or so. Like I said, Kathy used to deal with it, and my ex-wife before that. I've never really had anything to do with it."

"Can you give us any details about your ex-wife?" Metcalfe cut in. "Just in case we need to ask her anything?"

"I haven't killed her, if that's what you mean," Barker said viciously.

"Anything you can tell us would be helpful," Metcalfe replied smoothly.

"Her name is Sue Dashwood," Barker informed him, "assuming she's gone back to her maiden name, that is. She used to do a bit of work at the practice on our IT systems, although that was only a casual job for her. She was training to be a psychotherapist; I don't know if she ever finished. That's why I ended up having to pay her so much maintenance; she said I'd told her it was OK for her not to work and that I'd support her while she was getting qualified. I believe she's still living in London somewhere, but I don't know. I haven't seen her or spoken to her since the day we split up; everything was done through lawyers. It wasn't exactly an amicable divorce."

"Am I to understand it, then, that you were seeing Kathy while you were still living with your then wife?" said Collison.

"For a while, yes," Barker said awkwardly. "What of it? It's not a crime, is it? These things happen."

"Just trying to build up a complete picture."

"It seems to me that the details of my client's former marriage are of marginal relevance at best," Cohen observed. "We would much rather hear whatever it is that this tip-off concerns—the one which was reported in the newspapers today."

"I don't think that's something we can talk about right now," Collison replied.

Cohen stared at him. "I'm sure I don't have to remind you, Superintendent, that if you are aware of anything that is relevant to my client's defence then you are obliged to disclose it."

"Should this matter proceed to trial, yes," Collison acknowledged. "But right now your client hasn't even been charged. Anyway, even if we did have information relating to the Redman killing, we would hardly disclose it while your client is still considering his position as to a possible alibi for that murder. You tell us where you stand on that, and then we'll see."

"Then perhaps we could take a break while I take instructions from my client?" Cohen suggested.

"By all means," Collison agreed, looking at his watch. "For the tape, interview suspended at 1634 for Mr Cohen to take instructions from his client."

Metcalfe pushed the stop button and the machine beeped. He took the tape out of one of the two decks and gave it to Cohen. "You're welcome to stay in here if you like," he told the lawyer. "I can have some tea or coffee sent in."

"Is my client under arrest?" Cohen asked.

Collison hesitated and looked at Metcalfe.

"If it makes any difference to your decision," Cohen continued, producing a passport from his inside pocket, "Dr Barker wishes to state his willingness to assist you with your enquiries, as I am sure you will agree he has done so far. He is also willing to surrender his passport."

"In that case no, not at this stage," Collison conceded.

"Then with your permission, I'd like to take my client outside for a coffee and some fresh air."

"That may not be a good idea, Mr Cohen," Metcalfe demurred. "There's probably still a whole gang of press outside the station."

"We ran the gauntlet on the way in," Cohen said, "and I'm sure we can do the same on the way out."

"I have a better idea," suggested Collison. "Let me show you out the side way, through the magistrates' court. That door is never used normally when the court's not in session. You can come back that way too, if you phone the desk sergeant and ask him to let you in."

"Thank you," Cohen acknowledged. "That would be preferable."

Collison opened the door of the interview room and let Cohen and Barker go ahead of him as they walked down the corridor into the waiting room. He registered the tall, slim figure of Susan McCormick sitting there, and nodded to her in greeting. To his surprise she reddened and buried her face in her magazine. Suddenly Barker stopped still and Collison cannoned into him. They both staggered across the room, Collison clutching at the wall to stop himself falling.

"Hello," Barker said hesitantly, a strange expression on his face.

Collison looked from Barker to Susan McCormick and back again. The level of embarrassment in the room was tangible. Suddenly Barker laughed mirthlessly. "You were asking about my ex-wife, Inspector," he addressed Metcalfe. "Well, here she is. Susan Barker, née Dashwood."

Collison and Metcalfe gazed blankly at Susan McCormick, who still said nothing.

"Well," Collison said, attempting to gather his wits, "why don't we say one hour, Mr Cohen? I have another interview to be getting on with. Sergeant, will you see Mr Cohen and his client out through the side door, please, and be ready to let them back in when they return?"

"But what are you doing here, Susan?" Barker asked plaintively. "What's going on?"

"Come on, Colin," Cohen said, hustling him away. "Let's go and have a coffee and let the police get on with their job."

Collison waited for the door to close behind them, then turned to Susan McCormick.

"Why did you not tell us that you were Colin Barker's ex-wife?" he said curtly.

"I could say 'because you never asked me,' couldn't I?" she replied archly.

With the departure of Barker it seemed normality had reappeared—or maybe it was just because she had been given a few moments to compose herself while he and his solicitor left the room. "Don't worry, Superintendent," she went on with a smile, acknowledging the irritation on his face. "I'm happy to answer all your questions and a lot more besides, but first I have something to tell you."

"In that case we'd better get on with it," he said, looking at his watch. "We only have an hour. Will you come through to the interview room?"

Chapter Twenty-Four

"Now then," Collison demanded, trying to conceal his bafflement, "what on earth is all this about? If you're Dr Barker's ex-wife and your maiden name was Dashwood, how come you're now calling yourself Susan McCormick?"

"Well, I might have re-married," she said calmly, "but I haven't. I changed my name by deed poll because I didn't want to be known to all and sundry as the first Mrs Barker, and I didn't want to go back to Dashwood because it seemed like an admission of failure—having a husband and then losing him."

"Alright," Collison said. "We've got that cleared up, at least. Now, what is it that you want to tell me?"

"It's really very simple, Superintendent. I'm the person you're looking for. I'm your killer."

Metcalfe and Collison stared at her, and then Collison smiled. "I'm not sure what you think you're playing at, Ms McCormick, but you can try again. Whoever we're looking for is a man. For one thing, he rapes his victims."

"No," she said calmly. "It just looks like it. In fact they are raped by a dildo—this one in fact." So saying, she opened her large handbag and duly produced a large plastic phallus, laying it rather primly on the table in front of them.

"Of course, I had to get around the problem of there being no semen in the bodies, so I used a condom. I assumed that your forensic people would be able to find traces of the lubricant or spermicide or whatever, and believe that, as you have just said, they were raped by a man wearing a condom."

There was a long silence.

"Ms McCormick," Collison said eventually, "I am now going to caution you and turn on the tape recorder. DI Metcalfe?"

Metcalfe put two new tapes in the machine and switched it on. He made the preliminary announcements and administered the caution.

"Do you understand the caution?" Collison asked carefully.

"Yes, I do."

"I'm not obliged to ask you this," he went on, "but in view of the gravity of what I think you want to say to us under caution, would you like to have a lawyer present?"

"No," she replied. "I have nothing to hide. I want to make a clean breast of everything."

"Very well," Collison said. "Now, Ms McCormick, am I correct in understanding that you wish to confess to the murder of five women: Amy Grant, Jenny Hillyer, Joyce Mteki, Tracy Redman and Katherine Barker?"

She nodded.

"For the tape, please," Metcalfe urged.

"I'm sorry. Yes, I confess to all five murders."

"But what possible motive could you have?" Collison asked.

"The only one I wanted to murder was Katherine Barker, of course. I was sorry about the others. She deserved to die but they didn't."

"But you killed them anyway?"

"Yes."

Collison drew a deep breath. "Why don't you take us through it from the beginning?"

"I met Amy Grant on a train one Friday," she said. "She was a sad little soul—seemed completely lost, somehow. We got talking and I was soon pretty sure that she was gay and that she found me attractive, so I invited her to stay with me a few weekends later."

"So she stayed with you?"

"Yes. To begin with, when I issued the invitation, it was really just curiosity. I'd never been to bed with another woman and wondered what it would be like. But then I got to thinking about how much I wanted to get rid of that bitch Kathy. I'd been dreaming about it for ages, imagining all sorts of different ways I might do it, ideally slowly and painfully, but I always came to the same conclusion: that I would be the obvious suspect. After all, nobody else had a motive for killing her."

"And just to be clear," Collison asked, "your motive was simple jealousy?"

She laughed humourlessly. "There's nothing simple about jealousy, Superintendent. It's an all-consuming passion. Jealousy and anger have been my constant companions ever since he came home one evening and told me that he was leaving me for that cheap tart. Ten years we'd been married and then along she comes with her short skirts and high heels and entices him away. She could never make him happy of course, but he was too blind to see that."

"So when did you form the intention to kill her?"

"A little while after he left. I thought that if she was no longer around he'd come to his senses and come back to me. I thought I'd get over it, but I didn't. The anger got worse and worse, and then, quite suddenly, one day I just somehow knew what I needed to do."

"But you were scared of being caught?"

"Yes, of course. I'd be an obvious suspect, wouldn't I? Then I started to think that if I could kill someone else, a total stranger, and then later kill Kathy in exactly the same way, the police would look for someone who was connected to both murders rather than someone who could only be a suspect for one of them. Not long after I met Amy, I began to think that she could be the one. Perhaps it was even in my mind when I met her that first time on the train. Then I started to think about how I might do it."

"And you settled on…?"

"Chloroform. I thought it would be quick and easy. I quickly discovered that the practice hadn't changed any of their passwords since I used to work there, so I could still log on to the system. Then I went over late one night and found that they hadn't changed the code on the entry alarm either. So I logged on remotely, ordered the stuff and then went in a few nights later to pick it up. I was only just in time. It looked as though they'd put it out to be returned."

Collison and Metcalfe exchanged glances.

"Tell us how you killed Amy," Collison said.

"It was the Sunday afternoon. We'd had sex the night before. For all my curiosity, I'd been disappointed. It didn't really do anything for me. But she was transformed—seemed genuinely happy. Sad, really, that something so trivial could make such a difference to someone."

"Perhaps she didn't think it was trivial," Metcalfe suggested, struggling to keep his voice calm. "Perhaps she thought this was going to be the start of a serious relationship."

"Perhaps. I don't know." She shrugged. "Anyway, that afternoon I pretended to be looking for something—a box of books, I think—and asked her to come into the garage to help me. It's an integral garage so we could walk straight into it from the kitchen. Once her attention was distracted I came up behind her with a pad of cotton wool soaked in chloroform and clamped it over her nose and mouth."

"What happened then?"

"She started struggling and kicking like mad. It was a real shock. I thought that stuff would work almost instantly and she'd just keel over, but she didn't. She broke away from me and was about to run back into the kitchen so I grabbed something off the shelf—a hammer as it happened—and hit her over the back of the head. She fell down but she was still groaning and moving about pathetically, so I just watched and waited until I was sure she was dead. I left her on the floor of the garage and went back into the kitchen for a cup of tea. I was shaking a bit; excitement I think. It was a strange feeling knowing that she was lying next door, dead. I kept going back in to check that she hadn't suddenly come back to life or something. Then I realised there was a lot of blood everywhere."

"What did you do next?" Collison asked.

"I remembered the dildo and condom which I had ready, and soon after she died I raped her. I wasn't quite sure how long to do it for. Did it matter? Maybe not. I took her knickers and kept them, by the way. I'd already decided that when that bitch Kathy was killed I'd do the same with hers. It would be another point of similarity. Then I called Gary."

"Gary?" Collison said abruptly, and then again more slowly: "Gary Clarke?"

"Yes, Gary Clarke. He'd been hanging around me for weeks and the only reason I hadn't sent him packing was because I thought he might just be able to make himself useful. I knew I needed to kill Amy somewhere private and safe like my garage, but that then meant I would have to move the body after death, and for that I'd need help."

"But how did you persuade him to become an accessory to murder?" Collison said incredulously.

She laughed again. "Oh Superintendent, don't be so naïve. Sex, of course. Clarke was pathetic. He had no chance of finding a halfway decent woman to have sex with. He was desperate, not just for the usual physical reasons but also to feel adequate as a man. So I invited him round a few days before and prepared the ground a bit."

"And how did you do that?"

"I gave him a glass of wine and told him that I'd always found him attractive; that I felt he was a kindred spirit, who wasn't just looking for a normal, boring relationship, but something different and exciting. Of course he agreed straight away.

He'd have put his hand in a waste disposal unit if he thought it would get me to have sex with him."

"So you hatched a conspiracy with Clarke to kill Amy?"

"No, nothing like that. I just suggested that I should find something really dark and exciting for us to do together. Naturally the poor fool couldn't agree quickly enough. Then he tried to jump on me but I pushed him off and told him he'd have to prove himself first. To stop his whining I gave him a quick handjob and sent him home. When he came on the Sunday, I showed him what I'd done."

"How did he react?" Metcalfe asked, repelled but fascinated at the same time.

"He ran out of the garage into the kitchen and became hysterical. I played the innocent and said I couldn't understand why he was so upset as I'd done it for the two of us, like we'd discussed the other day. He started shouting that he'd never intended for me to do anything like this. Then he went into the living room, sat down and cried for ages. I got fed up with it all and went and had a coffee while he pulled himself together."

"And then?" Metcalfe prompted.

"Well, just as I'd hoped, once he'd calmed down he said that we had to dispose of the body somehow and try to forget the whole thing ever happened. I'd bought some things at a garden centre already so we wrapped her up in polythene and put her at the end of the garage, so we could clean the whole place thoroughly. I had a hose and brushes and lots of bleach, and we washed everything away down the drain in the middle of the garage. There was nothing to see afterwards, though I expect your forensic people would probably find something if they looked hard enough. Then once it was dark I brought the car in from the road, we put her in the boot, and Gary drove her off to dump her in some woods near High Wycombe where I used to walk a dog when I lived in Beaconsfield as a girl. I'd been back a week previously late at night to check it out and it was completely deserted—just the odd courting couple from time to time. I told him to undo the plastic first and lift her out of it. He brought that back in the boot and I put it in a black dustbin bag and took it to the dump a few days later."

"And he went along with all this willingly?" Collison asked.

"Yes, but he was in a dreadful state," she said scornfully. "He kept whimpering and saying how awful it all was. I think I'd convinced him that in some way I thought he'd asked me to do it. When he came back with the car I let him have sex with me on the floor in the living room. It was pretty frightful but at least it was all over quickly. I told him that the sight of the body had excited me. I pretended I thought it had excited him too."

This seemed to bring proceedings to a natural break. Susan McCormick sat with a slight smile playing around her lips.

"May I ask how tall you are?" Metcalfe asked suddenly.

"I'm five feet eleven. More like six feet, to be honest, though I don't like to admit it. Doesn't sound very ladylike, does it?"

The two detectives glanced at each other, still struggling to come to terms with what they were hearing.

"Perhaps I could ask you at this juncture, Ms McCormick," Collison said eventually, "what prompted you to come and make this confession? If what you have told us is true then it seems to me that the only person who could have incriminated you was your accomplice, Gary Clarke, and he's dead."

"I always thought," she replied calmly, "that once that bitch Kathy was safely out of the way, Colin would regain his senses and we would get back together again. I was going to give it six months or so and then approach him. But when I started driving over to his flat and watching from outside, I discovered that he'd already taken up with someone else. That's Colin for you, 'shallow' is his middle name. *And* he's always had a thing for Asian women." She snorted what might have been a sardonic laugh.

"But I'm afraid I still don't understand," Collison said helplessly. "Your plan had failed, yes, but that's not necessarily a reason to suddenly turn yourself in."

"It was the only way to show him that I really did love him, that I'd always loved him. After all, what greater proof can there be of someone's love than that they are prepared to kill for it, not just once but again and again? Then when I learned today that he was suspected of the murders I realised that I had to come forward straight away and clear him. Though why you should suddenly think he might have done it I really don't know…"

She looked at them in a faintly comical, mildly enquiring way, her eyebrows raised.

"I'm afraid we can't discuss our internal process," Collison said formally. Metcalfe stared at the table.

There was a knock at the door and Willis came in with another note.

"DC Willis has entered the room," Metcalfe informed the tape recorder as Collison read the note.

"Ms McCormick," he said after a moment's thought. "I need to suspend this interview for an hour or so while I deal with some other matters. I am going to ask DC Willis to show you to the desk sergeant to be taken into custody. Please ask for any food or drink, or anything else that you require. Before I switch off the tape, I would like to state for the record that it is currently my intention to charge you with the murder of Amy Grant. Further charges may follow. Do you understand? I am happy to repeat anything or offer any explanation you may require."

"I understand," she said calmly.

"Interview suspended at 1741." Metcalfe switched off the machine. He gave one tape to Susan McCormick, who looked at it as though uncertain what to do with it, and finally put it in her handbag.

"Bob," Collison said quietly, "would you please go ahead and make sure that our various visitors don't run into each other?"

"Right, guv," said Metcalfe, and left the room.

Collison stood back as Willis led Susan McCormick away. He followed them down the corridor and noted with relief that the waiting area was clear. As the two women walked away into the custody area, the sergeant jerked his head at the door leading into the magistrates' court. Collison opened it, and Metcalfe led Colin Barker and Stephen Cohen back into the waiting area. Without waiting to be asked, they filed back into the interview room.

"Thank you for your patience, gentlemen," Collison said as they sat down. "I don't intend to switch the tape recorder back on again unless you'd particularly like me to."

Cohen looked shocked. "You know the rules as to how interviews with suspects should be conducted, Superintendent."

"That's just the point," Collison replied. "I would like to inform you that we have just received some information which, while it has to be independently verified, leads me to conclude that Dr Barker should no longer be treated as a suspect for his wife's murder, for the present at least."

"For the present at least?" echoed Cohen. "Surely he is either a suspect or he's not. Which is it?"

"Please bear with me, Mr Cohen," Collison said wearily. "I am partway through another interview which I have broken off specifically to talk to you now rather than keep you waiting for what might prove a very long time. If you would rather I did things differently then I will happily do so."

The solicitor made no answer, but gestured grudging acceptance.

"I don't think that any good purpose would be served by Dr Barker remaining here this evening, Mr Cohen," Collison went on. "As far as we are concerned he is free to return home, though we may wish him to return tomorrow, as a witness rather than a suspect. DI Metcalfe, please return Dr Barker's passport to him."

Barker, who had been gaping soundlessly throughout this exchange, now regained the power of speech. "Does this have something to do with whatever my ex-wife's been telling you?" he demanded.

"Whatever your ex-wife may have told us is of course confidential, Dr Barker," Collison said blandly. "And, as regards the press outside, I would be grateful if you would refrain from any comment as you leave. I cannot dictate to you what to say or not to say, but I can tell you honestly that I believe it would greatly help the search for your wife's killer were you to remain silent at this point."

"All very mysterious," Cohen commented, "but in the circumstances, Superintendent, we will do as you ask."

"It's much appreciated," Collison acknowledged. "Bob, will you show our guests out, please?"

Chapter Twenty-Five

"You don't suppose, do you," Metcalfe asked Willis as they grabbed a quick cup of coffee in the canteen, "that she's come forward with a false confession just because her ex is in the frame?"

"To clear his name, you mean?"

"That and to show him that she's still so much in love with him that she's prepared to go to prison in his place, yes."

She stirred what passed for coffee reflectively. "Anything's possible, I suppose. But she did seem to know an awful lot about the killings."

"Nothing that didn't come out in evidence at the trial."

"Really? What about the fact that she didn't realise how ineffective chloroform was? That was never mentioned. We only found out about it ourselves a day or so back."

"That's true," he acknowledged grudgingly. "And she can explain how it came to be ordered by the practice and then disappear."

"I know it all sounds absurd," she said, "but it seems to hang together. She must be a very disturbed person. I'd love to have Peter's opinion."

"Yes," he agreed, looking at her uncomfortably. "Karen…"

"Give me a bit more time, Bob," she said quietly, giving him a smile that made him feel suddenly breathless. "Not long now."

"There's the guvnor," he said, glancing away from her with difficulty.

"Coffee, sir?" he asked as Collison approached.

"So that's what it is," Collison said with a smile. "Another mystery solved. No, but you finish yours. There's no hurry. I've just been trying to speak to the ACC but he's not in the office, so I've left a message."

"Is she genuine, do you think, sir?" Willis asked.

"Seems to be, but frankly I'm losing all grasp of reality on this case. I don't know what to believe anymore. There's always the possibility that she's making it all up, but she hasn't made any slips so far."

"I'm waiting to see how she deals with the fact that Clarke had an alibi for the Hillyer murder," said Metcalfe.

"To be honest, so am I," Collison concurred. "Right now that's about the only thing I can see standing between us throwing out her story or having to admit that we've been wrong about this case yet again."

"So, Ms McCormick," he said once the tapes were switched on and the preliminary announcements out of the way, "I'd like to remind you that you are still under caution."

"I understand."

"Before we suspended the interview you were telling us about how you came to murder Amy Grant. I want to now move on to Jenny Hillyer. You said that your intention was simply to kill one other woman before Katherine Barker, so why would you want to kill anyone else?"

"Yes, I did say that," she agreed, "and it was true at the time. But then I realised that two wasn't enough; I had to make this look like the work of a serial killer. I knew that I'd be most at risk when it was Kathy's turn, as I'd have to act whenever I had a good opportunity, rather than be sure of getting her somewhere private, like my garage. Doubly at risk, actually. First there was the chance of being surprised in the act by a passer-by. Second there was the risk of being an obvious suspect."

"So?"

"So I thought that once she was dead a few other women would need to die too, and it would be that much more difficult—who knows, I might even have been under observation as a possible suspect—so it was better to focus on the others first, establishing and strengthening the pattern all the time, and then make her murder, the real one, the last. I was hoping that perhaps the police might think the killer had moved away from London or fled the country."

"And Jenny Hillyer?"

"I met her in a pub in Belsize Park. She'd been waiting for one of these internet blind dates but he'd never shown up, or maybe he had and didn't fancy what he saw and went home again. She had a few drinks while she was waiting so she was a bit drunk already. I pretended to be waiting for a date as well, and bought her a few more. Then I suggested we go back to my place and call out for a pizza. She never made it into the house. We went in through the garage and I grabbed the hammer and hit her on the back of the head. She went down straight away and I carefully repeated everything I'd done to Amy, including making sure there were chloroform burns on her face."

"And then you called Clarke and he came over as before and disposed of the body?" said Metcalfe.

She laughed. "Ah, that's where you all went wrong, wasn't it? Because you thought he was actually the murderer you jumped to the conclusion that if he had an alibi for the night she was killed then he must be innocent. How funny I thought, when I read about it in the newspapers. What you should have been asking, had you known the truth, was whether he had an alibi for the next night, the night she was moved and dumped."

"And that's when he did it?"

"Yes, though he was in a dreadful state. He'd obviously been drinking heavily the night before and he was still massively hungover. Maybe that's why he didn't object so much that time. It also got me out of sleeping with him, though he came back a few nights later for his pound of flesh."

"So you kept the body in your garage for twenty-four hours?"

"Well, I didn't have much choice, did I? I rang Clarke and got no answer, then I tried again later and still no good. I was pretty angry actually. I didn't finally get hold of him until the following afternoon, and he sounded pretty shaky. I met him when I came home from work, though I'd tried cleaning up a bit already the night before."

"So having discovered that you liked killing, you went on with it?"

She frowned. "I'm not sure I liked it exactly. Frankly, I didn't feel much at all. I simply had a plan and I did what needed to be done to carry it out. Joyce was what you'd probably call a random victim. I met her at the hospital when I was visiting a friend who'd had a hysterectomy. We got chatting and I asked her if she'd like to do some private work caring for my invalid mother. She said she would, so I invited her to call round and discuss it."

"And Tracy Redman?"

"Rather sordid, I'm afraid. I saw a card in a newsagent's window and called to ask if she'd like to service a couple. I didn't even know her real name until I saw the press reports. She was going by Tiffany when I met her."

"So in each case the victim went to your house? As simple as that?"

"Yes, and in each case they never got further than the garage," she said dispassionately.

"Very well," Collison said. "We will of course be despatching a Scene of Crime team to your property."

"And I'm sure they'll find lots of supporting evidence, won't they?" she replied calmly. "I know it's almost impossible to get rid of it all, even if it looks really clean."

"Let's move on to Katherine Barker," Collison asked, ignoring her response.

"She was the one I felt nervous about. The only one I felt any real emotion about, actually. I was excited by the thought of doing it, but at the same time nervous about being discovered. The one thing that could spoil everything with Colin was him finding out that I'd killed her."

"And how did you go about it?"

"I started waiting outside their flat in my car at night. After a while I noticed a pattern of noisy rows late at night, ending with her storming out of the flat. The first few times he ran after her and they had an argument in the street and then finally went back in again, but after a while he stopped following her. So I did. She went to the same place every time, and often she looked the worse for wear. Too much alcohol, clearly. I worked out that if I drove off straight away while she was staggering around looking for a taxi I could get there first and wait for her. There was an alleyway that she had to walk through after the taxi dropped her, and there was usually nobody around; it was a pretty dodgy neighbourhood. I reckoned I could do everything I needed to do in about three or four minutes. It meant taking a big risk, but it was worth it."

"It sounds as if this was a rational process on your part— you planned it all very carefully?"

"Yes, and it was round then that I went to Gary's flat for the first time. You could have knocked me over with a feather when I realised it was our flat—mine and Colin's that is, the one I used to rent out. I kept quiet about that, of course, but a few idle questions were enough to establish that he knew Kathy. God, he even fancied her! Ridiculous though it may seem, the moron fantasised about her being secretly in love with him."

"She was an attractive woman," Collison pointed out mildly.

"She was a bitch!" spat Susan McCormick. "And a totally unprincipled bitch at that. She stole my husband. Even though she wasn't in love with him and he wasn't in love with her."

"At the risk of getting drawn off the main topic at hand," Collison said, surprised, "if Dr Barker wasn't in love with Katherine, then why did he leave you and marry her?"

"He *thought* he was in love with her, of course. Women like her are good at that. She made eyes at him and wore tarty clothes, and made him believe that a young woman really could find a middle-aged man attractive. Typical man; he might just as well have been locked on auto-pilot. Pathetic!"

It was not clear whether this epithet was being applied to the late Katherine Barker, her husband or men in general, but Collison decided to press on.

"Perhaps we'll back come to this point later. Tell me how you felt when you realised that by strange coincidence Gary Clarke actually knew your intended victim."

"At first I was panicked," she admitted. "I thought about calling the whole thing off. It seemed too risky. She'd even told him off about trying to contact her all the time, you know, making excuses to call her. It seemed likely that she would have mentioned that to someone, which would mean that the police might well come knocking on his door as a suspect."

"What changed your mind then?" Metcalfe enquired.

"I suddenly had a brainwave." She beamed. "I was looking at it all wrong; he was a ready-made suspect all by himself. I'd constructed a mythical serial killer who was probably inadequate with women, and he was undoubtedly that. He was well known as a fantasist, so people would be unlikely to believe anything he said—he used to tell silly stories all the time. Best of all, he knew Katherine Barker and was close to being obsessed with her. If the killings stopped with her, it might indeed look as if she had been the real target all along—but his target, not mine."

"Weren't you still taking a great risk though?" Collison asked. "If he was arrested and questioned, why wouldn't he just tell the truth and implicate you?"

"Two reasons. First, I think he had genuine feelings for me, despite the silly crush he had on Kathy. As far as he was concerned we were both committed to this special relationship together, albeit based, as it turned out, on killing. Sharing something like that brings you together in a strange way. I knew he wouldn't want to let me down."

"And second?"

"Second, we'd talked about one of us getting caught; we agreed that the other would keep shtum. I'd impressed upon him that he was likely to get exactly the same sentence as an accessory to murder as he would if he'd done the actual murders himself. So if either of us was charged, the best course would be to plead guilty and serve the time without mentioning the other. After all, these days even killers get let out after a few years, don't they?"

"And was he comfortable with that?"

"No, he was very unhappy about it but I had one more trick up my sleeve. I said that if either one of us was picked up, we should claim that we had been in bed together on the night of the murder, which would give either of us a perfect alibi."

"Yet you testified to the exact opposite. Why?"

"Because I realised he was the perfect suspect, like I said. I hid the stuff in the loft one day just after Kathy was killed, when I knew everyone was likely to be at work. I got the ladder from the flat; it was hard to reach but I was wearing heels and I was *just* able to get the bag into the loft. I knew that if you suspected him it would be one of the first places you'd look—it was so obvious."

Collison and Metcalfe exchanged wry glances.

"Then you'd have him 'bang to rights,' as you say. I thought he'd eventually realise things were hopeless and confess. When he stuck to our plan instead and tried to involve me in his alibi, I knew that by denying his story I'd just be making things even more open and shut for you. It would gel with what other people—like his colleagues—would say about him being a fantasist. So you'd have a man whom nobody would believe, with a bag full of murder evidence in his loft. Simple."

"Tell us about the night of Katherine's death," said Collison.

She shrugged. "It was all really just as I'd planned it. I waited outside the flat for a few nights until a row started, and right on cue she came staggering out. For a moment I wondered if I should risk just doing it there and then, but Lyndhurst Gardens is much too public, even after dark. You have occasional cars cutting through from Haverstock Hill to Fitzjohn's Avenue. So off I went and was ready waiting for her when she arrived. It was easy because she was very drunk. The only problem was that I got a lot of blood on my clothes, so when I got home I took off literally everything I was wearing and put it all in a bin bag."

"Where is the bag now?" Collison asked.

"God knows. I took it to the dump the next day. I expect it's in a landfill site somewhere by now."

"Did you see anyone else while you were…at the scene?"

"I think there was a homeless guy wandering around somewhere, but he looked as if he was pretty much out of it himself—either drink or drugs. He had a dog with him. I remember it barked at me once or twice, just out of curiosity I suspect."

"Would he have seen you with Katherine?"

"No, he'd gone off around the corner by then. My only real fear was that she'd scream and someone would look out of one of the windows at the back of the flats, but it was OK. She went straight down as soon as she was hit."

"I'd like you to think carefully before you answer this next question," Collison said. "Did you do anything different to the body this time? Something you'd never done before?"

She thought hard and then smiled. "Do you mean the fish food? Yes, that was naughty, wasn't it? Remember by this time I'd selected Gary as the perfect suspect, so I thought I'd just leave you one more clue. I took it from his flat."

There was a long silence while the detectives tried to think whether there was anything else to ask at this point. Collison looked at Metcalfe, who silently shook his head.

"Well, Ms McCormick, I suppose I should thank you for

being so open with us," Collison said at last. "We'll have a statement typed up for you to sign based on the tape recordings."

"Very well," she said, as calmly as though he had suggested popping down the road to buy a newspaper.

"Just before we end the interview," he went on. "I'm still struggling to understand your motivation. You killed five women in cold blood, having planned their deaths meticulously in advance. It is actually extremely rare for one woman to kill another woman. Usually they kill men—frequently abusive men. Was this really simply about jealousy?"

"It was a life for a life," Susan McCormick said, looking him straight in the eye. "I died deep down inside the day Colin came home and told me he was leaving. You make 'jealousy' sound petty somehow. It isn't. It gives you this constant, all-consuming sort of anger."

She thought for a moment.

"Actually, towards the end I'm not sure I felt anything at all. I just had this calm determination that she had to die. I knew it was the right thing to happen. I had no choice. It was as though it was predestined."

"But was he really worth it?" Metcalfe asked, voicing what they were both thinking. "Colin, I mean?"

"He was my *husband*," she said simply. "He was my life."

Chapter Twenty-Six

Simon Collison sat slumped in an armchair clutching a large gin and tonic. Caroline stood in the door, undecided whether to stay or return to the kitchen. He had been sitting in silence for some time. Finally, he looked up. "I've never been in the presence of a deranged killer before," he said matter-of-factly.

"What was she like?" she asked, intrigued despite her revulsion.

"Eerily calm and rational, as though everything made perfect sense but all in some parallel universe, some alternative reality. Very detached too. Kept using the passive voice. You know, 'she went down' rather than 'I knocked her down.' And then at other times she seemed almost proud of what she'd done. Both Bob and I ended up feeling quite disturbed, as though we'd encountered something beyond our understanding, like an alien or a time traveller or something."

She perched on the edge of the seat opposite, still watching him solicitously. "I suppose there's no doubt that it really is her? That she's not just covering for the husband?"

"We've considered that, of course. In fact, to start with that's what we both believed—or perhaps hoped. We couldn't accept that we could have got it so wrong about the husband. But no, it all fits. The chloroform in particular; it's the only sensible explanation of that."

"But couldn't he have done it instead of her?" she persisted. "Ordered it and then taken it from the practice?"

"He could theoretically, yes, but why would he? Being a doctor, he would already know that it was a pointless way to try to subdue someone. No, it had to be someone who didn't know that."

"Have you thought that maybe that's what you're being encouraged to believe?" Caroline asked dubiously. "I keep feeling that all the way through this case someone's been playing some strange, perverted game with you."

"They have," he said shortly. "Susan McCormick, alias Barker, alias Dashwood."

"Ah well," she said, surrendering, "at least you've solved the bloody thing, anyway."

He gave a short laugh. "But I haven't, don't you see? I was ready to arrest the wrong man yet again, against the advice of the DPP and the ACC by the way, and only the ex-wife's confession turning up at the magic moment stopped me from actually doing it."

"But she did stop you, didn't she? So maybe the whole thing will just be forgotten about."

"Not a chance." He shook his head violently. "Dr Barker arrived at the station in the full glare of the TV lights after a paper had printed a story that I was about to arrest him. And anyway, I did caution him and tell him he was a suspect. No, it's all a mess I'm afraid. I'm sorry, Caroline. I've let you down."

"You mustn't say that!" she exclaimed, suddenly angry. "You haven't let anyone down, least of all me. You're a decent, honourable man, and all through this investigation you've done what you thought was the right thing. You've always been like that, Simon, you know you have. Your integrity is one of the many things I love about you."

She knelt down and embraced him fiercely. He half responded in a distracted sort of way, and they remained silently for a while in each other's arms.

"It isn't your fault, you know," she said, more gently. "None of it was your fault."

"Thank you, darling, but that really isn't true," he said soberly as they slowly drew apart. "There were so many things we should have asked about but didn't. Why on earth did we never find out that McCormick was Barker's ex-wife? Why didn't we follow up the discrepancy between her story and Clarke's? Why didn't we make enquiries about the effect of chloroform? No, it's no good, dear; I screwed up. And ironically old Tom Allen probably *would* have found those things out because he's a good, sound copper, just like he found out about Clarke's alibi."

"Clarke's *apparent* alibi," she corrected him. "As to the rest, McCormick not being unmasked was because Dr Barker didn't attend the trial. The discrepancy was tested in court and the jury decided that Clarke was lying. And so far as the chloroform was concerned, if it was so obvious why didn't your forensic people comment on it?"

"All good excuses," he said with a smile. "I shall try to remember them for the morning. I have an appointment with the ACC. Somehow I doubt he'll take such an accommodating view."

The ACC was not alone. With him was a young man wearing shoes that were just a little too pointed and a suit that was just a little too blue. A quiff rose on the crown of his head, making it look as though he had forgotten to remove his comb that morning.

"Simon," the ACC said. "I'd like you to meet Mo Wallace from the Press Office."

"Nice to meet you," Collison said automatically. "That's an unusual name."

"Mo? Yes, short for Maurice."

Both the other men looked puzzled but then the ACC shrugged and continued, waving them into seats in front of his desk.

"Perhaps I could be one of the first to congratulate you, Superintendent," Wallace said. "A great achievement."

Collison looked at him warily. "Thank you but the investigation was flawed, you know. At the end of the day we were saved by the killer walking into the police station and confessing—a development we had no right to expect."

"Serial killers are often caught by accident," the ACC said, gesturing expansively. "Look at the Yorkshire Ripper. Anyway, let's focus on the matter in hand, shall we? We don't have much time."

"In what sense, sir?"

"Don't be dense, Simon. There's going to have to be a press conference of course. We're under intense pressure from the media already. You've probably come to the Yard straight from home, but the press are still camped outside Hampstead nick. They're all waiting for a statement."

"Speaking of statements," Wallace chipped in. "Can I just check whether we do now have a full confession signed by Susan McCormick?"

"Let me check with the station," said Collison.

"Don't worry," the ACC said crisply. "We have. I checked with Metcalfe. She signed it an hour ago."

"Excellent," Wallace said, making a quick note. "Well then, I think we're in very good shape indeed."

"Good shape?" Collison echoed. "Hardly. What do we say when they ask why we thought Dr Barker was the killer? Or when they ask why we didn't realise Clarke wasn't acting alone? Or why we never knew that Susan McCormick was Barker's ex-wife?"

"If those questions are asked, Simon," the ACC cut in, "and do not receive satisfactory answers then both you and I will be looking for new jobs. So I suggest you listen carefully to what Mo is about to tell you. You might like to make notes."

❀ ❀ ❀

An hour or so later, Collison put his pen back in his pocket and gazed reflectively at his notepad. "So that's the way things are going to be?" he said, with a slight inflection.

The ACC nodded.

"In that case, sir, may I ask that the two key members of the enquiry team—Metcalfe and Willis—receive some due recognition?"

"I can't put Metcalfe up to DCI. Not having only just briefed the Commissioner on the Andrews matter. He was livid, as you might expect. The best I can do is a commendation and a note on his file recommending him for early promotion."

"Fair enough." Collison nodded grudgingly. "Though, as I said, that was my idea not his."

"It was an error of judgment," the ACC said sententiously, "on both your parts. You are both senior offices and should have known better."

He allowed these words to sink in.

"As for Willis," he went on. "I propose promoting her to DS with immediate effect."

"Thank you, sir. It's well deserved. By the way, may I ask what is to happen about Andrews?"

"I spoke to DS Andrews yesterday afternoon," said the ACC expressionlessly. "It seems he will be retiring from the Met on grounds of ill health, also with immediate effect."

"So there will be no enquiry? No disciplinary proceedings?"

"Not for anybody, no," the ACC replied, pausing meaningfully after the word 'anybody.'

Collison became aware that Wallace had quietly slipped out of the room.

"It was felt best," the ACC continued, "that no mention of this incident should appear in Andrews's file. That way, there would be no problem about giving him a clean reference to assist him in his search for civilian employment. We have decided, therefore, that it is better to treat the conversations which I had with both you and him as strictly off the record."

"Which means no mention of it will occur on Metcalfe's file, sir?"

"Naturally, since officially the conversation never took place. Nor, of course, on yours."

Collison felt an absurdly unreal sense of relief. "Thank you very much, sir," he said simply.

He stood up and offered his hand. The ACC stood and took it.

"Now get downstairs," the senior man said with a smile. "Wallace is waiting for you."

"Now then, Superintendent," Wallace said, without actually rubbing his hands together, but in a tone of voice which suggested that he was. "I take it you've done a few press conferences before?"

"Just a few," Collison replied with a smile. In his present mood he found it hard to be irritated, even with a PR man.

"Well, I've never managed one of yours before," Wallace went on, "so perhaps we could agree on a few basic ground rules before we go in."

"Managed? I wasn't aware that press conferences could be managed. One needs to know the right things to say and not to say, of course, but you can't control which questions get asked."

"Oh, dear me, Superintendent," Wallace said pityingly. "We do seem to have led a rather sheltered life, don't we?"

He produced a two-page list of bullet points and handed it across. "These are the questions you will be asked and these are the answers you will give. By all means put things in your own words; it's important that everyone hears your voice, as it were. But the gist of it is here."

"But how can you be so sure that these are the questions that will be asked?"

Wallace smiled. "Well, let's just say that I will be exercising due care over which members of the audience to take questions from."

"But still," Collison persisted. "You can't possibly know in advance what they're going to say."

"Oh, but I do," Wallace said with another smile. "You see, I discuss it with them in advance. They know if they don't toe the line they won't get the inside story on the next case. In fact, if they're very naughty boys and girls, they may never get access to anyone in the Met ever again."

"Good God! Does that really go on? You hear about it, of course, but I never thought that it actually happened."

"It's my job." Wallace shrugged. "How do you think I justify my salary?"

"To be honest," Collison replied with a smile which he hoped robbed the words of any offence, "I had no idea."

"Well, in that case you're about to find out," he said earnestly. "By the way, please cancel any plans which you might have for this evening. You're going to be interviewed on the TV news."

"Which one? BBC or ITV?"

"Both, actually," Wallace said modestly. "Now, do get on and learn your lines. We only have about twenty minutes."

"The Metropolitan Police today revealed details of what is surely destined to enter the annals of criminal history as one of the most bizarre series of murders ever committed," Peter Collins read to Karen Willis. "Not only were the killings committed, most unusually, by a woman, Susan McCormick, but it is believed that the officer in charge of the investigation, Detective Superintendent Collison, deduced that the earlier murders had in fact been committed not by a serial killer, as had previously been believed, but by a calculating individual who wished to create a false trail to lead the police away from anyone who might have a discernible motive for killing Katherine Barker, the last victim."

"That's neat," Karen said admiringly. "I wonder who planted that 'belief'?"

"The enquiry team were able to charge and convict the killer's male accomplice," Peter went on, "though it was at that time unclear exactly how many people had been involved. When Gary Clarke's trial failed to elicit the full truth, it is rumoured that Superintendent Collison hit upon the bold and highly original stratagem of leaking to the press a false report that suspicion was now falling on the killer's ex-husband, Dr Colin Barker, in the hope that this would draw the killer, who had previously been married to the doctor and was still in love with him, to come forward and confess in order to save the man she loved, as in fact proved to be the case. Superintendent Collison was quick to praise Dr Barker for his assistance with the enquiry and to emphasise that the police fully acknowledged that he was never in any way a serious suspect concerning the death of his wife."

"Collison gets a good spread," Karen said, picking up a different newspaper. "There's a whole piece on him here, describing him as one of Scotland Yard's coming men, a high achiever who's been groomed for a senior position."

"And this one"—Peter picked up a third—"carries his TV interviews almost verbatim. It would appear that our Superintendent has woken up a hero this morning. Richly deserved, I'm sure, though it would be nice if there were some recognition for you and Bob Metcalfe, old thing."

"Oh, but there is," she said warmly. "Maybe not in the papers, though the boss did mention us both by name during the press conference, but Bob's got a commendation from the ACC and guess what I found out today: I've been promoted. I'm a Detective Sergeant now."

"Now that *is* richly deserved," Peter said delightedly. "We shall have to crack a bottle of bubbly—the Krug, I think, for a special occasion like this." He looked up over his glasses. "Or perhaps you'd rather go out? We could always stroll down to the Wells and see if they have a table free upstairs in the restaurant."

"That would be nice," she agreed.

"In fact," he said decisively, "why don't we do both? A bottle of bubbly here first and then a meal at the Wells."

"Wonderful. Yes, let's do that."

He swallowed hard and took the plunge, feeling his heart pounding as he did so. "I wonder if you might like to invite Bob to join us?" he suggested softly.

"Oh," she replied, feeling suddenly flustered, "do you think so? Well, alright then."

"It's just that I know you've become close working on this case for so long, and I'm sure he'd want to join in the celebration."

"That's a nice idea," she said uncertainly, "though I don't know if he'll be free. I could call him and find out."

"It must be a very special sort of relationship, working on an investigation together," he mused. "Perhaps like a bomber crew in wartime or something like that?"

"There's a camaraderie, of course," she agreed cautiously.

"I can see that. After all, you work very long hours together and you're part of a common purpose, sharing the same hopes and disappointments."

"Mmm."

He gazed uncertainly at her. "Forgive me if I'm being fanciful or unfair, my darling. I know I've been ill and it affected me badly. But is it my imagination or has something come between us? You've seemed so troubled recently. I thought it must be the investigation, but now that's over and I still feel there's something troubling you."

"I suppose there is," she said in a very small voice.

He forced himself to ask the question to which he had been dreading the answer for some time. "Is it Bob?" he said simply.

She knew now that there was no turning back. She had no ability to lie, either to him or to herself. "Yes, it is. Nothing has happened between us, I promise, but I really don't know whether

I'm coming or going, Peter. I have very strong feelings for him, very strong feelings indeed, feelings which I can't even explain."

"Are you in love with him?" he asked, knowing already what the answer would be and feeling a deep, yearning ache spreading within him.

"I feel instinctively that I want to be with him, that we belong together," she said helplessly, and then, slowly, "so yes, Peter, I suppose I am. I'm so sorry, my dear, really truly sorry. I never looked for anything like this to happen. I have been happy with you."

There was a long silence.

"How long have you known?" she asked finally.

"I didn't know," he replied sadly. "Not until just now. But I guessed. I just hoped I was wrong."

"Oh, Peter, I should have been honest with you sooner. I thought I was acting for the best but I should have known you'd work it out. You're so wise."

"It's not really a matter of being wise," he said. "Just of knowing you, which I do very well."

She was crying now, little jerky sobs that she was angry with herself for not being able to control.

"Come on, my darling," he said. "Let's be honest with each other and face up to the facts. We owe ourselves that, don't we, after all the wonderful times we've had together?"

"Oh Peter," she said dismally. "Oh, Peter."